PRAISE FOR ROCHELLE B. WEINSTEIN

"Readers who enjoy watching a protagonist's journey to emotional truths will appreciate this story of a woman struggling to determine how hers ends."

—*Booklist* on *This Is Not How It Ends*

"The journey to the inevitable ending still manages to take some fascinating turns along the way."

—*Library Journal* on *This Is Not How It Ends*

"An immediately and exceptionally engaging novel by a writer with an impressive knack for the kind of narrative storytelling style that rewards the reader with a story that will linger in the mind and memory long after the book is finished."

—*Midwest Book Review* on *This Is Not How It Ends*

"Weinstein has found her latest novel debuting at precisely the perfect cultural moment. *Somebody's Daughter* explores the disturbing rise in cyberbullying—and how women (and mothers) cope with unmerited guilt and shame."

—*Entertainment Weekly* on *Somebody's Daughter*

"A deftly crafted and thoroughly engaging read from cover to cover, *Somebody's Daughter* showcases author Rochelle B. Weinstein's genuine flair as a novelist for narrative storytelling, making it an ideal and highly recommended addition to community library Contemporary General Fiction collections."

—*Midwest Book Review* on *Somebody's Daughter*

WHEN
WE
LET
GO

WHEN WE LET GO

ROCHELLE B. WEINSTEIN

Text copyright © 2022 by Rochelle B. Weinstein
All rights reserved.

No part of this book may be reproduced, or stored in a retrieval system, or transmitted in any form or by any means, electronic, mechanical, photocopying, recording, or otherwise, without express written permission of the publisher.

Published by Lake Union Publishing, Seattle

www.apub.com

Amazon, the Amazon logo, and Lake Union Publishing are trademarks of Amazon.com, Inc., or its affiliates.

ISBN-13: 9781662501036
ISBN-10: 166250103X

Cover design by Eileen Carey

Printed in the United States of America

For Steven, Jordan, and Brandon, my inspiration. And for all the butterflies who danced around me while I dreamed this book into life.

CHAPTER 1

Deep down I already know the truth. Jude is about to propose. And I know I should do something to stop it instead of continuing our stroll through Vizcaya's gardens, but I don't. I tell myself the clamminess of his palm is due to the eighty-degree temperature, a consequence of tropical living, or simply a projection of my own fear, but it doesn't shake the feeling. I know. I can read it on his face. The apprehension. The anticipation. And I love him, I do, but there couldn't be a worse day for a proposal.

Guests flock daily to Coconut Grove's elaborate Deering Estate, crowding its ornate mansion and lush gardens. But today the visitors have all gone home, the sun scurrying toward the west, drenching the property in magnificent light. A handful of staff lingers, tending to the parterre, and there's Lloyd, security guard and trusted friend, making his rounds. Lloyd glances in my direction, a knowing grin strapped to his face, which only heightens my suspicion.

When Jude phoned earlier asking to stop by after work, the request wasn't unusual. His job at the hospital involves complex cases, and we often unwind with a stroll around the property where I work. I was happy to stay later, as I often do, but here we are, nearing the Fountain Garden, and everything is about to change.

I steal a sidelong glance in his direction as he meets my eyes. Jude. Tall and boyish. Thick, dark hair framing his soft blue eyes. And just as fast, I turn, so he can't see my worry. Two years in, and I suppose I believed I had more time to sort out the layer of indecision. It's not Jude's fault he doesn't know the significance of this date, and as we pass the newly planted rose garden, Jude stops and takes both my hands in his.

Jude is both nervous and sure of himself, and his stare brings forth a flare of longing, a burst of warmth I've worked so hard to tame. His devotion patched many of the holes left by that tragic long-ago afternoon. But the regret remains. And when he wraps me in his arms and I sink into him, I wish to preserve the feeling, his scent mingling with the flowers and nearby bay—being safe.

"You know I've fallen in love with you, Avery. And I know it's not just the two of us . . . The kids and I make a bit of a crowd."

My body stiffens. I've fallen in love with him, too. Against all odds. Even when I doubted it was possible. His eyes are so sure, so sure they see *me*. But he doesn't see me at all. It makes me want to burst into tears. Jude's already done the impossible, loving me when I didn't believe I could be loved. Awakening something in me I thought forever lost.

"We'll take it slow," he says. "We'll do it together. I didn't think I'd have another shot. But Avery, you surprised me."

His willingness makes me feel worse, the kindness burrowed deep inside his stare, and I'm burning with a different regret. The kind that comes from secrets.

This is Jude, I remind myself. And it brings forth a reel, the afternoons we spent walking the beach, competitive games of backgammon, the first time we made love. And his kids. Henry and Milo tossing macaroni and cheese at each other from across the table, ducking noodles and snarky insults from big sister Elle.

"Avery." He says my name, brushing the memories aside. I refuse to make another mistake. Not today. The last one left me ruined, cost me my most important relationship. But here I am, standing before a second chance, and I want it, and him.

He drops to one knee. "Avery Beckett, will you marry me?"

The words crash into me. I try to speak, but sound won't come out. Jude blinks. His face hopeful and expectant. Birds flock overhead, but the only sound I hear is my heart. It bursts from my chest, and I want to force it down, let him know how he surprised me, too.

"Jude."

He once told me he could read every emotion in my eyes. What he sees now has to be such a disappointment. Letting him down, causing any more pain than he's already endured, was never part of the plan. I can't look at him, knowing how my silence hurts. And when I try to turn away, the possibility of us fades from his cheeks, the earlier glow turning pale and dull. "Avery." His voice shakes. "Did you hear me? I want to spend the rest of my life with you."

I clamp my eyes shut, blotting out his sadness while remembering mine. The fire. The baby. Oliver. I want to open my eyes and let Jude in, all in, but I'm paralyzed with fear. The last proposal cost me everything.

I should tell him. And I want to tell him—I *tried* to tell him—but we were doing fine. *Fine*. Because *fine* came with no expectations.

"Avery, please say something."

But I can't. His offer of a commitment and a family comes on the same date I lost both. And seeing him on his knees doesn't only make me happy. It makes me terribly afraid it might happen again.

He slowly gets to his feet, time stopping around us. The garden sighs, a whisper of wind through the leaves.

He's so handsome and sure. I'm so lost.

You mess everything up, Avery.

I shake my head, shake the demons away, and Jude mistakes it for a more decisive response, and maybe it is.

Deflated, he takes a few steps back. He's slipping away. From me. From us. And I don't know how to stop him. If I disclose the truth now, he'll never forgive me. But saying yes and then hurting him later would be far worse. I understand that this could be it, the end, and it terrifies me to imagine another loss spreading deep within.

I watch him in slow motion as he tucks the ring into the pocket of his navy blazer, the one the kids and I picked out for his recent birthday. They were so excited to be a part of choosing; I had basked in the intimacy of picking out his clothes.

"I don't understand," he says.

I reach for him, out of concern, out of longing, but he pulls back. And I know how quickly this will change us. Had I been forthcoming from the start, he, of all people, would have understood. But I never imagined Jude and I would grow as we had, that he would dive under my skin and latch on as he did. And for a time, it was so much easier burying my past. But then we fell in love, and Jude saw in me what I couldn't see in myself. By then, too much time had gone by, and I lost the courage. It was too late. Unearthing these hidden parts of me will only make him angry, make him run. I am dangerous. I make people leave. My child, Quinn. Oliver. This way, at least I am in control of how we end. And leaving is always better than being left.

When I speak, it comes out a whisper. "I thought we were comfortable with the way things were . . . Taking it slow."

"And I thought we were happy—"

"We are," I say. While he couldn't repair the damage, he carved a space inside that meant I wasn't completely dead, that I could feel something, trust that broken promises wouldn't constrain me forever. But a proposal is a big ask. And even though the subject of our future had come up in recent months, I thought we were on the same page.

"And you're still unwilling—"

"It's not that, Jude—"

He faces me, steely eyed. "Then tell me what it is."

How can I tell him that deep down inside, I don't believe I deserve him? That I will only hurt him or, God forbid, one of the kids? How can I tell him that I am quite literally terrified to open up my heart, the risk of losing another piece too big? Ashamed, I break away, scanning the grounds for answers. There's the reflection pool with the lily pads,

4

the lofty palms, but it's the roses that catch my attention, their sharp, pointed thorns.

"I get it, Avery," he says. "I get that you're scared. So am I. When I asked Mallory to marry me, I never expected to ask the question again. To someone else."

Jude's wife's name erupts between us, reminding me of his vulnerability. It's because of her that Jude is a widower, and it's astonishing he's standing before me, willing to try again. But we don't have time to dwell on her absence, or my lack of response, because Jude's phone rings with the familiar tune that signals one of his kids is calling.

"Slow down, Elle," he says soon after he answers.

I admit, at first I assume this is another one of Elle's tricks, tapping into her intuitive hold on her father. She can sense when she needs to intervene, taking the necessary steps to keep us from getting too close. But then Jude's face drains of color.

"What did they take, Elle?" He rushes toward the museum's exit, and I'm not far behind, a jumble of worry running through me. Did someone break in? Are they hurt? Lloyd's strolling the perimeter, happily shuffling a cart with champagne flutes in our direction, and when he finds us sprinting across the property, sees my frightened expression, he abruptly stops, sending the glasses crashing to the floor.

Jude's voice spikes, but he remains calm. "Both of the boys? Listen carefully, Elle. I need you to hang up the phone and dial 911 . . . now. Don't do or say anything but make that call. I'll meet you at the hospital."

My heart's beating loudly, or it's his—I can't be sure—but something's terribly wrong. I'm reminded of the emergency all those years ago. "Are the boys okay?"

He doesn't answer right away, and my panic swells.

That's when he turns around and glowers at me. "No, Avery. Nothing's okay."

CHAPTER 2

Jude makes no effort to slow down, and I'm trailing him when we reach his car. "Let me go with you," I offer. And in his stillness, I see the anguish clawing at his face. If he gets in that car without me, I may never see him again.

"Go away, Avery," he says, slamming the door.

Worry snakes through my body, fear so visceral I'm helpless to tamp it down. Normally, this would be a nonissue. I'd join Jude, be right by his side, but our relationship just exploded. I could ignore the rebuff and follow him, but my legs won't move. *He doesn't want me there.* The car hums to life, and he pulls away. Which leaves me with a gnawing ache.

Lloyd abandons his tray, the shattered glass, and slinks up beside me.

"Please, not now," I say, turning my back to my friend. But he ignores me, and I'm forced to flee. Lloyd's no pushover; he follows me through the estate doors, and we're met with the opulent architecture from another time. I'm no match for his athleticism or determination. He's close behind on the stone stairs, and soon I'm pushing through the door to the roof.

"Avery. Talk to me."

"I can't, Lloyd."

He doesn't make a move to leave.

Up here, the air is lighter, the breeze flimsy and mild. The tightness in my chest releases as I drop to the ground and stare out at Biscayne Bay and the massive breakwater disguised as a barge. The waves crash into the limestone mermaids, their casings weakening against the salt. Lloyd takes a seat beside me, a line of sweat dotting his forehead. His nearness inches me closer to reality, though I don't want to be there. I want to be back in time, transported to a place where anything is possible.

The days leading up to June 13 are often difficult. Each year I say it'll get easier. I'll come to terms with what happened and let it go. But what just transpired makes a painful day even more complicated. I don't know which event to latch on to first.

Seven years have passed, but it still feels like yesterday. There was a fire. Oliver, my first great love, and I had been together in a cabin in the woods. I was carrying Quinn, our unborn child, inside me. When the flames erupted, Ollie carried us out, but there was nothing he could do. We lost her. And then each other.

Remembering that day, how I'd spent all those months protecting her, I feel a mounting dread, and I can't imagine something happening to one of Jude's kids. I grab my phone, though it's too soon for an update.

Please let me know if they're ok. I'm worried sick.

And when he doesn't reply, I send: I'm so sorry, Jude. Please.

"Talk to me," Lloyd interrupts, reminding me he's there, his dark eyes flecked with concern.

Lloyd is one of the few friends I've made in Miami. After the fire, I wasn't able to maintain friendships, let people close. I saw firsthand how openness could be a weapon used against you. How intimacy could pull you in and knock you down flat. Lloyd noticed the flaws in me early on, and he persisted. "I've never seen anyone prune hedges with as much precision," he'd said on the first day we met in the gardens. He was patrolling the grounds, the boy next door, with a full-toothed smile and big brown eyes.

Precision is crucial to my existence. The fire had been caused by one careless move, so now everything must be exact, just right. That way, I am in control. And the earth can't be tilted on its axis again.

Lloyd's waiting. His patience matches his grit. That's when I know I must reel in the emotions—something at which I'm normally adept. I offer my bare left hand instead.

"I don't understand. Did he get cold feet? He was so excited . . ."

I already know the pain I've inflicted, though it hurts worse to hear it from someone else's mouth. "He asked. Then Elle called." I pause, unable to explain the rest. It had happened so fast, and I deserved to be shut out. "There was a situation with the boys. They're headed to the hospital."

"Oh dear. Those poor kids." Lloyd knows all about Elle's erratic behavior. The way she aggressively pushes limits before relenting, vacillating between mouthiness and mild mannered. She is a frequent topic of our conversations. "I'm guessing she had something to do with this?"

I say nothing, because I'm feeling a million different things, mostly dreadful thoughts that end badly.

"But, Avery, you were going to accept, right?"

I shrug, staring off into the distance, momentarily rapt by a group of teenagers careening across the water on Jet Skis. Lloyd doesn't need to know that *yes* was impossible for me to say. Saying yes would mean opening myself up to feelings I'm not yet sure I can handle.

"You said no . . . to Jude?"

It's no secret that sweet Lloyd has his own crush on Jude.

"I don't understand. You love him."

"I do."

"Then why on earth would you say no? Are you sure you're okay?"

I lean into him, welcoming the concern, though really trying to defuse the situation. "I'm fine."

But I know I'm not. Today just shed light on my greatest weakness, my inability to wholly connect. I haven't been *fine* in some time.

His radio buzzes, and he stands. "Duty calls. Will you be all right?"

I smile up at him, holding in all that's about to spill out. "You know I love it up here. Go."

As soon as he's out of sight, I cave into myself.

The solitude brings it all forth, and I feel my body go weak and slack, just as it had all those years ago. Throwing my head back, I stare up at the sky, the hopelessness closing in, cluttering my brain with what-ifs and whys. I think about the kids. Milo and Henry are only eleven and thirteen; Elle is fifteen going on twenty-five. I shudder to think of something having happened to them. And Elle, what if she had a hand in it? How would she live with herself? My mind is going in circles, I can't stop the spin. I'm losing them all at once, and I never had the chance to really know them.

The wind picks up, ruffling my hair, and my phone sits beside me, absent of messages, ringless and mute. Settling back, I take in the view that I've stared at dozens of times. The property abuts the open water, and the setting sun gallops across the blue. The Italian gardens to my right, created as a Renaissance palazzo, are symmetrical in design, meticulously detailed. The afternoon blaze reflects on the water grottos and stone sculptures, and I notice one of the lavishly clipped hedges is uneven.

It takes all my self-control not to walk down there and fix it.

I love this estate. I once believed, like the man who had created her, that Vizcaya could be my refuge. James Deering, felled by anemia, constructed the sprawling property in Miami in 1916 to escape Chicago's frigid temperatures. I hadn't escaped the elements or frail health. Mine was a different form of healing. Here, I laid down the framework for a new life, a new identity.

I discovered this spot high above the grounds shortly after I'd fled to Florida and replied to the job listing for a horticulture assistant. Before, my life was in Crystal. A small, bucolic town in the North Carolina mountains two hours northwest of Charlotte. The application for the job stood out not for the work I was trained to do but, rather, the prompt asterisked at the bottom: *Tell us about yourself in one sentence.*

I was a collection of contradictions and subtleties, an escapee in search of a new path, but how would I arrange all that into one concise sentence? One that made proper sense? Who was I without the people I loved? And who was I without the sins of what I'd done wrapped around my neck, slowly squeezing?

So I went with honesty: *I'm not sure who I am anymore.*

That first day of work, I was dropping off my signed forms at the administrative office when I missed the fourth-floor landing and pushed through the door exiting onto the roof. It was easily one hundred degrees in Miami, a perfectly blue cloudless sky spreading for miles, and when I caught a glimpse of the vast size of the world laid out before me, I'd never felt so completely hopeful and at once so utterly alone.

Who am I? I ask myself. Jude's face is embossed in my mind—the disappointment—the *who the hell are you, I don't know you* glare.

I check my phone again.

Other than the picture of Jude's face smiling back at me, the screen is blank.

CHAPTER 3

Jude and I didn't exactly meet when we first met. I was strolling down the hallway of the Miami Beach JCC when he crashed into me as he rounded a corner. It didn't hurt, but I dropped my purse and all its contents—tampons, lipstick, my *bra*—onto the floor. That hurt. As did seeing the door marked "Grief Support Group" staring at us.

I knelt to pick up each mortifying item, and he crouched down next to me, his hands settling on the less precarious things, like the pens (so many of them) and my wallet. "Are you okay?" he asked.

"I'm fine."

Stuffing the bra back in, I thought about explaining. I didn't need to wear a bra; it was more of a formality for work, and I always took it off at the end of my shift. But I wasn't going to say all that to a guy who was heading through *that* door.

I felt myself blush. He'd later say (much later) how he liked the way the red in my cheeks had matched my hair. Apologizing, I gathered my things and tossed them into my purse before slinging the bag over my shoulder.

"Hello, Avery."

Following his gaze to the plastic name tag pinned to my shirt, I felt more heat rush to my cheeks. Unpinning it, I slipped the shiny snitch inside my purse, too.

"Will you be joining?" he asked, motioning toward the door in that pitiful tone reserved for people who are grieving. "We're just about to begin."

And that's how the lie took root and sprouted, witnessing this dejected man, simultaneously handsome and eager, cautious and unobtrusive. Long-hidden sadness crept up my skin, until I noticed his wedding band, wondering what part of him had been broken. And I knew at once, I couldn't go in there. I couldn't face the feelings. I didn't *want* to face the feelings.

"Oh." Then another set of *ohs*. "No. No. No . . . I'm not signed up . . . not this class . . ." And his eyes—neither big nor small, but just the right blue, watered down with unmistakable loss, sent me headfirst into a web of deceit.

Stealing a glance down the hallway, I explained I was there for yoga. "It's one door down." Which made perfect sense for why I was walking around braless. His eyes lowered, and I hurried past, grateful for the reprieve granted by the door marked "Beginners Yoga."

I hadn't thought about the man after that. Did we really meet if I didn't know his name? But I did wonder what it must be like to walk through a door, heart open, with a willingness to fix the kinks. Then a week flew by, and I was filling in for one of our garden tour guides, Brenda, leading a group of tourists, when I spotted him standing by the reflecting pool. I would've recognized his thick brown hair anywhere.

Myla, a guest and self-proclaimed flower expert because she had a garden back in Tokyo, was monopolizing the tour with endless commentary. It was a good thing Brenda was a no-show. I knew a lot more about the plants and flowers than she ever could, having worked on my father's farm since birth. But now Myla was interrupting my discussion on hydrangeas with a lesson on the soil's acidity.

"Yes, Myla," I politely agreed, "pH levels determine the hydrangeas' color. As you can see, our flowers reflect those differences with a wide variety—there's lavender and white, pink, and pale blue. Even green."

I found my attention shifting from Myla to the man and then to the three children surrounding him. The missing piece was glaring, and the realization made it impossible for me to finish explaining the myriad of colors. His eyes found mine, and he smiled.

Myla interrupted again, something about excessive heat and moisture playing a role in subtropical plant life, and I suspected she was referring to herself. This was August, and Miami was essentially crackling with a fiery heat. Her thin, yellow dress clung to her petite frame, and rivulets of sweat trickled down her neck, immune to the fan she used to cool herself.

"Let's take a bathroom break, everyone. Meet back in ten?"

I watched the group scatter toward the restrooms and snack shop, very much aware of the man's stare. The children, two young boys and a teenage girl, were exact replicas of their dad. The girl, tall and lanky, eyed me curiously as her father headed in my direction.

The boys climbed up on the ledge of the lily pond, and I called for them to get down. They were running and jumping, their laughter mixing with the breeze. The girl did an about-face. "Hey, morons, did you hear what the lady said? Get down."

The man whipped around. "Elle."

The boys were shouting, "Moron. Moron. Moron."

The girl, undoubtedly testing limits, twirled the dark ponytail that hung down her shoulder and said, "Well, they are."

"I'm sorry about that," he directed at me.

As an employee who had to maintain the integrity of the gardens and the safety of its guests, I carefully observed the boys frolicking around the maze of shrubs, skipping too close to the water. And as a woman who followed rules and understood dangerous outcomes, I couldn't ignore the worst-case scenarios littering my brain.

"Do you remember me?" he asked.

His voice pulled me away from the children, and I narrowed in on his features. The sun highlighted unshaven cheeks and eyes framed by the longest lashes I'd ever seen. He appeared less broken that day. Honestly, he looked like one of the Romanesque sculptures adorning the property. Strong and smooth. Chiseled but with a slight scar along his forehead.

"I'm Jude." He held out his hand. "It's nice to officially meet you, Avery."

I liked that he remembered my name, and I glanced over my shoulder as if we were being watched, unfamiliar with fraternizing on the job.

"Don't worry," he quickly added. "I'm not hitting on you. I'm in no way ready for dating again."

I'm unsure if his admission reassured me or disappointed me. There was something sexy and sad about this Jude. My fingers found his, and he squeezed. In them, I felt the awkward pleasantness of knowing more about someone than they knew of me. Could I have told him about my past then? I could've. But I didn't. I think if someone had asked what initially drew me to Jude, it was that he accepted his grief, dealt with his pain. Unlike me, who had buried it so deep, no one knew it was there.

"It's nice to see you again, Avery. Let's forget that curious meeting outside your yoga class."

A pang of regret shot through me, and I perpetuated the lie. "I don't usually carry so much junk in my bag."

He smiled, remembering. "I have no idea what you're talking about." Turning to leave, he quickly decided against it. "Hey, I was wondering, would you mind if we tagged along on your tour?"

I surveyed the boys, now wrestling on the ground, arms and legs flailing in the air, while the girl, who looked like a young woman, went back and forth between braiding her ponytail and watching us. He was going on, apologizing for their behavior, citing their ages, surprising me when he said that Elle was barely thirteen.

Taking a step back, I was about to argue how it wasn't a good idea, how tours required a ticket, and there was a cap on size, no more than ten—and Myla was probably the kind of woman who would count and report me—but I didn't want him to leave just yet. The boys ran over to us. They were intrigued by my ear pods and the microphone cuffed to my lapel that made me official. But Elle, she stayed a few feet away. And that made some things easier, despite the tug I felt in her presence.

"Sure, why not?" I said.

Jude was an attentive guest. He listened without interruption and asked questions without being patronizing, unlike Myla. He was especially interested in the estate's history, and when I shared the story of the now-famous robbery in 1971 when three thieves took off with $1.7 million in art and silver, Jude shut Myla down before she could interrupt. "I'd like to hear what our guide has to say about the subject. If you don't mind."

Myla waved him off, pursing her lips, while mine turned into a thin smile. "The trio was arrested in New York, but not all the property was recovered," I continued. "In fact, there's still a missing bowl that once belonged to Napoleon Bonaparte." This seemed to excite Jude's boys but bored Myla, who claimed she didn't come for the "mystery tour."

As we returned to the gardens, Myla asked a gazillion more questions, and I didn't even mind. It kept me distracted from Jude's loss colliding with mine, kept the feelings from crawling up and down my skin. The afternoon turned out to be a flash of what would eventually become my relationship with Jude Masters. The jubilant chaos of his younger boys, the cool indifference of his mercurial daughter. And me, drawn to a person not for what he could provide but for what he could not. A man in mourning meant a reasonable distance that kept me safe.

CHAPTER 4

That false sense of security worked for a while. Jude and I were two grieving souls tethered to separate ports. Until today. I guess I always believed that he would never want to remarry, that he'd promised Mallory. Just as I'd promised myself that I wouldn't utter *yes* again, give in to the uncertainty, and devastation, that came with a proposal. Only for a fleeting moment do I consider that I may have lost him for good. That my holding back means losing him forever.

Abandoning the view and heading down the stairs, I try Jude once more, desperate to know what's happening. I'm surprised when he answers, and I immediately ask about the boys.

He's talking to someone who I presume is Elle, telling her he'll be right back, before I hear a door close. "Elle left a bag of gummy bears in her room. Theresa found them when she was cleaning and put them in the pantry. The boys got into them."

"I don't understand."

"They weren't Publix gummies, Avery. They're from a dispensary."

I gasp. "Are they all right?"

"They're sleeping it off. They should be fine. Elle acted quickly."

A niggling doubt fills the air at the mention of Elle's competence. She isn't always the most responsible babysitter, as evidenced by the time Elle told Henry that wasabi was guacamole, and he swallowed an entire spoonful, tears streaming down his face.

Jude senses it, too. "You don't have to say it," he says. "I'm dealing with it."

"What can I do?" I ask.

"I don't know, Avery. What *can* you do?"

He's referring to the botched proposal, but I'm considering all the lies and half-truths. There's so much I can do, could've done, and when I don't answer, he says he has to go.

Relief and regret wash through me as I steer my car through Vizcaya's gates. I keep telling myself that the boys will be fine, which returns my heart to its normal rhythm. The regret is much more difficult to wash away. And there is so much of it.

I wasn't always like this. There was a time I could give and take love freely, without limits, but then came the fire. And when its flames took my angel baby away, I understood the depth of a mother's love. Losing Quinn left a barren hole, never to be filled. I may have survived the fire physically intact, but I was broken into a million little pieces. And when Oliver left, never quite pointing a finger—he didn't have to, I had enough blame for the two of us—our relationship could never be repaired. The pieces would never be put back together.

So I placed the feelings in a box—rage and grief, disbelief and denial—and buried them deep within, a hidden space where no one could get through. I left my home, my family, and every promise that had shaped my twenty-three years.

Until Jude.

After that first meeting at Vizcaya, Jude and the kids became regulars. It didn't help my regimented schedule to have the jumble of a young family interfering with my routine. But they persisted. They'd tag along on tours when I filled in for Brenda or sign up for community events at the gardens, and there was one day when they joined me in sunset yoga. The boys, freckled and energetic, would needle me with questions about the robbery and the whereabouts of Napoleon's bowl, and I found myself gradually opening up, enjoying their company. But Elle was different, or I should say, indifferent, always off to the side, observing, never quite fully there.

From early on, Jude's presence steadied me. I enjoyed having him around, though part of me fought hard against it. We took things slow, and I was careful not to overstep. He was cautious, too, a busy cardiologist focused on repairing hearts, those of his patients and the unseen brokenness of his kids'. In me, he had someone immersed in her work, centered on seedlings and plants, someone just as reluctant to dive back into the dangerous dating pool.

For a long time, I was *Daddy's friend*. We'd see each other a few times a week, a consistent schedule. Jude would continue the family visits to Vizcaya, where I would watch them roam the grounds, sometimes joining, other times giving them the privacy I believed they needed. After almost a year of this routine, the ring had come off, and I became *Daddy's girlfriend*. Jude decided I was someone he wanted the children to know better, which brought forth a resistance in me, one that kept me awake during our Saturday sleepovers. Could I be a parental figure to three kids?

Elle, in her typical Elle style, posed a real challenge. Some motherless daughters gravitate toward other women, a subconscious desire to replace what they lost, but not her. The temperamental girl, a head taller than I, continued to frown upon me from her mighty pedestal. Always testing, stoking the flames of my festering insecurities. Most of the time, she tolerated what she surely noticed growing between her father and me, and she'd alternate between interest and apathy.

As easy as it was for me to keep her at arm's length, there was a part of me, the part that lost Quinn, that deeply wanted her approval. I wanted her to like me, to accept some part of what I tried to give. There were the nights she'd sit beside me on the sofa, watching *The Marvelous Mrs. Maisel,* and we'd laugh together, and other times she'd roll her eyes at me as though I were from another planet. I wish it didn't hurt so much, but it did, leaving me to wonder what kind of mother I might have been. I kept trying. Manicures and pedicures. Trips to the mall for new jeans. And when she rejected my efforts, the wound widened, but when I received the occasional smile, I found myself believing in second chances.

Then our feelings grew. Mine and Jude's. And not even my second-guessing could stop it. If anyone understood how seeds rooted into the earth and sprouted, it was me. I found myself thinking about him when we weren't together, my heart playing over my mind's warnings. Even Oliver told me to go for it when I'd shared with him Jude's willingness to try again, to find room for me in his already-full life. Oliver was always practical, more so after we ended, and he'd have me making actual lists about what drew me to this new man. It wasn't that hard. Jude was genuinely interested when I shared about the earth, full of questions. And he'd bring me flowers because he knew how I understood them, enjoyed their company. He spoke so warmly of Mallory, maintaining her presence in the kids' lives, whether through school activities or their bedtime routine. And he never pushed. He let me sprout at my own pace.

"I like the way this feels," I had whispered to him after a long walk on the beach ended with us wrapped up in his king-size bed. The waves had been fierce that day, crawling around our feet, forcing us to skip over them. He'd held my hand, sharing about thirty-five-year-old Mallory, how a morning jog was interrupted by a rare form of heart failure, something Jude could have never been able to predict or prevent. Several years had passed since that fateful day, though his pain lingered, and the loss reached inside me and squeezed. And even though I recognized the familiar feelings, how they wistfully introduced themselves to mine, it was easier to focus on his.

"I like the way this feels, too," he'd said.

Our histories were intertwined by that point. He'd grown up in New York; I'd been raised in a small rural town. "No one's ever heard of it. Trust me." He'd fallen in love with facts and science, and my first love had always been flowers and foliage, the expectation of growth and promise. When he'd dig deeper, which wasn't often, I'd share about my mother, who died when I was a baby, or ex-boyfriends—he'd asked if I had any. "One," I'd said. "We ended . . . right before I left the mountains." Or why I never went home or talked about my sister, Willow. "This is my home," I'd say. "And my sister and I aren't close." Not anymore.

Pretending was a skill I had mastered. Containing feelings was easy when you had a breezy answer that held no weight. Because a terse response left little to the imagination, ceased any further questions. And if that didn't work, I could easily pivot, change subjects, recite a humorous story about my day, or force my tongue between his lips—anything so as not to have to go back there.

That afternoon in Jude's bed, his fingers brushed through the strands of my hair, landing on my bare skin. "I feel like I know everything and nothing about you."

He smelled of salt and sand, a scent so intimate all I wanted was him inside me. I turned over and stared into his eyes. We were naked, skin on skin, and I had forgotten how pure it felt, the thrill of being one.

I believed my lies. My mistruths. Whatever name you want to call them. I believed that I was capable of erasing a past I didn't want anyone to see. And for what it was worth, it worked. I let him in, and he traveled deeper than anyone else. The emotional wounds were there, he just couldn't see them. Or maybe he didn't want to. The one physical stain on my left leg, where the blaze had curled around my ankle and seared the skin when Oliver was carrying me out of the burning cabin, I attributed to a biking accident. No one ever asked for the details. But Jude was a doctor, and he knew what a burn looked like. He pressed.

"Strange," he'd said. "I've never seen a biking injury present like that."

I'd cupped his face in my hands, forcing his gaze away from my leg. If he'd peer into my eyes, I could distract him. "It's no big deal," I'd said.

"Are you sure?"

The question had been there in his stare. I'd held on as long as I could, and then I kissed him.

I'd gone over that conversation in my head dozens of times. Maybe if I'd told him that instant where I came from, what I'd done, we could have properly healed each other. But I was ashamed. Embarrassed. I needed him to see me in the way in which he'd often teased—his mysterious strawberry blond, the ethereal flower girl who spent hours in the garden, trimming the hedges into precise lines, pretending they were the grounds of her very own castle.

This fragile relationship blended into a tidy, neat package, contained and controlled. There were days I sank right in and others when I questioned whether I deserved even this. It was a schedule that worked, a rhythm we followed and understood. When I left decisions and discipline up to him, he saw it as my respect for parental boundaries, that I wasn't trying to be their mother, to take a place I never could. When I stayed long hours at the museum, picking up multiple shifts, he admired my work ethic. And when I insisted he spend time with the kids—away from me—he revered what he saw as selflessness. But it was something else. I let my secret history, my apartment, and all the boundaries that came with entering an already-made family set the tone. There was this bridge between us, and we'd dip our toes into the water, sometimes meeting in the middle, always returning to our own shores. And we believed nothing could ever hurt us again. When no risks were taken, there were no surprises, no disappointments. And perhaps Jude chose me for the very same reasons.

I should have known it wouldn't always be this way. I should have known that normal people grow together and that a man like Jude

21

would eventually need more. I wished I could give it to him, but Jude never really knew me, so how could he love me? And as soon as he found out, the possibility ever present, lurking dangerously in the shadows, he'd have no choice but to leave.

I'm at the intersection where turning right takes me to my apartment and left takes me to the hospital.

In my lowest moments, when the sadness seems like it will overtake me, Oliver always bolsters me, urging me to "fight harder."

I drop my eyes to the steering wheel and stare at my hands. There are rough calluses from kneading dirt with my fingers, tugging on weeds that didn't want to be ripped from their beds.

His words resound in my mind as I grip the wheel. *Fight harder.*

And I know what I have to do.

CHAPTER 5

It's ironic that the boy who broke my heart is the one who doles out advice and influences my decisions, but I've come to understand that while Oliver and I can never be together again (our ending, literally, explosive and irreparable), I still rely upon him to soothe me through the days. He often gives me the courage I need when I am most afraid; he's the calming voice, the person who knows me best.

I'm a bundle of nerves, and I mutter Oliver's mantra to myself. *Fight harder.* I'm not sure how Jude will react to my presence. After two years of dating, I've grown attached to his kids, and I can't shut those feelings off. I'm worried.

As I step through the doorway, I see the boys sleeping side by side, and I stop to watch them breathe. With each exhale, my concerns diminish, a steady calm pushing through.

Elle greets me with a glare, her dark hair falling loosely down her shoulders.

"How you doing?" I ask.

She shrugs, torn between escaping and crumbling. It's there in her swollen, tear-filled eyes and the way she stares at the door, ready to make a run for it. She's no longer the prepubescent girl biting back feelings and frustration. At almost sixteen, she's untamed and dangerous.

Seeing her like this, scared, chewing on her bottom lip, I'm reminded of the times she's been docile and kind and how, like with the ocean, I'd want to jump in.

But Elle is stormy and unpredictable like the currents.

Most of the time, I understand her pain. The girl lost her mother, and losses like that chip away at your senses, making the world one giant threat.

She watches me watching her, hesitating only slightly before dropping her long, waify body onto the upholstered chair and tucking her feet beneath her.

Despite my many shortcomings, I've always wanted to console Elle. No matter how often she's rejected my kindness, reminded me *you're not my mother*, no matter how awful I believe I'd be at it, I've longed to cradle her in my arms, longed to take away her pain. Do all the things I couldn't do for my own child. Instead, our tenuous relationship has been a push and pull of tireless effort as I crave and fend off her advances.

When Elle raises her head, blotches stain her cheeks. "This wasn't my fault. Theresa shouldn't have gone in my room, and she shouldn't have moved my things around."

Without their cleaning woman having access to her room, she'd be living in complete squalor, but I refrain from the obvious and proceed cautiously. "I know you didn't mean to put your brothers in danger, Elle."

"Well, duh, Avery."

Though having a bag of pot-laced gummies in her possession couldn't be good for her either.

"What were you doing with that stuff? It's dangerous." And when I see that I might have overstepped, I add, "I'm not trying to lecture you. I'm trying to help."

Our eyes lock. The blue in hers softens, as if she's opening a tiny door. And when that happens, I feel a shift, too, and I step in her direction.

24

But then Jude walks in, pausing when he sees me there. "Avery."

His aversion to my presence shatters whatever moment Elle and I were about to have, and a shameful disappointment descends over me.

I've arrived amid their standoff, and it appears as though Elle is losing. She tries to catch Jude's eyes in hers, to apologize again, but he stands his ground.

"I know you're sorry, Elle, but do you have any idea how serious this is?"

Elle's hands slip inside the pockets of her hoodie as she ducks her head. I'm not surprised by the empathy I feel for her. I know what it's like to latch on to something to make myself feel better. I know how devastating trauma can be, how the mind and the body find ways to comfort that aren't prudent. I also know what it feels like to have to escape.

But Jude is angling for an argument, and sympathy is nowhere to be found. "You haven't answered me yet. What were you doing with those gummies? And how many conversations are we going to have about this?" He stops, leading up to the zinger. "Do you know what this would've done to your mother?"

Elle flinches, holding back fresh tears. I flinch, too, the swipe slicing the air. Jude never talks to the kids like this, and I feel even worse knowing that his anger is manifesting in this painful way.

"All she did, every single day of her life, was worry about you kids. When you were a baby, a toddler, up until the day she died, she'd wake up in the middle of the night and check on you, be sure you were breathing, that your blanket was covering your feet." His eyes are brimming, his voice cracking. "This wouldn't make any sense to her, Elle. None. Everything she did was to protect you."

He waits while she searches the floor, fighting the message, fighting that immense love that was taken from her. I fall into a nearby chair, as though his speech was directed at me. What would he make of my inability to protect my own daughter? When he speaks again, he's definitive: "Hand over your phone."

Elle's teetering between surrender and rebellion, indecision lining her lips. There's no worse punishment for a teenager than a disconnect. She waits, thinking he might change his mind, but he's adamant. Defeated, she hands over the phone.

"You're grounded until you leave for your grandparents'. And as for your driver's license, I'm not sure you're responsible enough for that privilege, so cancel the appointment with the DMV. We'll revisit the subject when I see a change in your behavior."

Elle sulks, and I want her to feel my compassion that's bursting inside, but Jude continues. "Your mother would've done anything to be here with us. To watch you grow up. Anything. Think about that. Think about the life she gave you, what she would want for you."

Not only do I feel like an intruder, but I feel an unbearable sadness at their loss. Jude's touching on my deepest fears, my biggest mistakes.

A blush creeps across Elle's face as she turns in my direction. For a split second, it's as though she's pulled back the curtain and sees inside, and an understanding passes between us. But I'm wrong.

Her eyes grab hold of mine, and staring back is a mixture of rage and pain. She turns to Jude and yells, "What do you care about Mallory? You've already forgotten her." She lets the harshness sink in while I feel the knot in my stomach tighten, dissolving any inkling of unanimity. "I hate you," she says, scowling at him, at me, the walls, the ceiling. And then she storms out of the room.

Jude stands there, a distant, empty stare. Henry shuffles in his bed, which draws Jude's attention. I want to give him what he needs, comfort, but he doesn't want me here. I've made a mess of things, our spell irrevocably broken.

"I'm so sorry," I finally say.

He turns to me. "What are you sorry for?"

"You don't deserve this." And it's clear that there's nothing I can do to fix it. There's no fighting harder. "You should go after her," I whisper.

"She needs to cool down first."

He takes a step in my direction, narrowing the space between us. His white button-down is no longer tucked in, the navy blazer probably slumped over some chair, with the velvet box drowning in the pocket. He's close enough for me to feel his presence but too far to feel his touch.

"You shouldn't have come."

"I know."

"So why are you here?"

I search for the right words. "I was worried . . . I love you . . . I love the kids. What happened today doesn't change that."

"You can't even say what it was." And the hurt deepens the lines on his face. "It was a proposal. I asked you to marry me . . . to spend our lives together. So I'd say it changes everything, but you know what, this has always been your way." He takes a seat in the chair Elle vacated and drops his chin into his hands. His eyes are hollow, shoulders slumped. "I should've known this was a mistake," he says, shaking his head. "I can protect myself, but they can't. They need someone who cares. Who's willing to try."

He has it all wrong. The problem is that I care. Too much.

And I know there couldn't be a worse time, in the midst of a family crisis, for a confession, but it's now or never. I need to tell him the truth. Everything. Let him decide if I'm worth fighting for. Explain why I've been ill prepared to take the next step. See if there's a way we can make this work.

But then my phone rings, and *DAD* lights up the screen. I answer, ready to tell him I'll have to call him back, but I hear my sister's voice— Willow. My impulse is to hang up, but she's talking a mile a minute, something about Dad taking a fall. Surgery. "You need to come home."

Willow. We haven't spoken in ages, not since . . . Seven long years, and her voice feels like yesterday. She's using Dad's phone because I'd blocked her number. Made it impossible for her to reach me.

Jude watches me curiously, hearing the concern in my voice. "How did this happen?" And I see the man I love and all the things I can't give him. I see the past making its way into my present, and a phone call that only confuses me further. "Thanks for letting me know," I say before hanging up.

Jude's questioning me with his eyes, but I'm frozen in thought. Who am I kidding? Telling him now would be a drastic mistake, a giant leap not toward him but away. Away from Milo and Henry and Elle. Away from the love I want so desperately to give but don't know how.

"Is everything all right?" he asks. "You look like you just saw a ghost."

Hadn't I?

The unexpected phone call couldn't have come at a worse time, but it has me thinking long and hard. Maybe this is the answer. Maybe it's time. Maybe I need to go back, return to the scene of the crime, the place that holds all the tragic memories. Or maybe I just need to put the truth off a little longer. I've already ruined things here. There's no taking it back.

The decision floats from my mouth: "I have to go."

He straightens. "That's probably a good idea. The kids need rest, and your being here . . . it's just—"

"No." I meet his eyes. "I have to go. I have to go home. That was my sister." He doesn't make a move. "My dad's in the hospital . . . I have to go back."

A nurse pops her head in, sees Jude, and quickly darts out, but the door fails to close behind her.

I can tell he's torn, wanting to be angry at me, punish, but that's never been Jude's way. "I'm sorry to hear that," he says. And then he continues, avoiding my gaze, "It's probably good for you . . . for all of us." His hands smooth out his pants, and his eyes follow the motion. "You should go."

This morning, this very morning, he stopped by my apartment before he went to the hospital and crawled into my bed, kissing me from the tips of my toes to the top of my nose. He needed to touch me before work. He didn't want to leave. Now he wants me to go, and my heart can't take any more hits.

"You never talk about home. Whatever happened there, you probably need to fix."

"Will you just look at me, Jude?"

"I can't." He looks everywhere but at me. "Maybe this is for the best. Maybe we need a little break."

How could I argue with that after I'd refused the most important question he ever asked? I couldn't. Especially when he didn't know the person he was fighting for. And the loss creeps in, edging through every hollow in my body.

If I have any doubts about returning home and leaving Miami, they're compounded as I enter the hallway outside Milo and Henry's room.

Elle's standing there, back up against the wall, in her skinny jeans and lavender hoodie, face expressionless, with her eyes fixed in a faraway glaze. When she speaks, it's clear she's overheard our conversation. "Now you're leaving, too?"

She swipes at her cheek, and I know how difficult it is for her to let me see her vulnerable side. The accusation is so loaded, it unsteadies me. "That's not what's happening here, Elle." But I know how it must feel. To her. And I hate that I'll be yet another disappointment in her life.

When she looks up, she's blinking back tears. And before I can explain, she stomps off down the hall. I call after her, tracing her steps, but she's too fast, slipping through the elevator doors just as they're closing. Frantically, I tap the down button, willing the doors to open, but it's no use. They remain shut, closed off, reminding me of holding on and holding back. And I wonder why the ones who need love the most are so difficult to give it to.

CHAPTER 6

I'm sitting on the tiny balcony of my apartment overlooking the ocean. Oliver and I always talk on the anniversary of the fire, and today I need to hear his voice more than ever.

"Hey, Ollie."

"*Hey* back."

The towering palms sway in the breeze, and he asks how I'm doing.

"I thought by now, today would be a lot easier," I say.

"You've come so far, Avery. Why do you always forget that?"

I squeeze my eyes shut, blocking out the memory of Oliver's face, his eyes locking onto mine when he dropped to his knees in the middle of the chicken coop and proposed.

"Did you plant the flowers?" he asks.

Of course I planted the flowers. I planted them every year. "Buttercups," I say.

"Happy flowers." He seems satisfied. "They'll flourish in the Miami sun."

He's right, but that's not the only reason I chose that particular flower, and he knows it, too. They were childlike, small and bright. The perfect choice to honor our daughter.

Neither of us speaks. We don't have to. I'm sure we're lost in thought, thinking about the same thing. How beautiful she was, wrapped in pink. How tiny her fingers and toes. The perfect nose. She'd be seven this year, and I can imagine her skipping through the farm, chasing the animals. And I'm so angry at myself I could scream.

But Ollie wouldn't want to hear that. He was always so much more levelheaded than I.

There's no sense in delaying it any longer. "Jude asked me to marry him."

Oliver waits a minute to answer. "That's good, right?"

"It should be."

He wavers, and I wonder if it's sadness. "Did you say yes?"

"Would it be easier if I had?"

He doesn't answer.

"Tell me, Ollie. Tell me what to do."

"Do you love him?"

At once, the guilt seizes me. "It's different. I'm different." Ollie knows all my secrets. He knows how I blame myself, how it was my fault that we lost our baby. He, of all people, knows what I'm capable of, how much I fear hurting someone else.

"But do you love him?" he asks again.

"I love him very much." When I admit this to Oliver, I feel the tears forming in my eyes, as though I'm betraying him.

"Then what's stopping you?"

You. But I refrain from saying that aloud. Oliver doesn't like when I get weepy. He expects me to be strong and sensible. He says it does neither of us any good to delve into the past, to revisit old, loaded feelings.

So I change the subject. "I'm going home."

He pauses before answering. "Are you sure you're ready to do that?"

"I'm fine, Oliver." It's a whisper because I'm much more damaged than I'm letting on.

"I think it's a mistake," he says.

I don't know if it's the sky that's slowly morphing into night, the prospect of losing Jude, or the meaning of this day, but I'm tired. I'm tired of running, tired of pretending. It's all that weariness, but it's also him. Normally, I could shut the feelings down and curl inside my shell, escape to the beach, or work on the gardens, but not today. Today I blurt it out. "I wish I could see you."

There's silence. Then he says, "Don't do this to yourself. You're in a good place. You said Jude makes you happy."

His voice is sunshine against my cheeks, and I can't help but miss him. I miss the way he loved me. The way we once loved each other. And I know I shouldn't, not this much, not after all this time, but I can't help myself.

"Holding on to something broken won't get you what you want. I'll always be here for you, Avery, but I can't give you any more than that."

The last few hours—the proposal, the horrible memories, the kids—come crashing into me. I'm angry and I'm alone, and after all these years, none of it makes sense. "I still don't understand. I will never understand."

His sigh is deep, his tone unmistakably remorseful. "We may never understand, but we can't go back. We can't change it."

"I just wish there was some way you could understand how sorry I am." I picture his dirty-blond hair, the pale brown of his eyes.

"Look," he says, "it's okay to love someone, Avery, to let someone love you. You don't need my forgiveness. You need yours. And you don't need to go home to do that."

"But I do. Willow called. Dad took a fall. He's in the hospital. It's going to be a bit of a recovery."

Oliver doesn't respond. He knows I haven't been in touch with my older sister in years. I like imagining him being annoyed with her, too.

"I know I said I'd never go back—that place is just too painful for me—but I may not have a choice."

More silence.

"My dad needs me. And this thing with Willow . . . you know . . . and Jude wants nothing to do with me . . . So maybe it's time . . . Maybe I need to do this."

"I'm just worried that going back there might be too much for you. Why dredge up something that doesn't need to be dredged up?"

"Maybe that's just it," I reply, my voice rising. "Maybe I've been avoiding too much. Maybe it's time to face what's been holding me back. Believe me, I don't want to go back there, but maybe I have to do this."

I close my eyes and let our history unfurl. Memories of Oliver are always bright and colorful.

I tell him what I'm remembering, adding, "I'm so sorry I ruined our story."

We were at Elle's provocative age, fifteen teetering on sixteen, a time when it was natural to yearn for and fend off feelings that were coming close. Call it naivete, an unawareness of our sexuality, but when the time came, the sparks were impossible to ignore. With one kiss, he changed me, changed us.

It was fitting that the season was October, a time of transformation, when leaves fell from the trees and Oliver and I fell, too. We were at his sister's wedding atop a sprawling hill in a renovated barn with exquisite views. The party was simple and intimate, with rustic wood tables covered in golden tea lights and arrangements of pink, white, and peach ranunculus. The band played our favorite music, and fairy lights strung across the ceiling cast the room in a warm glow.

Oliver pulled me onto the dance floor. He was long and lean, and I just reached his chest. The band was playing Elvis's "Can't Help Falling in Love," and Oliver's arms came around me. I never understood the song or why it was such a draw, but that night I had no choice but to listen, and the lyrics crooned in my ear, telling me how Ollie and I were simply meant to be.

He leaned in to sing me the words, and it all began to make sense. That boy was about to upend my life. He was going to make the dreams I didn't know I had come true.

"Let's go," he said, grabbing my hand and leading me off the dance floor. My dislike for dresses meant I was wearing one of Willow's flowing silk blouses, a deep emerald green that complemented my hair. I loved the silky feel of it against my skin, how it was long enough to cinch at the waist. With Oliver's arm against my hip, the fabric brushing against my thighs, we pushed through the barn doors and out into the sprawling meadow.

Evening had descended as we stepped through the cushion of crisp air. "Are you cold?" he asked.

I wasn't cold at all. I was alive and with Oliver. Oliver, who knew parts of me I barely knew myself. How could I have missed these feelings? The music filtered through the doors and windows, Neil Diamond crooning "Sweet Caroline." Oliver found a spot beside a brilliant red maple, the rising moon silhouetting his face.

We were turned toward one another, not nearly eye to eye because I'd always have to strain my neck to admire Oliver. And even though I had searched his face a million times before, it was never like this, never this close, with this kind of thrill.

"Say something," I said, because Oliver was making me nervous. Sweat lined my palms, a thin film that made no sense. This was Oliver, I reminded myself. The boy I had spitball contests with, the one who trapped bugs in plastic cups with me so that we could dissect and classify them. I'd seen him with bloody gauze pads stuffed in his mouth after his wisdom teeth were pulled. I'd also seen him peel off his shirt and jump into Trash Can Falls that summer he spent weight training. And never in the last dozen or so years had we entertained the unlikeliest of feelings.

Until now.

"Something," he said.

I pinch him. "Not funny. What's going on in that head of yours?"

"You've done something to me, Avery."

It could've been the cool air hugging my skin that caused tiny bumps to crawl up and down my arms and legs, but I knew by the subtle warmth in certain places that the chill wasn't the cause of this reaction.

And then his fingers reached for my chin.

"This feels serious, Ollie."

"It is."

"Do we like serious?"

"I think we might. Because I like you, Avery Beckett."

"Well, duh," I said, over the pounding of my heart. "We've been best friends since I taught you how to tie your shoes."

"I taught you how to tie your shoes."

"No, Ollie, I taught *you*. Gym class. All the kids had on those Velcro shoes, and you were wearing laced-up black Converse sneakers, about to run toward the basketball—"

His hand came over my mouth. "Shut up, Avery."

I could taste the salt of his palm.

"You never shut up. You just keep talking and talking and talking. Nobody can get a word in."

And when he removed his hand, I couldn't help but keep going. "It was me who taught you how to tie your shoes, Oliver." Then I knocked on the side of his head with my knuckle. "You're always getting things confused in there."

He reached for my wrist on the way down. It was gentle, yet firm. Righting me with his stare. "I'll give you that one, but I've got something else I'll teach you."

Our eyes met, and I swear I became dizzy, like we were floating above the earth, spinning on the moon. Oliver was about to say something big. I could feel it in the pulsing energy crackling around us, our private Idaho under the trees and a handful of stars. I was whirling it around my head, the idea that Oliver liked me, really *liked* me, and we were heading toward something bigger than the sky.

"I'm going to change your life," he finally said.

I took a step toward him, gazing up, trusting this, trusting him. "How are you going to do that?"

It was a game, who could inch closer.

"One day, you're going to tell our children this story. Sure, you'll probably fib a little about some of the details, but you'll tell them, the four of them, maybe five, about that day your best friend fell in love with you—"

My cheeks burned. "You said you liked me. Who's fudging details now?"

"Oh, jeez, Avery." He shook his head from side to side. "You have no idea what you're doing to me."

Crimson leaves dropped from the tree like tiny hearts swirling in the air. One of them was mine. "When you got out of the car . . . in that dress . . ."

"It's not really a dress." I was shifting from one foot to another.

"I don't know who you are . . . You're someone else."

I angled my head, feeling a prickly heat inside. "Who am I?"

The intensity of his gaze meant he wasn't sure.

"Those boys. I saw the way they were all looking at you. When you walked into the room . . . when we were dancing."

Our bodies kept drawing closer. "You're acting crazy."

He was half smiling, teasing. "Look at me."

I did what he asked. I held Oliver's eyes.

"I didn't like them staring at you . . . I didn't like it one bit."

Our bodies swayed in rhythm, and he tilted my chin up toward his.

I knew everything about Oliver except this. His lips brushed mine, the taste of spearmint and salt and Coca-Cola, his heart beating fiercely against my chest.

I kissed him back, falling into him, parting my lips and letting him inside. He was no longer the little boy I once knew. He was a young man I desperately wanted.

His hands went up and down the satiny shirt, his fingers taut against the thin fabric. Kissing him hurt, a pent-up desire we never knew was there. And though we were crossing a line, everything about our coming together was normal and natural. Oliver saw me. He knew me naked before we'd ever touched. Tears formed in my eyes, though there was nothing sad about the moment at all. I'd never felt happier.

When he pulled away, the disappointment fell in waves. Now that we had crossed this line, I wasn't ready to stop. His kiss was water to a flower, and I needed more. He dried my cheek with the back of his palm, careful to hold my gaze in his. Then he pulled me into his arms, stroking my hair with his fingers. "Don't cry, Avery. I promise. This is going to be a really happy story."

CHAPTER 7

Two days have passed since the proposal, though it feels much longer. Jude and I haven't spoken, apart from a few short texts responding to my inquiries about the boys. Milo and Henry are home and healthy. But when I get the thumbs-up emoji after I apologize, again, I know the damage is done.

With my request for two weeks' vacation approved, I'm packed up and ready for the drive to my childhood home in Crystal. The only thing left to do is swing by Jude's for the rest of my things. Lloyd said it was a mistake. One that reeked of desperation. Whether he's right or wrong, I make my way over.

I waited until I couldn't wait any longer, until all the preparations were in place, every bag loaded into my trunk, spilling over to the back seat, which is why I'm standing in Jude's driveway at close to eleven in the evening. Arriving this late left little room to second-guess my decision. Not because Jude would want me to stay, but because I would want to.

The lights are out, except for the one on the porch, and I hesitate, wondering if I've made a mistake.

I text Jude that I'm outside, because it's wrong to use the key he gave me, back when he trusted me, trusted us. Soon he's at the door, wearing the familiar gray pajama bottoms I've seen him in a thousand times, his hair messy and uncombed.

"I just need to get my stuff," I say. "I'm leaving early in the morning."

He opens the door wider for me to step through.

"Are the kids asleep?" I ask, somewhat relieved when he says yes, making the goodbye a little easier.

"Elle, too? It's early for her."

"She's been sulking in her room for days. I changed their flight to see my parents. They're leaving for New York tomorrow."

"Are you going, too?" I ask.

"Medical conference." And I remember it was on the calendar. All these plans were. With the kids away, Jude and I were going to take our first trip together, though we never managed to finalize any details. I don't harp on any of this. Instead, I take in the surroundings.

I've always liked Jude's house. Not even Mallory's memory woven through the walls and furnishings changed that. It was a home filled with warmth and light, with high ceilings and a blend of old and new. Tonight, it's dim and disheveled. I spot backpacks and suitcases lined up along the floor. Giant pillows are tossed haphazardly on the gray sectional, and the matching throws are wadded up, waiting to be folded and fluffed. Weekends—the days when Theresa's off—are easy to recognize. And while Mallory's parents encouraged Jude to hire someone to live in, Jude firmly refused. They could handle it, he had said. He wanted to handle it. And most of the time, he did.

We don't talk as I follow him up the stairs toward his bedroom. The air feels cooler, the space modern but cozy, and I spot Milo fast asleep, buried in a tangle of sheets and blankets. Jude tugs on the covers, lifting his limp body, carefully draping him over his shoulder. As they pass, I touch the boy's mussed-up hair, wondering if I'll ever see him again, and I'm surprised by how that notion affects me.

Left alone, I walk toward the closet and the space Jude allotted for my clothes.

A slight row of colorful dresses and shirts flattens against the grays and blues, and I question how I ever thought I would fit into this life. Mallory's clothes were still there, hanging on hangers that would never be touched, jangling from time to time as a subtle reminder, so we'd made a place for my jeans and tops beside Jude's. The space was narrow and tight, and clothes got wrinkled from time to time, and even though he had mentioned boxing her things up, having her parents drive from Tampa to help, that hadn't happened, and I'd never push.

Avoiding the final step was natural and expected, so we left it alone, and having Mallory's presence circle around us never bothered me before. Tonight, it feels different.

Grabbing a few hangers—a favorite leopard-print top, white jeans that are probably too small—the clothes seem all so inconsequential when Jude and I are on the cusp of what might break us for good. I begin the process of removing my shirts from their hangers, folding the pieces on a nearby chair. I'm halfway through the jumble of an overcrowded closet when he returns, a blank expression I can't read.

He takes a seat on the edge of the bed, patting the space beside him. "You all right?" he asks.

I sit, staring ahead at the framed picture of Jude's family on the wall, everything I lost gazing back at me. "I should be asking you that question."

Jude details the last couple of days of Elle's lockdown, how she's been as challenging as some of his patients, alternating between sulking and trying to appease him. "And the boys . . . well, good thing they have no idea they were high. They're back on earth like the rest of us." He pauses to ask about my dad.

"He's a bit of a mess," I say. "Broken hip. Crushed hand. He's had two surgeries in a matter of days. When he gets back to the farm, he'll need to rehab."

"I'm sure he's glad you're going home . . ." And then, "A farm?"

A tingle of deception spreads through me. "I thought I told you about the farm."

"No," he says, rather pointedly. "I'd remember that."

He falls silent, and I can see he's struggling, trust and devotion slipping away.

It's hard to keep up with the history I've deliberately omitted. "It's a silly farm," I say, squeaking out a laugh. "Nothing like living here."

Then he does something that makes me feel even worse. "Maybe you mentioned it. I guess I don't remember." And he quickly pivots. "But it's good you're leaving . . . to the farm . . . not just for your dad . . . but for us, too."

He's vague, and I'm not sure what to make of it, but I'm hoping it means we have a chance, that my absence will provide much-needed time for us to reflect, with reconciliation a possibility.

He stares down at his clasped fingers, and I can tell this is difficult for him. Here's a man who's already lost so much. "I won't lie," he begins, "the last few days have been hell around here. Hell without you." His sadness coils around me. "I'm not ready to let you go, Avery. Not entirely. Maybe this break will help us figure out what we both want."

I'd been holding my breath, and it's a relief to let it go. "I like that idea," I say, taking him in, wanting to touch him when I know I can't. I'm leaving, and I have no way of knowing if he'll be waiting when I get back.

He glances my way, love and disappointment in one somber gaze. The emotions are still there. I can feel them through my clothes, touching my skin. I want to leave; I want to stay. I want him to wrap me in his arms and beg me not to go. "You know I never meant to hurt you," I say.

"But you did . . . hurt me."

"I thought we wanted the same things. I thought . . ." I stop and bite back the emotions. Because we do want the same things. I believe that in my heart. But I'm compromised in a way he doesn't yet understand.

I remind him of the night not too long ago when we sat on the deck behind the house, watching the moon light up the water. "We were talking about how happy we were with the way things were going. You said the kids were adjusting. I understood." I glance toward the closet door and all that remains inside. "I didn't think you were ready for more."

"I guess I didn't expect to feel like this. To find someone who understood my situation . . . who didn't ask for too much . . . who made me happy again . . ." I lift myself off the bed and kneel in front of him so that I can see his face when he continues. "I didn't expect to feel *this*, Avery. Not a second time. No one wants to go through that pain again."

When I open my mouth, all I can feel is the lump lodged in my throat. I barely make out a whisper. "I know."

"You don't. Because if you did . . ."

I search the floor, because I have no right to disagree when I've kept my losses so deeply hidden. "I didn't say no."

"You didn't say yes."

"I love you. You know that."

He blinks in disagreement. "I believe you. But it's not enough."

Enough. "What if I'm scared?" My voice rises, and I reach for his hands. "What if there's something deep inside of me so broken that it'll only end up making things worse?"

"I'd think you would tell me so I could help you."

"What if you can't?"

"I wouldn't give up until I proved you wrong."

I'm sure he can see right through me. He can see what happened in Crystal, lurking close to the surface. He can see what I did, the damage I caused. I want so much to believe in him, believe in us, but I back down. "You'd never understand. But I'm going to go home . . . and while I'm there, I'm going to try to make sense of it all."

One lie had led to another and then another, though I told myself they were sins of omission, half-truths. *There was a boyfriend. We broke up. My life was boring and uneventful except for the flowers and plants that brought me to life.* When I was really painting a portrait of a fraud. And the trouble with this approach is that when you pretend too long, you begin to believe your own tales. And because I don't know what more to say or how to fix this, I move in and touch his cheek with my hand. He leans into it, closing his eyes, and we are close enough to feel each other's breath. My lips inch toward his, and all I want is to feel his mouth on mine. His lips part, and then he retreats. "I can't, Avery."

"I know. That was foolish." Rising from the floor, I swallow the disappointment, the desperate need, and inability, to save us.

As I return to the closet, Jude stretches across the bed. I finish with the hanging clothes and move on to emptying my drawer—my section—making piles on the floor. He doesn't say anything. He doesn't ask when I'll be back. He lets me pack up the proof of our life together, and it fills me with sadness.

Downstairs, I rifle around the kitchen for garbage bags, stopping in front of the table, already made for tomorrow's breakfast. Jude is a planner, and he prides himself on his hearty breakfasts. Tomorrow won't be nearly as much fun without our cooking pancakes and eggs, watching Elle pick at the silly shapes we'd create for the boys. I notice the placemats I bought them for the holidays. Personalized, with each of their names. Jude. Elle. Henry. Milo. A perfect, even square.

I linger longer than I should. The house is rarely this quiet, and I take in the calm, memorizing the smell of citrus. That's when I remember the garden. Soon I'm outside, the humidity clinging to my skin. The landscape is lit up, the bay chopping in the distance. Jude had enthusiastically welcomed the addition to their home, and on weekends, the boys and I would take turns tending to the vegetables and herbs. I photograph each section, each plant, and scribble instructions into the phone.

I talk to the leafy greens and sprouting vines. I tell them that I'll be back. Even though I'm not sure I will.

As I lock the door behind me, the sadness descends. I jot a quick note to Milo and Henry, wishing them a fun summer, and leave it beside their placemats.

For Elle, I leave my favorite lipstick, the one that seems to go missing, only to magically appear in her bathroom drawer. I drop it beside her plate. A peace offering. Or perhaps because I'll miss sharing makeup with her, and it hurts more than I'll admit.

Returning upstairs, I see Jude's fallen asleep, his light snores filling the room. Between his busy practice and the demands of three kids, it's no wonder he's passed out. Peering closer, I notice how the recent stress has lined his face.

I'll miss hearing all the parts of his life—the copious amounts of homework that will have him up for hours, researching alongside the kids; the battles over wearing deodorant (Henry) and eating vegetables (Milo); and the stories of his patients (never their names), like the eighty-year-old men requesting Viagra when they really needed valve replacements. In small, beautiful ways, Jude's chaotic life has given me hope, a glimpse into what could be, and now I've jeopardized it all.

The last of my stuff is packed, and I drop the bags beside the bed, beside Jude. He's folded on his side atop the messy sheets, and I study the smoothness of his bare skin, the line where his shirt ends and a sunburn begins. I don't want to say goodbye.

Sliding onto the bed, I carefully curl into him so that our bodies fit. His breath falls in a steady rhythm, and there's relief in knowing he's at peace. I feel his skin against mine, his weight against my neck and shoulders, and nothing hurts, but everything hurts.

It happens without my trying. Sleep. First, I'm so focused on his body next to mine, wanting to remember every touch, every sensation, and then I'm dreaming. And when I wake up hours later, close to my departure time, I panic, freeing myself from his arms, careful not to rouse him from his own dreams. Maybe I am in there somewhere;

maybe it's a better version of me, someone who can give him what he needs.

I lightly touch his cheek and tell him I love him. I tell him I'm sorry. I tell him I wish I hadn't been such a coward, that I didn't ruin our shot at another chance.

But that's what I do. I break things. People. I make horrible things happen.

CHAPTER 8

It's dark and I'm on the road, the city lights reflecting in my rearview mirror. As I cross the Julia Tuttle Causeway and head toward the place where it all fell apart, the memories come flooding back.

Oliver was hesitant about going to his family's cabin. I was in my thirty-eighth week, my due date looming near, and Dr. Kramer told us if I went into labor at that point, I could deliver a healthy baby girl. Oliver thought it best we stay home, near our families, but I'd insisted. The mountains had brought us such joy, and I knew it would be the last time it was just the two of us. The cabin was nestled deep in the forest, and as we stepped through its creaky door, I remember twisting the modest diamond around my finger, the one he placed there soon after the proposal.

Oliver had been thrilled when I told him I was pregnant, lifting me up and twirling me into the air. We didn't need a ring to seal our union. He was mine, and I was his.

The first day at the cabin, we casually strolled along the nature trail, photographing the blooming flowers and plants, and later that night, we grilled burgers and sat by the fire, roasting s'mores, talking to my belly, to Quinn. We were letting her know about this beautiful world, about how much fun she was going to have there, hiking and tubing at the nearby lake. I felt fantastic during my pregnancy, the usual complaints from other mothers all but absent. And Willow. She was so excited. She'd always been like a mother to me, and I knew how Quinn's presence had her longing for her own children.

In bed later on, I was tracing the lines of Oliver's body. He kept telling me how beautiful I was, though I disagreed, saying, "I'm fat." And as we drifted in and out of sleep, he kept his hand on my belly, reminding me how I never looked better. I had brought a special candle with me. It was the amber scent that swirled around us the day we first discovered each other's bodies. And when I lit it on the dresser, he rustled my hair, reminding me to blow it out before bed. Oliver was always reminding me of things, especially during the pregnancy, but then he'd just end up doing it himself. Like he did that first night, extinguishing the candle's flame.

The next day, a late-afternoon storm descended, and we were naked, pressed against each other in bed, listening to the sounds of the rain. "It's coming through the window," I'd told him. But he was too busy touching me, running his hands along the length of my body. His mouth was warm on my lips, against my neck. "Mm-hmm," he mumbled as he left a trail of kisses down my chest, landing on my stomach. The candle lit up the darkened room, and Oliver's skin had a balmy glow. He was teasing me about ways to induce labor, nudging my legs open with his knee, and I playfully swatted him away. "We can't give birth in the middle of the forest."

"We love the forest," he said, finding my sensitive spot and pressing. Afterward, we were tangled in each other's bodies, Oliver wrapped around me like a vine. Our lovely cocoon was all I needed. I could've stayed like that forever. We dozed off, and when I felt him wriggling away, I held him harder, refusing to let go.

"Come on, baby. I have to blow out your candle." But I stopped him. And I teased him with my fingers, made it impossible for him to move. And after we'd explored our bodies a second time, exhaustion put us to sleep.

When I startled awake, my eyes popped open, met by a stinging sensation, an oppressive heat. Then came the pungent smell of ash and smoke, and a gusty wind shot flames across the cabin, a dragon roaring to life. Panic coursed through me, and it was an effort to breathe. There was fire everywhere. On the ceiling, on the floor, circling around us like a wild storm. The smoke clutched my lungs, and I coughed, sputtering words that fought to come out. "Ollie," I screamed, smoke lodged in my throat, shoving him with both hands. "Ollie, wake up!"

He sat up and immediately began to gasp. I saw it from a grainy distance, the candle that we'd left to burn. *I'd* left to burn. It had toppled over onto its side. And the wind, the wind had tossed the curtains into its path, engulfing them in flames until they danced along the walls.

He shouted.

We held on to each other. I held on to my belly. I prayed. I spoke to her.

Quinn, we'll take care of you. We won't let anything happen to you.

I felt my body being lifted from the bed as he carried me through the smoke-covered room.

Then everything went fuzzy and black.

I woke up in a hospital with my ankle bandaged, hooked up to an IV. Something about a third-degree burn that would leave a permanent scar, some loss of sensation. My father and Willow stood over me as though they wanted to say, *Thank God it's nothing worse,* but it was worse. Much worse than anyone could have imagined.

My arm, attached to an IV with an array of plastic tubes, prevented me from reaching for my belly, where I felt the weight of Quinn, though she was still. Too still. "Where's Oliver?"

Willow was a pasty white. Streaks of dried-up tears crossed her face. She took the seat beside me, lacing her free hand through mine. "Oliver saved you."

I remembered the fire. The flames. I saw the candle on its side, sparking a trail of debris.

Of course Oliver saved me. He would've done anything for me. For Quinn. Which turned my attention back to my daughter.

My dad cowered in the corner. Willow was about to say something bad. Very bad. I saw the way she blinked back tears, pressed her lips together. "Avery, honey—"

But then the doctor walked in, and she wasn't Dr. Kramer. Willow just squeezed my hand, and though she tried to hide it, I could feel her trembling.

"How are you feeling, Avery?" the woman asked. She had short, cropped hair and a sympathetic smile.

"I'm fine," I said. "But someone needs to tell me what's going on." At this point, it hadn't even occurred to me what could go wrong. Babies didn't die this far along in a pregnancy.

"Avery," the doctor said to me, lightly dusting my sleeve with her fingers. "We did all we could. Your baby fought hard, but she didn't make it. I'm sorry."

"What do you mean? That's not possible. She's right here . . ." And I tugged on the lines and clutched my stomach, feeling her there, but feeling nothing at all. "I don't understand." Then I began crying. Crumbling. Stroking my belly with both hands, believing my touch could save her, rub life back into her. The doctor pressed down firmer on my arm, but I flung her away.

"Avery, you've suffered what's called a placental abruption. The placenta detaches from the womb. By the time we got you here, prepped for surgery, it was too late."

She continued talking, but I didn't hear her. Something about a fall, hitting the ground.

"No. No." I was choking on my words. "She's alive . . . I feel her . . ." I looked toward my father, to Willow, but there was only pity, tears springing from their eyes. The doctor excused herself, giving us some privacy, letting us know that she'd return to explain the next steps. None of this registered. My baby. My beautiful Quinn. How could this be?

The door closed, and that was all I needed to begin wailing, sobbing so uncontrollably, I was sure I would die right there along with our daughter. We had named her. That's how sure we were of her existence. This would destroy Ollie.

"Does he know?" I asked.

They shook their heads.

I told myself we would get through this together. I told myself all kinds of things to make the next few hours bearable. I bargained. I begged. I made promises. I pleaded to anyone who would listen to make this a dream, to make me wake up from the nightmare. I went over every scenario in my head. I cursed. I questioned. How was something like this even possible?

Hours later, floating in a fog of drugs promising to numb the pain and sorrow, I was wheeled into a cold, sterile room.

Ollie was there beside me, his fingers holding tightly to mine.

He kissed me on the forehead. "I'm right here, Avery. You're one of the strongest women I know."

I cried. "I can't do this, Ollie. I can't say goodbye."

"I know, honey." He was fighting tears, too.

"Please don't leave," I said. "Stay here with me."

"I promise, Avery. I'm right here. Always."

The memory makes me wince, and I grip the steering wheel tighter, focusing my eyes on the road, careful not to let the emotions distract me. I knew this was going to be a difficult journey home, back to the place and the people who cracked me apart. When I'd fled to Florida all those years ago, I'd had no plan to return, had never looked back.

I'd packed up my things, hurling them into the car, and watched my family's farm, the place that had raised me, disappear in a plume of dust.

Sometimes, late at night, when I can't sleep and the thoughts plague me, I imagine returning, wondering if I'll recognize the beauty that was once there, or will I only see the ash?

CHAPTER 9

I pass through Broward and Palm Beach, and the terrain becomes lifeless and barren. Stretches of flat land frame the highway, straw-colored grass, burned by the heat. I'm just a few miles from Fort Pierce when the sun begins to tiptoe across the sky, and I reach across the front seat for my bag and sunglasses.

It's then that I sense movement behind me, an unnerving sensation that I'm not alone.

When I glance over my shoulder, my heart skips, and the car swerves. Slowing down to get a better look, I'm sure I'm seeing things, because I know I don't own a red sneaker, but there's one in my back seat.

And the red sneaker is attached to a leg.

And the leg is connected to a body.

And the body is partially hidden by the bags of clothes I'd thrown into the back seat.

I gasp, pulling into the rest stop I was just about to pass.

Elle. Elle is in my back seat.

The car comes to a stop, and I release the seat belt to get a better look. There's no mistaking—it's her. She's sleeping, sprawled out as though she belongs there, and I'm quite honestly terrified for her to wake up and realize she's miles from home. With me.

I slap the steering wheel and whisper-scream *"Shit"* into the universe. I'm torn between letting her sleep until we're too far to turn back and throttling her. Exiting the car, I open the back door and wiggle in beside her.

"Elle."

She grumbles.

"Elle." I nudge her gently on the leg, knocking one of the bags to the floor.

"Go away."

That's when I catch a whiff of the alcohol coming from her breath.

"Elle." This time I press a little harder. "It's Avery. Wake up."

She squirms, slowly crossing from sleep to a hazy awareness. "What do you want?"

"You're asleep," I say. "In the back of my car."

She pops up, startled, another bag rolling off her and onto the floor. Her puffy eyes blink from the sunlight, and she slowly surveys her surroundings. And as reality sets in and she sees the sign outside the window, "Kennedy Space Center Ahead," the confusion turns to something else. She rights herself just when one of the bags flops on its side, revealing my favorite purple panties.

"I think I'm going to—"

Springing into action, I open the car door. Elle's body slumps over the side, and I do what I know any parent would want me to do: I hold her hair back while she vomits partly on herself and on the parking lot.

"It's okay," I say. "Let it out."

She's gagging, and I empathize, knowing how awful it feels, though a rite of passage and necessary punishment. At thirty, I still can't stand to hear the words *Long Island iced tea*.

When she's done, I reach over the seat for my water bottle. "Here, take a sip."

Elle straightens, but not before glaring at me with what I've come to know as the look of utter disdain.

54

"Where the hell are we?" she asks.

I aim the bottle closer to her mouth, stuff the panties back inside the bag.

She pulls back, wrinkling her face with a snarl. "I don't share drinks with people."

People. "I'm the one who should be averse to sharing."

Begrudgingly, she takes the bottle and airdrops the remaining liquid into her mouth. There's vomit caked to her neck and the collar of her white T-shirt, so I hop out of the car in search of paper towels, because I'm quite sure Elle won't get them herself. But she surprises me, exiting the car, too, and we walk silently toward the restrooms.

Elle enters a stall, whacking the door as hard as she can. I use the unplanned interruption to go to the bathroom, and we meet at the sinks. This is not how I had planned my return home. Not with a stowaway and not with one I can't figure out. Her appearance also brings chaos to my perfectly timed driving schedule. Do I go back? Would Jude come to fetch her?

I finish washing my hands while Elle tries to clean her shirt with a brown paper napkin, but all it does is leave a much-darker smudge.

"You can't tell Daddy," she says.

We're having the conversation through the mirror, and I wad up a napkin and toss it through the opening beside the sink.

"I can't keep this from him, Elle."

"Yes, you can. Just drive me home, and I'll go to my room like nothing ever happened."

"Elle, you saw where we are. Cape Canaveral is fifteen minutes away."

She stares at her fingernails. They're almond shaped and covered with checkerboards, courtesy of her nail salon, Vanity Projects.

I show her my phone. "It's eight thirteen. If we turn around, Waze says we'll be home around twelve twenty."

She does the math. "We're *FOUR HOURS* from home?" Thankfully, the private-school education has paid for something. "What the hell, Avery? Where were you taking me? This is like kidnapping! I'm supposed to be flying to New York . . . away from all this . . . away from you!"

I'm not at all surprised by Elle's outburst. Her moods are tiny eruptions I've eventually come to predict. "I didn't do this, Elle."

She finishes attempting to clean her shirt and exits the bathroom as if she can exit from me, but she can't, and that's becoming more and more apparent, judging by the agitation pinned to her face.

She stops in front of the vending machine, and I get an insight into being her parent. "I don't have any money," she pouts, holding up a tube of lipstick, *my lipstick*, the only thing she brought with her. Which means I'm digging inside my purse for change. After feeding the machine the coins, she presses the button for a Red Bull with one hand and coats her lips in Rouge Coco with the other.

"You shouldn't," I say.

"But it's such a pretty color," she says.

"I'm talking about the Red Bull."

"Seriously, Avery, why would I listen to you?"

"Get water," I advise her. "Or Gatorade. You'll feel a lot better."

But she does what Elle does best, ignores me, and she flashes the Red Bull in my face as she walks past me, smacking her lips, without as much as a thank-you. I find another machine with snacks and buy some pretzels, knowing the salt will help. Despite her churlishness, she's still pale and sluggish.

When we arrive at the car, Elle tries to get in the back seat, and I give her the *I'm not your Uber driver* glare, so she unenthusiastically gets in beside me.

"I need to call your father."

Her hands cover her face, her voice muffled. "I can't believe this is happening to me."

I want to remind her that there are two of us in the pages of this thriller, but I stop myself, attempting a different approach. "You want to tell me how you ended up in my car?"

She settles back in the seat, legs and arms crossed. "Not really."

"I know you'll find this hard to believe, but I was once your age. I know how these things work."

"Oh my God, Avery. Are you really going to start with the *when I was your age* conversation?"

"Let me guess. You thought it would be cool to sneak out of the house . . . see your friends before leaving town . . . sneak a few drinks. But you forgot one thing. Your keys. Or maybe you couldn't find them because you were so drunk? Your dad always locks his car, but mine was open, so you camped out. Except you had no idea I was leaving town at the crack of dawn."

She refuses to look at me, choosing to stare out the window at the people strolling in and out of the rest stop.

"What I can't figure out is if that lipstick was the gift I left on your plate or the one that went missing last week."

Her foot taps steadily against the floor, causing her entire leg to shake. I'm not even sure she notices, because the rest of her is so intent on composure. She's wrestling with whether to answer. "I saw you and Daddy spooning. Ew. If that's what you're wondering."

So she snuck out after we'd fallen asleep, taking the lipstick I'd left for her. Somehow, that gives me some small satisfaction.

"You have to take me home," she hisses.

I'm not sure where this comes from, what soulless part of me reaches this decision, but I'm not turning back. Maybe it's how she's talking to me, crueler than usual, or because I'm the judge and she must face the consequences of her actions, but I pick up my phone and dial Jude.

When he answers, his voice is groggy with sleep, and the momentary valor gets tripped up in old worries. *This is somehow your fault.* And regrets. *You're not who I thought you were.* It's too late to hang up.

"Hey," he says, surprised to hear from me. "Everything all right?"

Elle opens her window and hangs her head out, munching loudly on the pretzels.

"I'm sorry to bother you. I've just . . . I've hit a little snag."

"Are you okay?" And his voice and its concern feel nice.

"It has a name. This snag." Then I breathe in deeply. "It begins with the letter *E*."

It doesn't take Jude long to figure it out, and I fill in the blanks. I half expect Elle to reach for the phone and start arguing, blaming me, but she's shoving pretzels down her throat, feigning interest.

Jude yells and swears, and it's better that Elle can't hear him. Even if driving her back was an option, she'd miss her flight to New York, and Jude would be on his way to his medical conference.

"She can't stay at home unsupervised," he argues. And before I mention Theresa, he's already arguing that's not an option. "No way."

"I can drop her at the Jacksonville airport," I offer. "She can meet her brothers in New York."

He's weighing possibilities, and I'm trying to be helpful, but we reach an impasse where neither of us speaks. That's when Jude comes up with an idea. "Hear me out. I know this is a lot to ask, especially in light of our situation, but maybe you can take her to Crystal with you?"

No. No. My stomach does a flip as I imagine Elle riding beside me, blaming me every single passing hour for her misery. "But Jacksonville's right here."

"She can fly out of Charlotte."

Elle brings her head back in the car, dropping the empty bag of pretzels between us, while my peaceful solitude detonates. "We're ten hours away, Jude."

That's when Elle starts shouting. "*You're* ten hours away. I'm not going anywhere near North Carolina."

I'm thinking: *How can you ask this of me? The girl wants nothing to do with me.*

"Maybe this is the punishment she needs," he says, echoing my earlier sentiment. "I know I shouldn't be asking this. It's a lot, and she got herself into this mess . . . but I don't want to make it too easy for her. If you take her to Crystal, she'll be forced to sit with her actions for a few hours. Then I'll send her bag with the boys, and she can meet them in New York."

A few hours is two or three. This is ten. My mind buzzes with all the ways in which this is a punishment for me, not just Elle.

"Put her on," he says.

I toss Elle the phone, and she stares at it like it's infected with *E. coli*. I want to tell her to hurry up, to move things along, because her little stunt has already put me behind schedule, but she continues to leer at me, not making a move. "Elle. Take the phone." Cautiously, she draws it into her hands, holding it far away from her ear.

It doesn't take long for Elle to begin making excuses and disagreeing. Swearing, too. Her defiance is effortless, sharp words that shoot from her tongue, leaving me feeling sorry for Jude. It's obvious when he tells her that she's joining me on my trip, because she suddenly shuts down and does the unthinkable. It's like slow motion, but there it goes, my cell phone, flying out the car window. And as though to prove her point, she rolls the window back up so that we can muse on what she's just done.

"No, you didn't." Deep, angry breaths fuel my response, and I clench the wheel. "You didn't just throw my phone out the window."

Elle is pouting—though at least she's not yelling anymore—and I jump out of the car to salvage what's left of it. Even with the case, there's a gash at the center of the glass. Shards loosen and fall to the pavement. The power is on—there's Jude's face, marking the conversation—but the phone is frozen. Stuck. Like us.

I count to five before speaking. "Elle, besides that being my personal property you just destroyed, it was our navigation."

"Your navigation."

She wasn't going to make this easy. "While you were doing all that sneaking around, did you happen to sneak your phone back from your father?"

She frowns, followed by her signature eye roll.

"Elle, if we're going to do this, at the very least, you need to acknowledge me when I talk to you."

"Your car doesn't come with navigation?" she asks, derision coating every syllable.

"No. It doesn't."

"Well, it's really not my problem you haven't made it into the twenty-first century."

It's pointless to argue with her, and I don't try because her insults sting. I start the car, slowly inching into the oncoming traffic. We'll have to stop at the nearest gas station for a map and a pay phone (do they still exist?) to let Jude know why he can't reach us.

One glance at Elle, and I know we have a long road ahead of us. It's useless to sugarcoat the adventure we're about to embark on. Two damaged women without any direction.

CHAPTER 10

Florida might be a painfully long and boring drive, but imagine being seated next to a cranky, hungover almost-sixteen-year-old who can't decide if she hates you or needs you. Elle and I don't speak; she's curled on her side, staring out the window, and eventually falls asleep. I steal glances at her from time to time, studying her expression, the peacefulness that belies her maddening disposition.

Two years isn't long to know someone, but I've spent enough time with Elle to witness her transformation from spunky thirteen-year-old to the willful child-woman sitting beside me. In her stillness, I empathize with her pain; I could almost give her a pass for being, at times, difficult or bratty. Adolescence is hard under the best of circumstances, but losing one's mother turned that awkwardness into stormy unpredictability. And Elle didn't have a big sister guiding her through life's pivotal moments. A house of boys wasn't the easiest place for a girl to bloom.

I'm reminded of a day Theresa called in sick, back when Jude and I were flirting around labels like *relationship* and *boyfriend*. My boss, Delilah Ford, a patient of Jude's, generously offered the kids access to the museum estate, and that afternoon, they showed up from school, racing from room to room until my shift ended.

In the beginning, the museum was a nuisance for Elle. A place she couldn't understand or appreciate, but then she stumbled upon the bedroom of every young girl's dreams. I was fixing the flower arrangements in the mansion when Elle whipped past me. "I'm hiding from the boys, Avery. Don't give me up."

It was a silly game of hide-and-seek, and Elle was on the brink, caught between innocence and arrogance, knowing everything and nothing. Her brown hair fell long down her back, the breezy look that made her appear older than her years.

The Cathay bedroom was a favorite of mine, too, its elegance drawn from chinoiserie, French for "Chinese-esque," a European style infused with Asian influence. The focal point was the dreamy canopy bed made of saffron-yellow silk, draped in layers of foam green and pale pink. The surrounding walls were decorated with whimsical painted landscapes and flowery silk.

Details. I had a habit of collecting them. Laying them out and spending inordinate amounts of time studying their individual parts. It served me well in avoiding other subjects. As I approached the bedroom that afternoon, paying no mind to Elle's game, I was astonished to find her having crossed over the rope and thrown herself across the bed's fine upholstery.

To the students there on a tour, Elle looked like part of the decor, a model posed on her side with her back to us, as though she belonged there. Delilah had fired other employees over less than this, so I dropped the flowers I was holding and hurried the kids along to the next room while I backtracked, careful not to step over the red velvet rope. "Elle, honey. What are you doing? Guests aren't allowed in here."

That's when I noticed the red stain on the back of her shorts, at the same time she sat up, wiping tears she didn't want me to see. "My mom and I were going to redo my room together."

She stood, having not a clue about the blood, and I was careful to be attentive and delicate while making sure there was no aftermath left on the bedspread. And when she crossed back over the rope, I placed an arm around her shoulder and she leaned into me, long enough for me to think that maybe this was something I could do, that maybe she'd grow to like me. Her brothers rounded the corner, yelling and giggling. "We found you, Elle! We found you!" But then Milo pointed at Elle's shorts, and someone laughed, and through the busy milieu, Delilah appeared.

Delilah's a mother of five. So when she saw Elle's backside, I didn't have a chance to intervene. Before the comforting words could leave my mouth, before I could assure Elle that all she was feeling was normal, Delilah took over, rendering me useless, forced to pick up the flowers I'd dropped one by one. It was Delilah who had eventually led Elle into the ladies' room. It was Delilah who had explained what had happened, what was about to happen, and what it all meant.

I knew she hadn't intended to make me feel inadequate, but she did. She later told me how a young girl needed her mother, and if absent, another mother, especially for that moment when she learned she's no longer a child but a young woman. Delilah pointed out that I lacked maternal instinct, the nurturing capabilities that only a mother knew. And while it stung, seeped into my core, I didn't argue with her generalization. I let her prattle on because somewhere deep inside, I already believed that to be true.

After that, I let Elle sneak inside the Cathay bedroom from time to time. It was the only thing I could give her—our lone private secret. It was wrong, and I could've gotten in trouble, but it was wrong for little girls to lose their mothers, for Elle to lose her special bedroom, to have to face a rite of passage with a stranger.

There was a dramatic shift in Elle's demeanor after she had her *Are You There God, It's Me Margaret?* moment. Jude and I had discussed it when we were alone, though who was I to offer an opinion? I was merely a glorified gardener, someone who shared fun facts about the earth and plants with his kids and let them play in the dirt.

Jude was a man of explanation and variables. Like his patients, no two diagnoses were ever the same. There was history and circumstance that influenced symptoms and treatment. What I saw as a surge of emotions flowing from Elle at precisely the same time she got her first period could easily be explained as a young, grieving girl who had just lost her mother.

But then her behavior worsened, becoming reckless and rebellious. She'd talk back, argue any subject; her grades began to slip. And when Jude found a joint in her dresser drawer after she'd arrived home from the beach with bloodshot eyes and a silly grin on her face, their home went from somber to explosive.

I didn't know how to react to Elle's indifference; the boys were slightly easier. They were rowdy and rambunctious—I could appeal to their innocence, latch on to their casual playfulness.

But Elle. She was an enigma to me. Her moods shifted like the wind. Surly and sarcastic one moment, then abruptly turning pleasant and mild. Some would call it emotional whiplash, how she lured me in with her full-toothed smile, only to bite me with her sharp tongue.

By the time we hit the tail end of Florida, Elle is alert, sober, and questioning how much longer. I toss her the atlas I bought when I filled up the car with gas and borrowed a stranger's cell phone. "We're crossing into Georgia," I point out, because I'm entirely unsure if she knows the location of the states.

She's eyeing the map, taking off her sneakers and stretching her long legs up on the dashboard. "Why didn't you fly? Why would you want to drive all this way? And why do you need a map to get to your own house?"

I'm wondering if her reproach—disguised as small talk—means we're capable of having a civilized conversation. And I quickly imagine us on a road trip, a modern-day *Thelma & Louise*, where we argue and bond over troubles and challenges, discovering a deeper will that connects us. On our make-believe trip, she'd tell me about her friends and maybe a boy, and I'd tell her about the trees and shrubs that line the highway, how the land will blossom—turn lush and green—as we inch closer to the mountains. But it's just that. Make-believe.

"I like driving," I say. "There's a freedom to it."

"Sure. Just rub it in, Avery."

Our pivotal moment evaporates as Elle's punishment flares up between us. Now wasn't the time to relish driving when Elle had her privilege taken away.

"I'm sorry. I forgot."

"Well, I didn't."

I realize the less I say, the more engrossed Elle becomes in the map. She traces a finger along the thin spaghetti lines that snake through each city. "What good are these maps if you can't look at them while you're driving?"

She had a point, and I wink at her. "That's what I have you for."

There's a small triumph when she buries her head in the pages and finds us the best route through South Carolina, and we're actually agreeing when Katy Perry's "I Kissed a Girl" comes on the radio.

She's mouthing the words, though I can feel her eyes boring into the side of my face. I wonder what she sees. Not the slight woman with strawberry blond hair and fair skin, the one with the fine lines forming around her eyes. Does she see an enemy? An adversary? Someone who's trying to replace her mother?

No doubt she spots the pimple on my chin, the kind that tend to crop up when I'm under stress. If she had her phone, I'm certain she'd snap a picture: My dad's gf has adult acne ☺ GROSS.

She's staring so intently, I have trouble concentrating. "What?" I finally ask.

"I don't know," she says. "I guess I never paid this much attention to you before." And then, "You should do keratin. It'll really make your hair smoother, get rid of that bird-nest thingy—"

"What thingy?"

"You know, that *thing* at the back of your head."

"No, Elle, I don't know." Which prompts me to reach for my hair with my free hand, feeling the messy bun I've twirled in a rubber band.

"With keratin, you just wake up and your hair is stick straight. You don't really even have to brush it."

I like the beachy feel to my hair.

Katy finishes singing, and Elle returns to the radio, changing the stations at a frenetic pace, the Coffee House channel not holding a chance. "I'm not some horrible person, Avery," she says. "Allison and Jenny said they'd be much worse if their mother was . . . whatever. But I can't expect you to understand."

Elle's not a child. I can't treat her like one. So I decide to tell her the truth. "I lost my mother, Elle."

She fidgets, and I can tell by the way she blinks her eyes and pulls her arms closer into her body that she wasn't expecting this.

"How come you never told me?" she asks.

I honestly don't have an answer. Maybe telling her was letting her in, and I was trying to keep her out. Besides, it's not like she ever asked. And what should have brought us closer, connected us, usually had the opposite effect. She promptly turns away and stares out the window, the large billboards passing by. And I continue. "She died when I was a baby. Six months old." I leave out how my big sister filled in, and then I lost her, too. Elle lets this sink in, the air in the car taking on a heaviness. "I never knew her . . . and I'm not comparing my loss to yours . . . I'd never do that, but don't say I don't understand. I know why you'd think drinking and smoking would help."

She gazes at me, probably running this information of mine through her brain's fickle teenage channels.

"*Everyone* does it, Avery. I was one of the last in my grade to try any of it."

"You're too young." And I'm careful to add, "You know how your father feels about that stuff. He loves you, and he worries."

"What about you, Avery?"

I feel her eyes on me, probing. "What about me?"

"How do you feel about me?"

I should be able to answer this question without hesitation, but instead I wrestle with conflicting feelings. I want to love her. I also want her to love me. But we've made it an art form, keeping each other distant.

"Elle, I know it's been difficult for you. For us. But I care about you. And I worry about you, too."

That's when a car pulls up alongside us with a boy in the window, holding up some sort of sign. I'm still blushing from telling her my feelings, a tiny disappointment creeping in at her lack of a response. But Elle's already moved on, intrigued by the boy, and soon I see her drop her legs to the floor.

"Did you see that?" she asks, not waiting for my response. "That kid's sign?"

I hadn't.

"It said, 'If driver stops short, you can break both legs.' I wonder how many people he shares that with." She seems genuinely excited about this. People helping people. People being kind. People caring about *her*. "That's so crazy," she says, "but it's probably freakishly true."

Miles later, we're deep inside South Carolina, and I'm thinking this isn't so terrible. Elle's handling the map, switching channels from Khalid to Coldplay, and we debate Selena Gomez versus Hailey Bieber. But then I hear sirens. My stomach drops, and though I haven't been speeding, I slow down. There's no single sound that makes a driver more religious than that of sirens. *Please just pass us.* But he doesn't. The dread shoots through my body, until there's no doubt: we're being pulled over.

The officer, gray haired with a Santa stomach, walks over to my window, and I already have my license and registration in hand. Before retrieving my information, he glances inside the car, homing in on Elle, who's sitting up weirdly straight, refusing to meet my eyes.

"Young lady," he says to her, not me, "is everything all right here?"

Elle's chewing on her bottom lip, turning it a deep red, and that's when I spot the back cover of the atlas. She's ripped it off, and it's folded in her fingers.

The officer returns to my information. "Is this your daughter, Miss Beckett?"

I clear my throat of unkind objections, shake my head, and grab the paper from Elle's fingers. Scribbled across the page in Rouge Coco: *HELP! I'VE BEEN KIDNAPPED!*

The anger rises in my throat, and it takes all my self-control to cram it down. The officer signals for me to get out of the car, and I glare at Elle as I open the door.

"I think there's been a bit of a misunderstanding, Officer." I'm fuming, but I manage a friendly calm. "She's my boyfriend's daughter."

"Ex-boyfriend," Elle shouts.

"It's complicated. We're taking a break."

Elle mumbles under her breath, but it's loud enough for us to hear over the cars racing by. "She said no when he asked her to marry him."

Officer Bob, that's what it says on his uniform, is beginning to lose his patience with us. "This makes for an exciting story, but can you get this ex-boyfriend of yours on the phone for me?"

Elle cowers in shame while I respond, "I wish I could, Officer." And it dawns on me that Elle's little stunt may raise more suspicion. "My phone broke." And then I turn in her direction and force a stiff smile. "Elle, do you think you might be able to tell this nice man that I didn't kidnap you?"

She stares at me with prideful vengeance, our earlier camaraderie stripped away.

"Young lady," he directs at Elle. "I'm going to have to ask you to get out of the car until we can come to some understanding."

There's no mistaking the tremor in my voice when I address Elle as she unbuckles her seat belt. "It's not funny. Tell him I didn't kidnap you."

Surrendering, Elle throws her arms up in the air.

"Whoa," Officer Bob says. "Keep your hands still and where I can see them."

She drops them into her lap and makes no move to exit the car. When she speaks, defeat laces her response. "I'm here willingly. Sort of."

Officer Bob is irritated. I'm sure he has more sinister people to stop, but then I catch the makings of a smile. Amusement. "You know, Miss—"

"Elle," I say, "Elle Masters." I'm pointing at his pad, where he's jotting something down. "That's two *l*s."

"Falsifying a report is against the law, Elle Masters."

She sinks into the seat. "I'm sorry for the trouble, Mr. Officer." She sulks. "I didn't mean it. I thought it was kind of funny."

"Wasn't funny, young lady. Kidnapping's a serious offense. We take it seriously. Where you two headed?"

"North Carolina," I say.

"New York," she replies.

He smiles, and I notice the sympathy in his light eyes. "I have a daughter about her age, Miss Beckett. But if you don't mind, I'll need to contact a legal guardian. You understand."

"Sure." But I wish he wouldn't. Not because there's anything to hide but because Jude is not going to appreciate yet another phone call. This time, from a cop.

I give him the number while Elle sinks even farther into her seat. She can bury herself deep into the cushion, but it's not going to change the outcome.

And maybe he takes pity on us, because when the call goes to voice mail, Officer Bob changes his mind and hangs up without leaving a message.

"I'll let it go this time. No more shenanigans." And lastly, "Good luck. I think y'all are going to need it."

When he's nothing but a dot in my rearview mirror and my knuckles hurt from gripping the steering wheel, my rage boils over. "What the hell were you thinking? How could you do something like that? I mean . . . I don't even know what I mean . . . but if you pull a stunt like that again, you'll be walking to North Carolina."

And then the strangest thing happens. Elle laughs, and instead of being annoyed, I laugh, too. And soon we're both belly laughing like a couple of hyenas, tears spilling down our cheeks, neither of us able to stop because it feels so darn good.

Shortly after our diversion, Elle withdraws again, attentive only to the map on her lap.

We stop for an early dinner at Shake Shack, and I go in to use the phone to give Jude our latest ETA. He informs me that because of a storm in New York, all flights in and out of the major airports are canceled. "Is it okay if she stays with you an extra day? She'll fly out first thing Tuesday morning."

Part of me wants to say no, but I tell him, "It's fine." Because I know I've already made so many mistakes, I just want to make it up to him.

Back on the road, we climb through North Carolina, and I try not to dwell on how Elle will respond to this change in plans, pointing out the mountain laurel and rhododendron as though we're at Vizcaya and she's wandering the grounds. Her presence eases my return, making it so that I can't harp on the old memories, miss what I had once loved so much. The conversation leads to a semi-interesting exchange

70

on symbolic meanings, how in late-nineteenth-century England, before cell phones, flowers were a means of communicating.

"Back then it wasn't proper to share one's personal feelings. Not like today."

"Is that why you're a gardener?" Elle asks, straight-faced, not missing a beat. "Because you're not good at expressing yourself?"

Concerned about the direction of the conversation, I keep the symbolism of impatiens—motherly love—to myself and let Elle take the lead. Natural surroundings have a way of changing people, and the beauty climbs inside her and erases some of her edginess. She can be funny when she lets her guard down, and without Jude, without the boys, she has my undivided attention, which she seems to enjoy. We touch on safe subjects. *Bubble Boy*, the show she starred in at school before summer break, and how she loves theater, the thrill of live performance.

The farther we drive from our old lives, stripping ourselves of our masks and shields, the better I come to understand how Elle and I are more similar than I thought. Hard to love, hard to give love. And though it isn't easy to admit, having her beside me is a necessary distraction, because as my hometown comes into view, an uneasiness wraps around me and squeezes.

Crystal shines as the afternoon sun bathes it in light. Flat land gives way to winding, mountainous terrain, and even Elle is rapt as she watches the expansive views unwind before her. First-timers are always astounded by the beauty.

I used to see it that way. Every vista awed me, but that was before the fire, before I saw burnt leaves and had touched flames.

There's the sandwich shop at the edge of town, where Oliver and I packed lunch before heading to the falls. And the road where he got a flat tire and we spent hours making out in his truck before help arrived.

And there's the turnoff to his house by the school. I wonder who lives there now.

"So what do you do in Crystal?" she asks, taking in the clapboard houses and the small-town, country setting, so different from everything she knows at home. "It looks boring."

"What are you basing that on?"

"Is there a mall?"

"It's not Miami, Elle, if that's what you're asking. But it has a lot to offer."

The memories inch closer. Here, I'd fallen in love and fallen apart. It's why I chose to drive for hours instead of flying. I needed time to cross into the past. To return to the place that had changed me in ways I could never undo. But now I'm here, and I'm feeling every emotion I hoped to forget.

CHAPTER 11

Elle asks me how much longer, and I return to the present. "Eight minutes."

I know. Oliver and I had timed it. The windy path descends to the carved wooden "Beckett Farm" sign. When I pull through the stone columns to the long gravel driveway, it's not quite evening, and the bright sun, along with the drop in temperature, tickles my skin. Towering trees line the road on each side as though they're welcoming us. The cicadas buzz while Elle watches the scenery unfold around her. I make a sharp turn toward the main house, a traditional two-story farmhouse with a wraparound covered porch and sweeping views.

Elle slowly exits the car, as though she's afraid to step on this strange new earth. She looks around, taking it all in, likely drawing comparisons but remaining mute.

"You grew up here?" she finally asks, unable to hide her disbelief. It's a modest home compared to the custom-built sanctuary Elle inhabits down south, but it's perched on one of the most beautiful stretches of land in Crystal. Backing up to the forest, there are miles and miles of terrain against a jaw-dropping cluster of mountain ranges.

"I did." And I'm surprised by how much pride I feel when I say it.

The property holds a deep history and charm, and I realize how much I've missed it. The white exterior and black shutters need a fresh coat of paint, but at least Willow's done a reasonable job tending to the landscaping—she hasn't killed anything.

Elle's studying her surroundings, and I convince myself that's a good sign, that she might be impressed with the magic of the sun slipping beyond the trees.

Then she jumps, swatting something in the air. "What the hell—"

"Stay still!"

"What is it?" She jerks back.

The tiny insect bursts with light, and Elle is, quite simply, astonished.

She follows the lightning bug's path, fascinated by the intermittent glow.

"How does it do that?"

"You've really never seen a firefly? Not even at your grandparents' house up north?"

She shakes her head, asking a second time, "How does it do that?"

I think back to all the fireflies that flew into my and Oliver's orbit, swirling around us, reminding us of miracles. Oliver would whisper in my ear, *It's love. It happens because of love.*

"It's a chemical reaction. Luciferin in the fly's abdomen mixes with oxygen, producing light." She eyes me curiously, so I go with a different version. "It's a mixture of cells and chemicals and oxygen in their bodies."

She smiles weakly, eyes trained on the fireflies as more appear to be circling around her.

"Cool," she says.

"Let's go inside," I tell her. "Your dad's probably wondering how we're doing. You'll see plenty of fireflies from the deck."

She doesn't argue. She breaks away from the luminous lights and even helps me retrieve my bags from the car.

"What time's my flight?" she asks for the fourth time.

Things are running so smoothly between us that I'm hesitant to tell her the latest snag in her travel plans. "About that, Elle."

She waits for me to go on as we reach the door. Then I change my mind. "You should call your dad and let him know we're here. He'll tell you everything."

Though we rarely locked the door up here, there was always a spare key beneath the potted peonies, and I reach around to find it. My senses overload with images of Willow and me picking the petals and lacing them through our hair. Remembering our laughter, I turn the knob and step through the threshold and back in time.

As I drop my bag to the floor, the house feels smaller, the furniture faded, the distressed wooden floors holding all our memories. Everywhere I look, there's a past I'd callously abandoned, and I feel a pang of what that had to feel like for the people I left behind.

I don't have to close my eyes to hear Willow screaming as we fought over the TV remote, wrestling ourselves onto one of the cowhide rugs, burying our bodies in the fuzzy fabric. And there's the lingering smell of fresh pine and balsam filling the air.

Here on the farm, our childhood had been simple and idyllic. We'd wake up to the sounds of roosters crowing and horses whinnying, with goats and cows grazing in the fenced-in pasture. Mornings, Dad would sit in his rocker on the front porch, sipping coffee, and we'd climb up on his lap, rubbing our cheeks against his tickly stubble. After school, Willow and I would spend hours chasing each other through the fields, each season bringing forth a new surprise. Summer's leafy fruits and vegetables; winter's dusting of snow, when we'd build snowmen and smash each other with snowballs; fall's stunning parade of color; and spring, my favorite time of year, planting seeds, watching our brood grow. I needled my father with questions about how it all worked. How seeds carried the promise of new life.

And when the sheep and cattle gave birth, I knew how badly I wanted to be a mother.

Moving a few steps farther into the country home, I see the table made of wood planks where we shared family meals. Willow and I'd experienced every emotion at that table, Dad nearby, sometimes joining in, other times refereeing. We'd laughed until apple cider shot through our noses, argued, pointed fingers when clothes went missing from our closets, played with our food when sad or unwell. Back then, Willow was a fixer of sorts. A modern-day Glinda, the good witch. She'd spend hours at the table, mixing spices and herbs, collecting crystals, believing that she had supernatural powers, that her crazy concoctions could heal the sick or neutralize threats.

And it was that meddling nature that led Willow to betray me in the worst possible way. And the rift between us took on a life of its own. Not even her witchery could bridge the gap.

"Avery." Elle's voice slices through my memories, drawing me back to the present.

"I'll show you to your room. There's a phone in there."

I lead her upstairs and down the narrow hall lined with family photos. Our footsteps echo against the cedar, and we're greeted by the squeaking sound of that one saggy spot on the floor near the end of the hallway. When we reach the room reserved for guests, I open the door for her to squeeze through. She makes no effort to hide her disappointment. The room is smaller than her one at home, with two wood-paneled twin beds made from trees that were grown on the property. All the rooms in the house have a theme, and this one is bears. Identical red duvets drape across the crisp white sheets, and several plaid pillows covered with hand-stitched bears are stacked along the headboards. There's a nightstand between the beds with a lamp that has two bears wrapped around the pedestal, and against the far wall, a dresser with a small TV. Like every room in the house, the adjacent window allows for generous views.

"I get it," she mumbles to herself, but loud enough for me to hear. "You're into bears."

"We can put you in the cow room."

She doesn't find my comment funny and heads toward the phone.

"I'll be back with some toiletries . . . and something for you to sleep in."

She doesn't say thank you, but she doesn't scream at me either. And before leaving her to make her call, I pick up the remote for the fan and set it to "ON."

"I don't need the fan," she says. "Can you just turn the A/C down?"

I brace myself for what is about to turn Elle apoplectic. "We don't have air here."

And before she pelts me with an offensive response, I quickly escape.

My room is diagonal to hers, and when I push through the door, I expect the memories to crash into me. And they do. Of being here when I was pregnant, in love with Oliver, a full life ahead of us. I'm caught off guard by the weight of it all. Taking a deep breath, I consider retracing my steps to Elle's room and grabbing the phone out of her hands. Jude would tell me what to do. He'd reassure me that I was okay.

I collapse on the bed with the yellow and blue plaid bedspread and throw pillows with ponies and stallions. There are framed pictures of horses on the walls and the same lamp as the guest room, but with a stand made of pewter horses. Over the years, there were noticeable changes to the space, modifications that reflected my childhood. I had filled it with my own personality, evidence of Oliver and me, but now most of that was gone.

I hear Elle. She's yelling so loudly, her voice bounces off the walls. I turn over on my side to make it go away, to make her go away, but all I hear is her fury over being "stuck in this dump for two nights. Without air-conditioning!"

That's when I see his words, and my heart stops.

AVERY BECKETT, YOU ARE BIGGER AND BRIGHTER THAN THE SUN.
OLIVER & AVERY TLF

After all these years, the inscription still overwhelms me, his messy handwriting blinding. There's no way to avoid it, to avoid us.

We were seventeen, impassioned by youth and desire. Oliver had scribed the message across the white wood wallpaper with a thick black Sharpie. My father had been enraged, screaming at us for disrespecting his home. Today, the permanence of Ollie's love makes me grateful and sad all at once.

I'd challenged my father when he charged into my room, ordering me to *fix* the wall, which would've meant stripping the wallpaper our mother had picked out.

"What? You don't believe we'll be together forever?"

Ignoring my casual dreaminess, he shot through the room with a sponge and some cleaning fluid that promised to neutralize stains, and I, indignant, stood in his way.

Summoning all my teenage melodrama, I'd yelled at him: "You can't erase us, Daddy!"

It hadn't occurred to anyone that Oliver and I wouldn't last forever, just as my dad probably hadn't thought about life without my mother. My obstinance brought forth something powerful in him. It was a battle of wills, a shouting match that concluded with my sister intervening, convincing my dad with some trope on young, foolish love. "We'll cover it with the horses," she said, pointing at the stack of pillows I'd outgrown and taken to leaving in a pile at the bottom of my closet.

"Couldn't he have written it somewhere else?" my father asked.

My dad liked my boyfriend, he was part of the family, but it didn't stop him from walking over to my cluttered desk and handing me a piece of lined paper. "Next time give him this. Tack it on your bulletin board for eternity."

"Fine," I said, knowing full well it wasn't. Willow had smirked in the corner because she understood. Oliver chose that spot for a reason, and it wouldn't have served me well to divulge to my old-fashioned father that it's where we'd lost our virginity. Where we'd bared our souls and bodies to one another.

We'd sneak inside when Willow was working, Dad tending to the fields, Oliver tending to me. We'd curl around each other in the bed, with the saying hovering close, having no way of knowing what we were in for. Oliver had written those words for the times he *couldn't* be with me. When I'd lie in bed, alone, in the dark, he'd remind me every single second that I was loved.

Dad didn't end up erasing the message that night, but he did blow out the candle beside my bed, sending a pleasant scent through the air that whisked me off to sleep. Today the memory forces me to roll over onto my stomach and bury my head in the pillow.

CHAPTER 12

After delivering a lifeless Quinn, I plunged into a deep despair, letting no one close. If I couldn't keep my child safe, what kind of monster was I?

The days immediately following were spent tending to the physical wound, where I watched the doctors remove the burnt tissue and cover the ankle with a skin graft. The emotional wound couldn't be treated with an ordinary dressing. When they released me to my father and Willow's care, I was a shell of my former self. Refusing contact with the outside world, I fought my sister's well-intentioned but pointless consolations and evaded my father's pitiful stare.

I had caused the fire.

I was to blame.

It was a regret I'd live with for the rest of my life.

And if I'd thought Oliver was going to be a source of shared grief and comfort, I was wrong about that, too.

I was pretty far gone. Barely eating, barely sleeping, staring out at the views that once gave me peace. I was dead inside.

In and out of fitful sleep, I could hear him blaming me. I could hear him screaming at me for not letting him blow out the candle. I screamed back. I apologized. I begged him for forgiveness. But how could Oliver ever forgive me?

He couldn't.

And I couldn't forgive myself either.

That's when Willow took things into her own hands, dialing the number of the psychiatrist they'd referred to us at the hospital.

And in that one phone call, my sister ruined everything.

Willow might have thought committing me to a facility after the accident was necessary, but all it did was destroy what was left of my relationships. With my family and with Oliver. I was holding on for dear life, and she had it in her head that I needed to start fresh. And after a three-week stay at Oak Haven, I returned home to find Oliver gone. His parents, too. And with nothing left for me there, I packed up my things and threw them into the car while she tried to stop me.

"Avery, please don't do this," she had begged.

"Don't tell me what to do," I said, tossing bags of clothes into the trunk. "You sent me away. What do you care?"

"Avery, you needed help. I did it because I love you." Her voice spiked, and she became hysterical. "Where are you going? You can't just leave!"

"I can, and you can't stop me."

"What about Dad?"

I had enough sense to know this would devastate him, but he'd understand when I explained that I had no choice, that leaving was my only option. And that's what I did, biting my lip to stop the tears, and nothing prepared me for the disappointment that crossed his face as I pulled away.

But I drove off.

I had no idea where I was going, only that I needed to get away, from Willow, from Crystal, from all the painful memories. There was no way to know this decision would land me hundreds of miles away, or span for years, but at the time, I wasn't thinking about any of that.

I was thinking of escaping, putting as much space between me and the pain as I could.

And when I'd settled in Miami and some of the anger subsided, Oliver found me, and we'd talk from time to time.

We were connected for life. And that's just the way it was.

I'm jostled from the memory by the sound of the front door slamming.

I wait patiently, my pulse picking up speed. I hear Willow before I see her. It's late, and her footsteps fill the house. I could always tell when she was near. My big sister, as petite as I, found ways to make herself noticed. She'd clunk into a room with thick wedges or cook by way of clanking pots and pans like cymbals. There was nothing soft-spoken about her. She was loud and made her presence known.

Five years separate us, but back then, Willow and I never let the age difference interfere with our closeness. Losing our mother created an alliance that transcended sisterly bonds. And like most siblings, there was a dominant one, the yin to the yang. Willow was laughter and personality, daring and bold. But she was also maternal, the person I turned to and the warm body I'd crawl beside when the nightmares came.

Our father relied upon her, too. She had dreams of going off to college and working in a big city, but caring for us and managing all aspects of our lives was paramount. And while she didn't have the same affection as I did for the get-your-hands-dirty farm life, she had a knack for the business side, which she assumed with ease. That's why she never left. Her loyalty to our father, and to me, took precedence. And when my life blew up, her arms spread even wider, though they couldn't repair the damage and, in the end, contributed to it.

If Willow is a sparkly firework, her collision with Elle in the hallway is a volcanic eruption of potty mouths. *Who the fuck are you? Well, who the fuck are you?* Whether or not they exchange names, I'm not sure, but I hear Elle offer up how she's my ex-boyfriend's daughter. "Trust me, I don't want to be here. I'm supposed to be in New York like a civilized person."

Willow's response is just what I'd expect from my sister. "Hope Dad is as charming as his offspring." As their faces appear in my doorway, I'm struck by the fact that this is how I'll reunite with my sister after all these years.

"Avery," she begins, a smile taking root. "You came."

Hearing my sister's voice returns me to childhood. And that's when the room begins to tilt. The way she says my name, it's laced with history and apology and perhaps a tinge of regret. The tension that spilled through the air moments ago recedes as two sets of eyes fix in my direction, two women who wholly confound me. Elle towers over Willow, her arms crossed defiantly, entirely uninterested in the reunion she's about to witness. Willow, on the other hand, is visibly shaken. Seeing me again as I'm seeing her, there's an arsenal of loaded feelings, ranging from joy to remorse. I take my time getting up, lingering for as long as I can.

"Avery," Willow repeats, whispering my name. This can't be easy for my sister, who has minimal self-restraint.

But Elle quickly interrupts. "If I'm stuck here until Tuesday, I need clothes, Avery. And a toothbrush."

Willow spins around, breaking our stare. "Whoever you are, could you just give us a minute?"

It's not what she says but how she says it that gets Elle's attention. She slinks out of the room. "Whatever."

Which leaves us alone. Willow and me.

Years have separated us. Time we'll never get back.

We're cautiously assessing each other, though a stony expression (mine) and damp eyes (hers) give us away. We've been mistaken as twins, but everything about me is richer in Willow. Her hair is a deeper strawberry blond, her eyes a milkier brown. Her laugh is silkier, her voice thicker. At thirty-five, she resembles a girl in her twenties, no sign that our being torn apart from each other had any dire effects. That's when I spot the diamond on her finger. And she sees me see the diamond, and a shadow of worry spreads across her face. Her other hand comes down over it so that I don't dare see that my sister has moved on, that my sister is getting a chance at happily ever after.

"I'm royally pissed at you, Avery, but shit, it's good to see you."

I should tell her that it's good to see her, too, but I stop myself. I hate her as much as I love her. There are miles between us, though it's only a couple of feet. Neither one of us dares draw closer. "I've missed you so much," she finally says.

Willow is also the more emotional of us. In addition to her weird little habits, like burning sage and brewing mystical tea, she thrives on discussing feelings and the whys of any given situation. That's the reason I had to cut her out of my life. As it was explained to me in one of the rare lucid moments after the fire, Willow was trying to do what she thought was best, but how could she know? I *had* what was best for me. Oliver. Quinn. Until it all blew up in my face. I refused to accept what she was saying. That Quinn was gone. That Oliver and I were through. And in that one phone call, she'd betrayed me.

"Can I hug you?" she asks.

I back away.

"No," she argues. "Don't do that. You have no idea what your leaving did to us."

I gulp down the emotions. "I know exactly . . ."

She eyes me solicitously. "You don't. You couldn't possibly . . ."

She mistakes my silence to mean she can come closer. The air between us crackles, and her thin arms wrap around mine, familiarity crawling up my nose. Willow. A hint of fresh cotton. Peaches. Our youth. And I slowly succumb, my body, hardened, now softening. Her tears collide with my skin, and the sensation is welcoming, frightening, too. She is my home, my earth, and I'm not sure how I let this go as far as I have. I want to pull away, I should pull away, but I also want to fall deeper. I want to close my eyes and collapse there in her arms. She would know what to do with the scary feelings; she'd protect me. She always knew how.

Until she tried to fix something she couldn't. That's when I pull away.

"Dad'll be happy to see you," she says, unable to take her eyes off me, afraid I might disappear.

"How is he?" I ask.

"He's okay. His blood pressure has been a bit high, so they're monitoring him. And he's been giving the staff a hard time." There's a hint of amusement in her voice. "You know Dad doesn't like to rely on anyone for anything. Helplessness isn't in his DNA."

I smile at the thought, familiar with my father's stubborn streak. This had to be playing on his last nerve.

"I'll go see him tonight."

She checks her watch, though I already know from the clock with the horse tails for hands that it's close to eight.

"It's late. Both of you need rest, and you can visit with him tomorrow." She lets a moment pass before adding, "You should know . . . he's fragile. This fall really got to him. He's been insistent about seeing you, talking to you. Didn't you get his calls this morning? We tried you . . . from his phone."

I let the reminder that I'd blocked her number go. "Elle threw my phone out the car window this morning. You wouldn't have been able to reach me."

"Lovely girl," she says.

I let out a deep sigh. "She has her moments."

"He's really missed you, Avery. It's been hard for him."

I envision my strong-willed father steering Georgie, his prized tractor, through the fields, yearning for the sounds of his girls singing "Thank God I'm a Country Girl" at the top of their lungs. I can't wrap my head around his being stuck in a hospital bed far from his land, but there's an accusation in what she's saying. I'd been blamed for many things, but I was not the cause of my father's decline. I may have shut Willow out, but not him. I'd kept the lines open, we'd spoken, he'd visited Miami twice, and I'd walked him around Vizcaya, where he, too, fell in love with the gardens and history.

Sure, he tried talking sense into me, tried luring me back home for a reconciliation. It wasn't so much my leaving that rocked him. When he buried our mother, it became his sole responsibility to teach us life's lessons, to ensure our safety. So when I'd left that candle lit, after he'd told me the dangers dozens of times, my father believed he had failed, too. And though he tried to put the pieces back together, to put me back together, he couldn't. Nobody could. And that's tough for any parent.

Elle reappears with a light tap at the door. "I'm sorry to interrupt the merry reunion, but I need to take a shower. Is there hot water?"

Willow abruptly turns. "What is with you and your attitude?"

I observe these two willful women, admiring the way in which Willow has complete freedom to stand up to Elle when I can't. "And how long are you gracing us with your presence?" she asks.

"Believe me, Willa—"

"Willow."

"Whatever. I never wanted to come here in the first place."

Scurrying past Willow's glare to keep this confrontation from escalating, I whisk Elle from the room. Motioning for the linen closet, I hand her two towels with bears on them. "Leave me your clothes to run through the wash, and I'll find you something of mine to sleep in. There's shampoo and soap in the shower."

She cringes. "I'm not using some stranger's soap, Avery. You don't even know how long it's been there."

I return to the linen closet and find new soap and shampoo. I'm sure the brand won't be good enough for her, but at least they haven't been touched by humans. Willow's watching, jaw agape at this exchange, and because I'm somewhat helpless and desperate, I silently implore her not to intervene.

With Elle situated behind the bathroom door, the water running, I search my suitcase for a change of clothes.

"I think we have some of our old Halloween costumes in the attic," Willow says. "The devil or witch might suit her."

I pick out a pair of leopard pajama pants and a matching tank.

"You don't understand her," I say.

"You don't seem to understand her either."

"She's angry. She lost her mother. Stuck on a road trip with her dad's ex is the last place she wants to be."

"You sure have changed. Now you're making excuses for blatant disrespect."

Irritated, I leave the room, dropping the clothes onto Elle's bed. When I return, Willow sits on my floor, yogi style, waiting for me to open up.

There's nothing zen about the loaded feelings between us, and I remember her driving me, against my will, to the facility far from home, far from Oliver. She tucks a strand of hair behind her ear and the diamond reappears, and this time she doesn't try to hide it.

Willow and I once talked about marrying best friends. We were in Dad's bed, out of breath from jumping up and down in one of our pillow fights, discussing a double wedding at the farm and honeymooning in Hawaii, which, for two farm girls, was the most romantic place on earth. But then I fell in love with Oliver while Willow assumed the role of pseudo-wife and mother, taking care of Dad and me while managing the farm.

We didn't end up meeting and marrying best friends, but at least one of us had the promise of a ring. After a massive search of the cabin's rubble, they never did find the diamond Oliver gave me.

When I don't initiate conversation, Willow searches the floor, and I notice my sister has a tiny sprouting of gray in her reddish blond hair.

The progression of time saddens me, our youthfulness beginning to fade. "I told Dad not to tell you," she says, looking down at the ring.

"It's fine," I tell her dryly. But it's not. I once had a ring and all that it promised. And I can't stand my selfishness.

"Cole?" It's not really a question. Those two had been dancing around each other for years.

The light in her eyes dims. "When you left, Cole was done with me, too."

I'm brought back to that morning, driving off the property, Cole on the side of the road.

"You'll have to meet Jackson," she says. And then she remembers Elle. "The Satan child said she belonged to your ex." She waits for me to answer. "That's good . . . I think . . . You're putting yourself out there—"

"I'm not talking about this with you, Willow," I say.

"You're still mad."

I don't answer.

"So being here doesn't mean you've changed your mind . . . about what happened?"

We lock eyes, and all the pent-up anger rises to the surface. "You had me committed, Willow."

She snaps back, as though I've slapped her. "I saved you!"

"You sent me away . . . That last shred of hope . . . you destroyed it."

"Avery." She reaches for my hand, but I snatch it away.

"Don't."

She gets up off the floor, seemingly about to flee, then turns back around. "Why'd you even bother coming?"

"I don't know. I'm sure it was a mistake."

There's no denying the small part of me that feels a tender relief at being home, but my anger toward her has numbed me for so long, it's difficult to let in.

"We're going to have to discuss it," she finally says. "We can't go on like this. We're sisters. We were best friends. And for what it's worth, this is killing our father."

And I'm sure she doesn't mean it, but her poor choice of words boils my blood. She's right. We were best friends, as close as any two sisters could be, and she should have come to me before she made the call to have me sent away. We could have talked about it. Instead, she'd blindsided me, barging into my room, my bag already packed. The decision was a breach of our trust, and I don't know how she expected me to forgive so easily.

"You hurt me, Willow. You, of all people—"

She comes closer. Our faces nearly touching. "I did everything for you your entire life. How could you think I'd ever want to hurt you?"

And before we can say anything more, she turns and storms out of my room.

CHAPTER 13

The atmosphere in the house simmers, and I close my door to avoid another eruption. When it feels quiet enough to venture out, I poke my head out into the hallway, relieved there's no sign of Willow, and check on Elle. She's showered and clothed in the pajamas I'd picked out, tucked in the bed farthest from the door.

Having her here in my childhood home feels strangely intimate. Willow had once said you never know someone until you travel with them, how they behave when away from the familiar. Seeing Elle like this, out of her comfort zone, I begin to understand.

"Are you sure you're not hungry?" I ask, because the last thing she ate was a Shake Shack burger hours ago.

"I'm fine."

"Don't you want to see the sunrise in the morning?" I motion toward the other bed.

"I don't sleep near doors or windows."

I hadn't recalled this behavior at home. And that's when I see that the window, which I'd opened earlier, is closed. "You may get hot."

"Good, then when someone climbs through your window, they'll get to you first."

I study her closely to see if this is another one of her jokes. It's not. And instead of finding her comment absurd and just plain rude, I ask, "Is this something that really worries you?"

"No," she answers. "Maybe." She's pulling on the comforter, positioning pillows and stuffed bears so that they form a wall around her. "It's no big deal."

But it is a big deal. Elle, with all her spunk, is afraid, and the vulnerability touches me. I know I should say something profound, not too deep, something that would make her feel better without drawing too much attention. But I don't. Instead, I take a seat on the opposite bed, then lie down, making myself comfortable while listening to her breathe. And I understand, as her breaths get even and I'm sure she's asleep, that being here is probably all she needs.

I doze off, and upon opening my eyes, it's well after midnight. Elle's sleeping soundly, and I tiptoe out of her room, shutting off the light. The house is dark and quiet, except for the melody of insects filtering through the open windows. Memories appear with each of my steps, and I avoid returning to my room, not quite ready for sleep, not ready for Oliver's words shouting from the wall. Instead, I venture downstairs.

Entering the kitchen, I open the drawer where Willow keeps the tea and chuckle because she's labeled each of the packets. *This is for constipation. This helps with insomnia.* I look for the one that helps with the dull ache inside, settling on *This will make you happy!* The citrusy flavor soothes, and I catch myself thinking about my sister's engagement. I'm sure hers went smoother than mine, this Jackson procuring a yes.

Unlatching the patio door and stepping outside, I take a seat on the chaise, inhaling the fresh air. Part of me wishes we could do it all over again, the part of me that gave in to Jude even when the rest of me pushed him away. A memory slithers through, one I'd held on to the tightest. It was early in our relationship, and we were relaxing in the backyard while the kids were visiting Mallory's parents in Tampa. He was reading a medical journal, and I was flipping through the pages

of one of the latest bestsellers that Reese Witherspoon had guaranteed
would stay with me long after the last page. I couldn't get beyond page
three because Jude was so close, his half-naked body interacting with
mine. At some point, he suggested paddleboarding.

Jude's home backs up to the bay, with a view almost as beautiful
as that at Vizcaya. On any given afternoon, there are boaters and Jet
Skis coasting across the open water. That afternoon, the winds were
mild, the bay smooth and flat. But about half a mile from the house,
the weather deteriorated, gray clouds gathered, and the temperature
dropped. Weather patterns were known to shift rapidly in Miami. A
perfect day could quickly turn to claps of thunder and violent lightning.

Before we knew it, the rain came tumbling down, battering the
water. Trying to paddle while balancing myself against the gusty waves,
I fell from the board, hitting my head against the fiberglass. There was
a painful thud before I dropped into the water. Oddly, I wasn't afraid.
When you've caused a senseless accident, you expect fate to intervene,
dole out your punishment. I had waited for something like this to happen for some time. I was only sorry Jude would have to witness it, carry
the burden. But I'd be lying if I didn't admit that there was a moment
when the water pulled me under, and I thought, *This is it. This is how it's
going to end.* And I gave in to it, letting the darkness wash away my sins.

Jude acted fast. He pulled me up, setting me down on top of the
board. I was breathless and cold, the rain slapping my chest and cheeks,
and he led us to shore, the other board left to drift out to sea. I assured
him I was all right, though there were doubts, always doubts. My head
throbbed, and all I wanted to do was close my eyes and sleep. At the
time, the weight of what I had carried pulled me deeper and deeper into
a fog. I couldn't be sure if it was the injury that weakened me when the
tide pulled me under or something else.

When we reached Jude's dock, the rain had stopped, and the sun
reappeared, erasing any proof of what we'd just endured. He bundled
me in a thick white towel, like I was wrapped in a cloud, whispering

"I'm right here" as he drove me to Mount Sinai's ER. There they administered several tests before admitting me into a room.

"Is this really necessary?" I asked after I was cleared. "I'm fine."

"You blacked out," he said. "One night. For observation."

My cheeks burned from the warmth of his attention, but mostly because I wondered if he saw the helplessness in my eyes, the way I slipped through the water effortlessly, like I was meant to be there. And it reminded me of the fire, of Oak Haven, Willow leading me through its awful doors.

But he wasn't Willow. And that wasn't Oak Haven. And having him save me felt like breathing fresh air. So when he teased, "I wouldn't mind observing you," that fresh air spread further inside, and our eyes met, neither of us able to look away.

"What I don't like . . ." But he stopped himself, the blue of his eyes revealing a familiar ache. "Forget it. It's nothing."

But I longed for him to say more, and he eventually did: "You scared me out there."

He held my stare, and I reached over and touched his face with my hand. "I'm okay, Jude."

Jude had saved me. Plucked me out of that water even when I wasn't sure I wanted to be saved. There was no other way to describe what happened that afternoon, other than two people who had known the power of loss, both understanding the fear and worry that go along with it.

At the feel of my touch, Jude's head dropped, and I stroked his salty hair with my fingers.

I was falling for this man. Literally, falling. He kept me going, his voice a trickle of hope I hadn't wanted to see. And I knew if there was no Oliver, no guilt and shame, I'd have dove headfirst in any water and swam right up to Jude. But there was something about that first love, and sending it up in flames, that kept me teetering along the edge.

From there, I gradually let him in, as much as I could, knowing the risk, believing the ruse would continue forever. Because once someone saves you, there's no turning back, even when you don't want to be saved.

I return to my room and curl into a ball, wrapping the covers around me.

Deep in sleep, I dream that I'm back at Vizcaya, and there's a wedding taking place in the gardens. The joyful couple faces each other beneath a canopy of bent trees, smiling into each other's eyes. The bride's beautiful, clad in ivory silk with a cathedral-length train. And when the grainy film becomes clearer, I recognize the woman's beaming face. It's me. And I'm crying.

The release feels natural, the tears, pent-up joy and sorrow, but then they become louder and louder, startling me awake. Propping myself up, I swipe at my eyes, but the tears aren't there. The sobbing is probably from Willow watching one of her Spanish novellas.

It's almost three in the morning, but now I'm awake and alert, hopping out of bed and tiptoeing down the hall. The cries aren't coming from Willow's room. They're coming from Elle's. At first, I knock lightly on the door, and when she doesn't respond, I open it a crack. The room is bathed in darkness, the only light from the moon streaming through the closed window. I can make out the pillows and bears surrounding her in her Fort Knox, and her feet are covered the way she likes them, but as I inch closer, I realize she's tossing and turning, lost in a dream, crying out.

"Elle." I nudge her gently. She turns on one cheek, the cries becoming louder. The moon catches her skin, and I notice the line of tears. I want to wipe them away, but I'm worried my touch will frighten her. So I sit beside her, lightly rubbing her back. The smell of coconut floats off her skin; her shirt is soaked in sweat.

Has she had these dreams before? Has she cried out, and nobody heard? Back home, her room is on the opposite end of the house from her dad's. Maybe Jude heard her and cared for her while I'd slept through it all. Because of that thought, I remain seated beside her, fatigued and concerned. And as though I'd willed it, her body begins to relax, her breaths evening out.

Here's a girl who's endured a terrible loss and hides it beneath her tough facade. Being in a strange home far away from her dad and brothers has to be a trigger, and a feeling comes over me, heartbreaking and hopeful. It's the memory of Quinn, and I'm imagining the songs we used to sing to my belly, songs meant to comfort her, familiarize her with our voices. I try to keep it at bay, the melody, but it's useless, and I hum the words so as not to wake her.

"It's going to be okay, Elle." It comes out a whisper and a promise. "I'm right here."

CHAPTER 14

The chirping outside my window rouses me awake, and it takes a moment to orient myself. I recognize the squawk of the northern mockingbird, and his high-pitched screech does little to quell the uneasiness stretching through my body.

I recall last night, sitting with Elle until the wee hours, long after her breathing returned to normal and the whimpering subsided. When I returned to my room, I imagined being a mother, and all the risks and responsibilities involved.

Jude and I never talked about having our own children. He already had three. But he knew I was of the age where some women fixated on their biological clocks. And still, whether it was intentional or not, future children were a subject we'd avoided. Now, it alarms me that in the early hours of morning, the idea became a flicker of light.

Slipping off the covers, I head toward the window and the long-range views of the mountains and fields. Today is overcast and gray.

Tucking my fears away, I march into the hallway, knocking directly into Elle. She's even prettier with sleep in her eyes and makeup-free, flawless skin. "Geezus, Avery. Watch where you're going."

I'm slightly taken aback by her cruelty, though I shouldn't be. The moment we shared last night was mine, not hers. My eyes follow her to the bathroom we're sharing, and I wait patiently for her to finish up.

"How'd you sleep?" I call out.

"Fine," she replies through the door, having absolutely zero recollection of my kindness. And then, "I need to get to a store today."

A rumbling inside Willow's room means she's heard us, and soon she and I are standing outside the door, crowding the hallway. "I'll take her," she offers. "You need to go see Dad."

"I can take her after."

I notice we're dressed in identical white T-shirts and black pajama bottoms, though neither of us acknowledges the coincidence.

"It's fine," she says. "It'll give us a chance to get acquainted."

One of the many facets of returning to your childhood home is reliving your adolescence and the nagging insecurities that come along with it. Imagining Willow and Elle alone together leaves me to wonder where the conversation will turn. Would they commiserate on their complicated relationships with me?

Elle appears, dewy and fresh, her dark hair pulled back in a ponytail, no signs of last night's grim episode.

"Get dressed," Willow announces. "I'm taking you to our favorite diner, and then we're going to get you a few things from the store."

Elle winces as though a truck just barreled into her, but she doesn't argue. In fact, I'm sensing she's afraid of my sister, which doesn't surprise me because my sister has this motherly, authoritative way about her, and it draws people in.

"It'll be nice to get to know each other, right, Ella?"

"Sure, Willa," Elle deadpans.

The house creaks with the sounds of three women circling around each other, careful not to get in each other's way. Elle is in the kitchen, dressed in her freshly cleaned outfit from the day before, when she asks what our plans are for the rest of the day. Willow explains how Crystal isn't Miami. "The nearest Target is fifty miles away." Which confuses Elle.

"We're going to Target? For my stuff?"

Willow ignores the insult while Elle looks to me for some form of validation. "It's one day," I remind her. Then, to avoid further protest, I hand her my credit card, and her eyes light up. "Don't go crazy," I tell her, quickly adding, "and Elle, there's a library there. Maybe you can get ahead on your research." There's a summer project to contend with. The students had to choose an influential leader from European history and create a newspaper around his or her life. The lead article would identify whether the individual was a hero or a tyrant. She chose Napoleon.

"The library?" she says with a laugh. "Do people really do that? The internet, Avery. Everything we need is on the internet."

It was a stupid suggestion, though I imagined it might give her something to focus on other than her complaints. And I don't want to read too much into it, but she said it. She said *we*.

A light drizzle dusts the mountain as I make the short drive to the hospital. After charging my phone overnight and praying for a small miracle, it's useless, the device is dead, which means I'll have to stop at Verizon on my way home to buy a new one.

It's been close to three years since I've seen my father. I know this because his last visit to Miami predated Jude. I'd had to back away, refuse his requests for future visits. At first, I chalked it up to my busy work schedule, and then it turned into heated arguments. He kept pushing for a reconciliation with Willow, and I refused.

When I find my father in his room, resting beside a man who shouts, *"Take cover—they're coming for us!"* every four minutes, I wonder how anyone can rehabilitate here. His right hand is bandaged and elevated, and I move in for a closer look. The fall may have battered him, but the last few years have aged him, and I feel the immediate pang of regret. Our father, solid and strong, appears tired, slightly worn. His hair is a shocking mess of white, eyebrows a bushy gray. His cheeks are sunken, spotted with purple blemishes and days' worth of growth.

"Dad," I whisper, my voice thready.

He slowly turns in my direction, his green eyes murky, no brightness implying he's pleased to see me.

I take a seat on the bed beside him. "Pop, it's me, Avery."

"Avery?"

"I came in from Florida to see you," I say, nervous about his condition. "How are you feeling?"

When he answers, the dullness feels as though he's talking to a stranger: "I'm hanging in there. How are you?"

With caution, I take his free hand in mine.

That's when he squints, as though he can't see me clearly, and then he says, "How's that granddaughter of mine?"

I'm not prepared for the mention of Quinn and search his eyes. "Dad?"

"How old is she now, honey?"

My heart beats loudly in my chest, making it difficult to speak.

"Quinn." He squeezes my hand. "She was such a beautiful little girl."

"Dad," I begin, but where to go from there? I never considered how Quinn's death may have affected him. Too caught up in my own misery, I didn't have much left for anyone else. But I see now how losing Quinn, and then me, took so much out of my father. And while I'm sure he's medicated and disoriented, his confusion merely confirms how much my father loved her, how he still mourned, and how I abandoned the people who were merely trying to love me.

His eyes open and close, and a nurse pops in to check his vitals. "How we doing, Jay?"

"He seems confused," I answer.

She's untangling some of the plastic lines pumping drugs into him, explaining how they're treating the pain along with a minor infection. "He's probably reacting to the Dilaudid."

Or the truth.

When she leaves, I study him while the man beside us belts out "God Bless America" as though auditioning for a Broadway musical.

Yet Dad sleeps. The changes in him over the last three years—the timeworn skin, the deep lines—are visible, and I wonder how much of it is due to the fall. Perhaps I'd missed the gradual decline from hero to aging adult, and this just saddens me all over again.

He flutters his eyelids.

"Daddy?"

It takes effort for him to turn in my direction, and when he does, his eyes momentarily pause.

"Quinn," he says it again.

I swallow. "It's me, Dad. Avery."

Click. That's how quickly things change. The man beside him croons the last line of the song, his arms dancing in the air, and my father returns.

His eyes widen, his gaze firmly on my face.

"Avery." It's a whisper of recognition.

Relief replaces the earlier worry. My father is here, smiling his generous smile, and it smooths away the deep lines in his cheeks.

"I'm here." And I drop myself into him, feeling his arms come around me.

"You're here."

I sit up. And that's when I see the tear slip down his cheek, all his happiness in the lone drop.

"Look how beautiful you are, Avery."

"Willow said you fell."

"That sister of yours . . . Can you hand me some water?"

I bring the cup to his mouth and hold it while he sips. "Everything's so darn dramatic with her."

I don't agree with him, though I should. "She's worried about you. So am I."

"She has me drinking her strange concoctions . . . rubbing ointments on my wrists."

That explains the flowery scent coming from his skin. "You smell nice," I tell him.

Dad's roommate wields an imaginary shotgun into the air, mouthing, *Pow! Pow! Pow!*

Dad barks back, "Hey, Patrick, can you knock it off while I talk to my daughter?"

No one's more surprised than I am that Patrick complies. "Sorry, Chief."

Which allows Dad to detail how Georgie whipped him into the air. "Like we were at some rodeo."

Mention of the faithful tractor he first took me up on when I was barely able to walk brings a string of fond memories to mind. Growing up, we'd ride side by side on Georgie, tending to the fields, the fresh smell of new growth (and manure) creeping up our noses. I was often my father's sidekick. Willow complained about the stench, the dust and the dirt that caked beneath her fingernails, while the cornfields and farmworkers became another source of comfort. As our father had taught us, the earth was a garden with countless treasures. It was where life began and ended.

"Pop," I begin. "Don't you think it's time to let someone else take over? Like Cole?"

Cole wasn't just the boy who crushed on Willow forever. Cole Manley was our foreman, a big brother of sorts, a steady fixture on the farm as long as I can remember.

He doesn't argue, because he has a different suggestion. "I was hoping you'd reconsider."

I back away, taking my hand along with me. "You know I can't."

It's a knee-jerk reaction, an automatic response to a terrible idea. Crystal would always be home, but I couldn't live there.

"Sure you can," my father argues, unable to understand how that dream got quashed in the fire. "You're here. You're not leaving again . . . are you?"

This is not confusion or the result of medication. Dad is clear about his intentions. The farm was always going to be mine, and for a split second, I imagine staying. I imagine immersing myself in the land that I love, with the people I loved, but then I stop. "I'll stay as long as I can, Pop."

"And that's it? You're just going to go back to that place again?"

"Vizcaya? I love it there. You liked it, too."

"This is your home, Avery Beckett. You belong here. It's time you come back. For good."

"Please, Dad." And the look of disappointment that passes across his face rattles me, so I agree to think about it, because there are things you say and promise to those you love, even when you know you can't see them through.

This seems to appease him, for now, and he sits back comfortably in the bed. But the idea settles not so comfortably within me, and I can't push it away.

Dad distracts me from my thoughts with details of the accident, how Cole found him, his hand pinned beneath one of Georgie's wheels.

"You could've gotten killed," I say.

And he looks as though he wants to say something more, but he stops himself. "I hate being stuck in this darn bed all day, and they're pumping too many drugs in me."

I don't disagree, but I have to trust what the doctors prescribe. Besides, the drugs may have him momentarily disoriented, but they also wipe his memory clean, and I'm sure he doesn't want to be reminded of Quinn again.

"It's temporary," I say apologetically, because it's trite and clichéd. *One day at a time* means no end in sight, only another tomorrow. There are no catchy phrases to make suffering go away.

"You'll be out of here soon, and I'll be at the house to help."

"I've missed riding with you," he says. "Your sister and I, we tried it a few times after you left. It just wasn't the same." His eyes drift but then quickly return. "She never loved the farm the way you did."

Seeing how upset this makes him, I promise him that I'll be here to go on one of our walks around the property. "Just the two of us."

"Have you met Jackson?" he asks. "You'll like this fellow your sister fancies. He's good for her."

I tell him I haven't, and we dance around the elephant in the room. Cole.

"How come you didn't tell me she had a boyfriend?"

He sighs, that cheerless expression returning. "I never know what to say to you, Avery . . . what will help or just hurt. Your sister's given up so much for this family, and I think now it's her turn."

Before I can offer my opinion, he drives the point home.

"You realize that, don't you, Avery? Willow's given up a lot."

"What's that supposed to mean?" I ask.

But he doesn't answer, and the conversation returns to the farm, normally the safest subject, though today it's cause for concern. Apparently, he's purchased additional land, adding acres to the property, and he wants me to come back. "Beckett's one of the largest providers in the area, serving some of the largest chains." And as he shares the details, his good hand comes over mine, and I want to be able to give him this, but I can't. I squeeze his hand back. It's frailer than I remembered, and though I'm happy to see the farm prosper and grow, it means he's been changing, too, and the years I've missed deeply sadden me.

"Never mind all that," he finally says. "Tell me, how are you doing?" The question is inevitable. You can't rip apart a family and mourn as deeply as I have without being asked. That's why Miami was an effort-less decision, a place where no one knew my secret history.

My father knew that I was broken just enough for Willow to have me committed to Oak Haven. He argued against it, but he didn't know all the details, the final straw that had Willow packing me up and throwing me into her car. Neither she nor I had ever shared the story of that day. It would have just upset him worse.

"I'm doing all right," I answer, unable to meet his eyes, while he follows it up with a flurry of queries, none relating to boyfriends, marriage, or children. It's a gaping hole we skip around. Sometimes the things people don't say hurt worse than the things they do. It's just the way of grief and loss. People think they're doing you a favor by avoiding the tougher subjects, but the silence only makes the absence bigger, deafening.

"Have you had a chance to talk to your sister?"

"We had words."

He shakes his head. "You two . . . I'll never understand. Two buds meant to grow side by side . . . but this thing . . ." His voice trails off before he can finish.

After our mother's death, Willow and I were all he had. The disso-lution of our close, loving relationship had to have wrecked him, aged him in the frail way I'm witnessing now.

"I'm sorry," I say, meaning it. "If there was a way to leave here without hurting you, I would've found it, but this was what I had to do. Everything here . . . it's just too hard . . . There are memories I want to forget. Need to forget."

"The leaving, that I understood, Avery. What you went through . . . no one should ever have to go through that. But you and your sister, the two of you could've figured out a way to work it out. You need each other. You always have. And I'm just afraid if you don't fix this with her . . . if you let it go on too long . . . well, you have to heal your first family before being happy in another."

This is not my father talking. "Who's gotten to you?" I ask playfully. "Or is that the drugs?"

"Just call it an old man's intuition. I'm worried about you, Avery."

"Don't be," I say. "I've got your blood running through my veins."

"I would've never left the farm," he says. "When I lost your mama, I stayed and took care of you girls."

His eyes lower when he thinks of her, and though I have his blood in me, I see how I didn't have his strength. Not at all.

He reaches over and smooths my hair with his hand. "Darn if you don't look just like her." I let the compliment sink in. My mother, from what I saw in pictures, was a remarkable woman. "She'd want you to be happy, Avery Beckett."

CHAPTER 15

The Verizon bag sits beside me on the front seat, the new phone fully charged, when I make the turn toward the farm. The clouds have passed, taking the rain along with them, the sun burning my eyes. My father crowds my mind for most of the drive back. And my sister's engagement has me curious and a bit unsettled. My hands need to dig, to cut, to shape something beautiful. When I pull up to the house, I know just where to start.

From an early age, I could tell I wasn't like most girls. I saw nothing wrong with carrying around a shovel instead of a pocketbook, paying no mind to the stinging blisters that accompanied a day of picking fruit. Most mornings, I rarely slipped on shoes, preferring to run through the knee-high fields in my bare feet. While Willow was trying on various shades of colorful lipsticks, I was often unkempt and untamed, rolling around in the hay in my faded overalls, catching spiders with my bare hands.

When it came to school, the strict schedule became an insult to my breeziness. I preferred flowers to fractions, plants to punctuation, and interacting with my classmates uncovered raging insecurities. When the kids enlisted me in conversation, I fumbled with the language, as though there was some secret code I wasn't privy to. I wasn't versed in nuances or small talk, not when I'd spent my free time with plants and animals that couldn't talk back. They were the only friends I needed. And I need them now.

Willow may have attempted to maintain the landscaping around the house, but it wasn't to my liking, and I enter the shed in search of my tools. My gloves are no longer nicely folded and washed in the drawer I left them in. Today they're thrown high on a shelf, balled up, worn and dirty. When I fit my fingers inside, I feel Willow's lingering presence. I don't bother changing. The T-shirt and jeans I wore to see my father are perfectly suitable for working outside, though I throw on some sunscreen and a wide-brimmed hat.

The flowers are dry, the bushes, too. I begin flushing them with water from the garden hose and ripping out the ones that can't be saved, dropping them in a large plastic bag. Taking out the shearing scissors, I trim the hedges, careful to keep their fullness. Willow's never been particularly good at maintaining order. She could be rushed and messy, evidenced by jagged, crooked lines. The seedlings she's planted in the spring are struggling in the summer heat. It's time to plant the azaleas and *Asclepias*.

A dragonfly flaps his wings, flying in circles, and I stop what I'm doing to admire his fluttering. He lands on a leaf, and I study his elongated body and transparent wings. I'm intent on keeping still, so as not to frighten him away. He's a he, I know, because of the bump beneath his abdomen.

He eventually scurries away, so I return to shearing and watering, and my mind drifts to Oliver and the other garden we'd started on the property. I feel my ex here, as though we never parted. It didn't matter that we were only teenagers back then. Our feelings were big. They had the power to live on forever.

Willow liked to tell people how she plucked Oliver from the earth for me.

The way she tells it, I was nearing my first birthday when Dad packed us up in his truck for a trip to the farmers' market. Hal, the owner, was short on blueberries, so Dad loaded up a few cartons and decided to make it an adventure. And an adventure it was. Willow, even though it might have been impossible for her to know these details at the age of five, rattled them off with a clarity that had everyone convinced otherwise.

My sister described me as a perfectly happy baby up until my mother died. Then I became colicky and headstrong. "And you kept throwing your bottle on the ground every time Daddy would shove it in your mouth. You clamped your eyes shut and hollered this blood-curdling scream that made the entire market stop what they were doing and stare. There was this one little boy, he was about your age. Squishy-baby age. Pink lips, a cap of sandy-blond hair, pale-brown eyes. He was playing on the grass with a big green ball, and every time we'd stroll you away from him, you'd shriek.

"Dad was exhausted, trying to get you to take the bottle, so I brought you over to the boy, and like some spell, you stopped crying. You were mesmerized. And wouldn't you know, you shoved that bottle in your mouth and began sucking until there wasn't a drop left. Your eyes never left that boy's face."

I used to love hearing this rendition of meeting Oliver, surrounded by rolling hills and a spray of trees. How even then, he knew how to calm me down, hold my attention. Everyone on the farm said the aneurysm that stole my mother from us when I was an infant had a pitiful side effect: me. My father said I cried and cried and cried because I missed my mother, but Willow said I was making my presence known in the world.

Willow claimed our meeting that day was destiny. *Her hand* in our destiny. And Cole would taunt her, chalking it up to blueberries. So when Willow looked it up in one of her weird books, she was delighted to read that blueberries symbolize eternal optimism. She'd smile. "The blueberries and stars aligned."

Sometimes I thought she made the whole story up. As exciting as it sounded, her claims of kismet and karma, the story felt overexaggerated. Ollie and I were simple. Our finding each other and falling in love was easy and without fuss. We were two people meant to be together, no matter how many thick clouds tried to get in our way. He'd say I was more interested in his green ball, but he was wrong. He reached inside me, and I reached back.

From that day forward, I don't remember a time in my life without Oliver by my side. With Willow and Cole, we became the fearsome foursome, always looking out for each other. But then June 13 arrived, and all the fates and blueberries in the world couldn't save us. And what Willow didn't know was that I also looked up blueberries. They meant a weakening of spirit, not always followed by a complete recovery.

A shiver passes through me, though my skin is warm from the sun. I drop the shears, survey my work, and swipe at my forehead.

I worry coming back was a mistake. It has me thinking about Oliver in ways that I shouldn't, and if I'm being really forthcoming, I worry Oliver will show up again and upend everything.

CHAPTER 16

By the time Elle and Willow return from Johnson City, I've convinced myself I have nothing to worry about, that there's no possibility Oliver's coming back. I'm tossing the garbage bags filled with dead flowers and weeds into the dumpster when I see them coming up the drive, dust kicking up in the air. But then they stop to watch the horses frolicking in the field, so I go inside and grab a drink, and that's when I decide to call Delilah.

"How much vacation time do I have left?"

"I'll have to look, but if it's your father . . . you can take as much time as you need, Avery. Summer's always slow around here."

I tell her he's okay and getting out of the hospital in a few days, but add, "I think I have to stay a little longer. He's going to need an extra set of hands."

She tells me not to worry, but I do worry. Because I really don't want to be here, but I don't want to be there either.

Minutes later, I see them exiting the car from where I'm sitting on the deck. I'm sipping one of Willow's teas, which I'm, surprisingly, enjoying. This one is honey lavender and promises to combat stress. Elle's hefting several Target bags, looking mildly pleased as she takes the steps up to the house. I recall my sister taking me shopping, sprinting through the store with the zest of a marathon runner. She had a knack for finding the best deals, the perfect accessory to liven up my dull wardrobe. And even though we are at odds with one another, I feel a rush of appreciation that she can be there for Elle, as she'd once been there for me.

Willow finds me lazing on a chair; she's skittish, as if she's interrupting, which has never been my sister's way. Normally, she'd pounce on the seat beside me, all but landing in my lap like an overeager puppy. Today, she chooses to stand.

"How was she?" I ask.

"Delightful."

I thank her for taking her. "Just let me know what I owe you."

Her eyes won't meet mine, and she refuses my offer. "You don't owe me anything, Avery." And the way she says it takes on a dual meaning. Because I owe her a lot.

"Tell the truth," I say. "How many people did she insult in the store?"

"Not a one." She drops down a few seats away. "She was surprisingly well-behaved. How's the tea?"

"It's good," I tell her, though its stress-reducing capabilities are challenged in her presence.

"So she behaved herself?"

"It's amazing how a little discipline"—and then she pauses—"and the presence of an adorable and sweaty young boy, can change the trajectory of . . . well . . . everything."

I can tell by the sparkle in her eyes she's up to no good.

"We ran into Cole's nephew Luke on our way out this morning. You know he helps out in the summer . . . maybe you don't . . . but he's been a fixture the last few years . . . a good kid. It was quite remarkable how polite that girl became in the presence of a boy saddling up his horse. He invited her to a small gathering at their house tonight."

A movement behind Willow catches my eye, and there's Elle, inching her way toward us. Her hair is tucked behind her ears, her lips slathered in pink. You'd have to be blind not to notice how pretty she is.

Willow gives me that mischievous look that marked our childhood.

"Oh no," I say. "You have no idea the trouble she's gotten herself into. The only reason she's here is because she snuck out, got drunk, and ended up in my car. I found her in my back seat by Cape Canaveral. A party is the last place she's going."

Cole's house sits on the opposite end of the farm. We'd spent hours traveling back and forth between the two. My sister shrugs. "If you have her under house arrest, she's not exactly leaving the property."

"Maybe you should keep out of it," I snap.

Elle draws nearer, and I can already see how her features have softened. I've grown accustomed to her various expressions: the "I want something from you," the "I can't stand you." Right now, what she wants is significant, her blue eyes big and pleading.

"I went to that library place," she begins, "like you asked." She stands over me until her head blocks the sun from my cheeks. "I took notes." She reaches into her pocket for a folded piece of paper and waves it in front of me.

"The answer's no," I say, though I'm mildly impressed.

"You don't even know what I'm going to ask," she says, pouting, folding the paper back into her pocket. "How come I do favors for you, but you can't reciprocate?"

"How is doing research on your assignment a favor for me?" I ask, annoyed. "Do you know how much it cost me to get a new phone today, Elle? No upgrade. No insurance. Four hundred dollars. And I never heard as much as an apology from you."

"I'm sorry, Avery, but that's really not my fault. You should have insurance . . . Everybody has phone insurance."

I let the insult go. "Did you learn anything new? Anything you can use for the project?"

"A shit ton," she grumbles. "And didn't you hear? We found Napoleon's million-dollar bowl hiding in plain sight in that Jacksonville, Tennessee, place, right in HomeGoods." She snaps her fingers in the air, so close I can feel the sarcasm glide off her fingers. "Poof. Magic."

I roll my eyes. "It's Johnson City."

"Whatever. It's all the same."

"Let's talk about it after dinner. You're going to need to make a decision so you can start the project, hero or tyrant."

"It's like the first day of my summer vacation, Avery. Chill."

"That's why she's drinking honey lavender," my sister says, making me sorry I left the wrapper on the table.

"Did you thank Willow for taking you, Elle?"

She looks to my sister. "I did. And I think you owe her an apology. How could you lose touch with her for all these years?"

My eyes land on Willow, and they're not kind. I'm struck by the unanimity of these two. Fourteen hours in the car, and I'm Elle's target, while less than half the time with my sister has them forming some weird pact.

"You told her?" I ask, panic rising.

"She didn't breathe a word," Elle replies. "And I tried. But this is all kind of fascinating, Avery. This other dimension to you."

My sister's remorse is there in her solemn eyes. She wrongly assumed I'd shared my history with Elle and her father. I imagine the awkwardness when she realized I'd kept it to myself.

"I think Elle and I reached a respectable understanding today," says my sister. "Haven't we, Elle?"

This isn't easy for Elle to admit, but she does, offering a smile.

"I'm still not letting you go to the party."

"Come on, Avery. It's not a party. What else am I gonna do tonight?"

"You can work on your paper, for starters."

A band of chalky white clouds floats across the sky, eclipsing the sun. I feel a tightening slither through me, and Willow sees it, too. "The best way to tame a city girl is to send her to a farm."

These are the kinds of decisions that frighten me. It's probably no big deal to let Elle travel less than a mile from the house. The Manleys are an all-American, honorable family—they play board games and volunteer at the homeless shelter. What would Jude want me to do? The thought of calling him to ask scares me, but it would be nice to hear his voice. "I have to ask your father. He grounded you, remember?"

"I know," she says, "but you'll put in a good word for me." And before I can respond with some witty comeback, she's marching toward the house, leaving me alone with my sister.

"How was Dad?" she asks.

Once, I could share anything with Willow. She was my secret keeper, the one I trusted above all others, but she lost that privilege when she betrayed me. So I don't tell her how Dad mentioned Quinn.

"He's getting old," I say. "It's tough to see."

"It's good you're here." A moment passes before she begins again. "Look, I wanted to tell you about the engagement. You'd blocked my phone calls. I figured if you wanted to know about my life, you'd let me in."

There was nothing easy about our estrangement. Even though I'd initiated it, there was an emptiness without my sister that nobody could fill. Those first few weeks, the urge to pick up the phone and cry to her, hear her comforting voice, was uncontrollable. And then I'd remember her abandoning me at the facility, and the anger would wipe out the loneliness. After a while, I got used to it. Used to her absence. And I'd pretend I didn't have a sister, until there came a time when I believed it.

"I always thought it would be Cole, you know? Sure, we played this game of cat and mouse, and he knew that you and Dad were my priority. I just thought . . . I don't know . . . I thought at some point, it would happen for us . . ."

I'm listening, but there's no mistaking the foreboding feeling that's creeping up on me.

"But it didn't. I guess he waited around long enough, until he couldn't wait any longer." She tries to meet my eyes. "I chose this life. I chose you."

I know she means this with all the love that will fit in her heart. My sister needed nothing more than to take care of us, but I have a strange suspicion that I had a hand in this. "I guess it was a good thing I left, so you could finally have a life."

"How can you say something like that?" Her voice is louder. "And why won't you look at me?"

I raise my eyes to hers, though it wouldn't make a difference; she's always been able to see through me. "You didn't choose me, Willow. You handed me off to strangers."

Elle reappears, dancing toward us, marking the end of this conversation. She tosses the cordless phone in my direction, and I'm just grateful she's not throwing it over the mountainside. "Daddy wants to talk to you, Avery."

Willow gets up, striding toward the house. Each stomp of her steps tells me she's pissed.

I sip the tea, washing away the ache stuck in my throat. Taking the phone in my hand, I feel a tiny jolt.

"Jude."

"Avery."

It's one single word, but the way he says it, I know he feels the same.

I get up off the chair and walk toward the wooden railing, holding the phone close to my ear.

"You okay?" he asks.

That could mean a host of things. Am I okay without him? I'm not. Am I scared I might lose it again? A little. And we dance around the pleasantries, though the charged silence suggests a longing that's hard to miss.

Jude's at a conference, so I'm careful not to keep him too long or disturb him with more to worry about. Maybe it's because of that, or because I want Elle to like me, but I find myself convincing him that it'll be fine for her to go to a small gathering. "It's our foreman. They live on the property. Cole's like family." Or might have been had I not intervened. And before I've even finished explaining, I can tell what he's thinking. Not about letting Elle go, but about how much of my life is a mystery to him. And when he answers, the distance flattens his voice.

"I want her home by nine," he says. "She has an early flight."

"That won't be a problem. I promise."

And I suddenly feel worthy of trust, of not mucking up someone's life.

Before we hang up, he adds, "Thanks, Avery." The appreciation is there, though it can't erase what I've done. I miss him. I want to tell him I love him. And I want to show him the farm, walk him through the pasture in the dark of night and have him kiss me under the moonlight.

So as not to confuse myself, or him, any further, I say goodbye, then return to Elle, who's waiting anxiously for his response. "Guess you're going to your first hoedown," I say. "Yeehaw!"

She makes her way in my direction, and I swear she starts to throw her arms around me before she remembers herself and backs up. "OMG. What am I going to wear?"

I remind her we're on a farm. But then Willow returns, mentioning the bags from Target, and now it all comes together. The two of them had already picked something out, and I can't be mad, even though I want to be. And if I won't let Willow be *my* big sister, she's going to assume that role for Elle. Before Elle skips back inside the house, I hear her *thank you*, and I take note of these glimmers of decency, where she is light and at ease. That's what happens to people when they visit the mountains, ground themselves in the earth. Simplicity spreads through the limbs, like stems bending in the wind, flowers scattering their petals. Even if she is conflicted about me, about being here, something about her is changing. No matter how she fights against it.

CHAPTER 17

Willow and I are seated in the Polaris, the farm's all-terrain vehicle, waiting for Elle to come out. "She's been in the bathroom for hours," I say. And when she steps out the front door, looking like a gorgeous flower child in jeans and a flowy white top, with pink and ivory petals strewn in her windblown hair, my sister and I smile. I recognize, at once, Rouge Coco on her lips.

When we arrive at Cole's, the big bear of a man with kind brown eyes lifts me off the ground and twirls me in the air. "I heard you were back," he whispers into my ear. "This place hasn't been the same without you."

"It's good to see you. I've missed you." And I may not have realized it, but being in his arms reminds me how much.

"This must be Elle," he says, dropping me on my feet. She seems nervous, but she's smiling, careful to use her manners.

An attractive woman approaches, blond, with legs dipped in cowboy boots. I don't recognize her, but Willow makes sure to scurry away, leading Elle outside to a group of kids, one of them strumming a guitar. Surprising no one but me, Cole introduces Skye as his wife, and I do my best to hide that surprise, fumbling with my greeting. A lot has changed since I left.

"You're married," I say.

"Yep." He wraps an arm around Skye's shoulder, pulling her close. Skye smiles up at him, clearly taken, but when Willow returns, I have enough sense to know things on the farm aren't as cozy as they'd once been. She hurries us out of there, barely saying goodbye, giving me no time to answer Cole when he asks how long I'll be staying.

Retreating to my room, I'm thinking about Cole and Willow, about the morning I left. The look on Cole's face. The phone vibrates, causing me to jump, and I see it's a text message from Jude.

> I know I shouldn't, but I miss you. Thanks for taking care of Elle.
> I hope you're taking care of you.

I start and stop no less than seventeen responses before settling on: I miss you, too.

Because I do. Missing him, loving him, those fundamental things haven't changed.

And I think about him being so far away in a lonely hotel room, and I wonder if he chooses the bed closest to the door or farthest from the window.

Willow pops her head in, asking if I'll join her outside for a drink. I'm not in the mood for a fight, but I go.

She pours each of us a glass of wine from Grandfather Winery, a pinot gris with a light, fruity flavor, and as we head out toward the deck, she tells me how she recently spent the day there. "Nicole asked about you."

I like Nicole, the owner. I remember she was one of the few people in town who didn't treat me like a pariah.

Willow takes the seat closest to the empty firepit while I sit on the opposite side in the rocker.

The sun creeps across the sky, and Willow fiddles with the thin silver necklace wrapped around her neck. "Tell me what happened with Elle's dad."

"Tell me about your fiancé."

This is what we used to do when we were kids, back when we'd climb into each other's beds, unbreakable.

Tell me about Oliver.

Tell me about Cole.

Back then, the names were familiar, but now we're all strangers, and everything is off, especially us. It saddens me to think I had to leave for her to find love. And it probably saddens her that I was once where she is. In love and ready to share my life with someone.

"You first," I say.

"Are you sure? Because we don't have to do this. Not if it's too difficult for you."

I set the glass on the table, and it makes a clinking sound. "Go ahead."

My sister glows when she tells me about this Jackson Prescott, and I'm left to wonder how it was for her all those years, taking care of others at the expense of her own happiness. They met at the barn. Nothing fanciful or romantic. No herbs or scented oils involved. He was the gangly young man delivering Amazon packages, and over time, he accepted her offers for soda and bottled water.

Soon they were meeting for coffee, which turned into dinner. By then, Willow was smitten. "I was so wrapped up in taking care of you, taking care of Dad, the business, I didn't take care of me." And she doesn't give me a chance to apologize, if that's what she's looking for. "Do you know what was in the first package he dropped off? You'll never believe it. The book *Mighty Attractor*. And don't shake your head. I can't make this up. 'How to manifest your dreams into reality.' Manifested that man right into my fucking life."

"You actually bought that book?"

"I did." She smiles. "And it worked."

"I'm happy for you," I tell her, our eyes meeting.

"I don't regret it, Avery. None of it. I loved being your big sister, caring for you as I know Mom would've wanted."

When she says it like that, I feel horribly sad. For her. For us. And I don't refuse it. I let it sit. Because there's an equally relieved part of me, knowing some good came from all this.

"I know you're wondering what happened with Cole. *Everyone* wonders what happened with Cole. I'm not really sure. That day he told me he loved me . . . I was too scared to say it back. And it shifted things. Our game of push and pull had run its course. I pushed too far, and I finally pushed him away." She pauses. "That's when I fell harder for him. You had left, and it took me a bit, but I showed up at his house, and he came to the door all messy and sexy, you know Cole, and I just—"

She drops her head and stares at her ring. "I guess it was too late. Something in him was different. I saw it right there in his eyes. I was too late . . . and then I heard footsteps. It was Skye. She was there with him, and I made up some excuse for my visit. Something so stupid I don't even remember. I came home and drowned myself in one of my concoctions that promised to mend a broken heart."

"Does that kind of tea really exist?"

She laughs. "Yes. It's called vodka."

I can barely face her. I'm calculating the timing, the guilt coursing through my veins. "You didn't tell him . . . You never tried to explain . . ."

"He was with Skye. He chose Skye. But I'll admit, I loved him. I'll always love him. You never forget your first—"

"You slept with Cole?"

"Duh, Avery. Our relationship . . . whatever you want to call it . . . wasn't conventional, but man, that boy was sexy as all hell. And I had needs, girl."

I let this sink in. "You didn't tell me."

"Do you remember how we used to go off to unload hay? Let's just say we unloaded a lot of hay."

My jaw drops a little.

"Sometimes I want to ask him what happened. It was like one minute"—she snaps—"everything changed. No closure. Don't get me wrong, I'm happy with Jackson. I love Jackson. But Cole . . . he'll always be the one that got away."

Her voice trails off, and I start to say something, but she talks over me. "He found Skye . . . and it happened for me when it was meant to happen."

But I don't believe that. I feel, somewhat, to blame.

"And I want you to meet Jackson. You have to meet him."

I sip at the wine and tell her I will.

And because of this, and because the wine is loosening me up and the farm brings forth a multitude of emotions, and because she's always been my person, I peel away the top layer. "Jude and I are taking a break."

"I need more than that. Who is he to you?"

Willow always gets right to the heart of any matter. Her brain isn't cluttered like mine. I don't know who Jude is to me concretely, but I know the way he makes me feel.

"There was this one day I mustered up the courage to go to a grief support group at the JCC . . . and that's where we met. We collided in the hall . . . and then I chickened out. I couldn't do it. I pretended I was there for yoga, the first of many stupid lies."

This is a delicate subject for us, and Willow pours herself another glass.

"No one there knows what I've done. About the fire."

"Not even Jude?"

"How could I tell them?"

"I don't know. Maybe because that's a part of who you are."

"That's just it. I don't want to be that person. He didn't need to know. Nobody needed to know. He might've never loved me. Not someone who could do what I did . . ."

"It's not all of you, Avery, but it explains so much. It's the part of you that makes you human."

"Yeah, well, it really doesn't matter anymore. He asked me to marry him . . . and now we're done." I don't continue, leaving her to wonder.

"I don't understand . . . What did you say?"

I catch her eyes in mine. "I didn't say anything."

"He loved you enough to propose," she says. "Isn't that worth something?"

But we both know she's being kind. A relationship could never survive this lack of transparency. I take another swig of wine while a breeze shakes the trees, rustling the leaves. "Proposals don't always mean possibility."

Willow seems to recognize her mistake, instinctively twisting the ring on her finger. I'd had a ring once, too, and the realization sinks in. The divide between us narrows and widens, and she takes another step. "None of us thought you'd ever get over him. It was a relief when Dad told me you were in a relationship."

And I'm relieved she doesn't say Oliver's name.

We inch around the sensitive subject when she says, "I know how difficult this must be for you, being back, so close to these awful memories." She wants to say more, come right out and ask the question she's burning to ask—*Do you still talk to Oliver?*—but she stops herself.

"I've been thinking about Mom a lot lately. With Dad being in the hospital . . . getting married," she continues. My sister's a lightweight. One sip of wine, and all her feelings pour out. I wait for her to make mention of one of her healing oils, how she's single-handedly saved Dad from further doom with turmeric, but she doesn't.

"When she died, you became mine. And I did everything I could. You know I did. And I hated what happened to you. She would've hated it, too."

Mention of our mother is never easy. I had no memories of her. But hearing Willow's concern, her willingness to give up so much of her life for me, tricks me into believing I knew my mother all along. And she is right here, sitting in front of me. Her love was just as fierce and strong, and for as many years. Except, when she sent me away, I didn't feel it at all.

"She was the reason you fell in love with the land. You were so happy out there."

When we were kids, Willow would talk about our mother all the time, often repeating the same stories over and over, about the day I was born, how excited she was to meet me, how she paraded me around the farm, greeting the horses and cattle and fields of flowers and crops as if they were friends. And they were.

"She had this deep laugh. And when she was pregnant with you, it became louder and more annoying. I'm sure anyone in earshot made fun of her, but it was pure joy, that laugh. We were so excited for your arrival. I would tell stories to her belly at night. To you. You were already my best friend."

It's difficult for me to identify with this strong attachment. A mother who loved me as much as mine did, whose one final show of that love was bringing me into the world, only to be snatched away. But Willow disagreed. "Mom's final act," she'd say whenever the subject came up, "was giving us each other to love."

There are pictures of our mother on the walls. A stranger, but without whom I would not exist. It was really Willow who triggered a feeling of motherly love in me. She was the one who filled every memory, provided a protective cocoon, so I didn't feel that other loss.

The crisp wine slides down my throat, and Willow continues talking. That's what she does best, and I have a sense she's making up for lost time. "All I wanted was a baby sister. And you'd let me dress you in pink, frilly dresses and do your hair and makeup."

"You're the reason I have an aversion to the color pink."

She casts her gaze downward. "I guess you only want to hold on to the bad stuff." And then her eyes plead with mine. "I'm sorry, A. I thought . . . I know I did it for the right reasons . . . I was just so scared for you. I didn't know what else to do."

I think about my behavior when they brought me home from the hospital. Sitting in the back seat of my father's truck, staring out the window, the farm alive and flourishing, while I was barren and wilting. I couldn't eat. I couldn't sleep. The only small comfort I found was in Oliver, the only one who understood the loss.

She reaches for my hand. "You know I did it because I love you . . . I did what I thought any mother would've done for her sick, grieving child."

There is where we disagree. And a slow-building resentment begins to spread, reminding me of the first night I slept in that cold, sterile room, far away from her, far away from everything safe and familiar.

Hearing her apology, the way she justifies the decision, only makes me angrier, sealing me off from any form of forgiveness. "You think our mom would've sent me away? Forced me to go to some hospital away from here, away from home?" What I should have said is that the only mother I'd ever known, the one who had assumed that job by default, had failed me. No one asked her to do it, but I expected her to help me through, squeeze the pain away, but she didn't.

Willow sinks into the cushion. "I did everything I possibly could, Avery. Dad was too distraught . . . It fell on me . . . I had to do what I thought was best. You say that Elle is tough to break, shielding herself from the world because of her scars, but you're just like her."

I feel the tiny cracks in my veneer. She's slowly breaking through.

"I don't expect you to understand this," she says. "I'd do it all over again." I turn away from her as she prattles on. "Except this time, I wouldn't make it so easy for you. I wouldn't let you go to Florida. I'd follow you, make it impossible for you to stay away."

"Stop it, Willow." My palm comes up, a shield between us. "I had to go. You, of all people, know that. There was nothing left for me here."

She doesn't immediately reply. She's carefully watching me.

When she breaks her silence, she says, "You had us. Me and Dad. And you had the farm and all the people here who care about you. They still do."

"Trust me, you wouldn't have wanted me." Reaching for the glass, I bring it to my lips, then stop. "When something like this happens to you and Jackson, show me how easily you wade through it. You can't make sense of it, Willow, because you never understood me and Oliver."

She intercepts the glass and sets it on the table, so I'm forced to look at her. "How can you say that? If anyone understood you and Ollie, it was me. Every bit of happiness he gave you, I felt. Everyone in this town wanted what the two of you had."

My voice is robotic, unfeeling, from years of practice. "I know you mean well, but nobody could've saved me, Willow. Not even you."

"It was an accident, Avery. You get that, right?"

Denial was Willow's signature, an overzealous need to banish fault in her baby sister. As young children, when I was caught red-handed eating the brownies baked for the sick neighbor, when I spilled the grape juice on the white bathroom rug, Willow found ways to defend me. So fierce was her loyalty, she offered excuses—my age, my losses— and her efforts lessened the impending punishment, but I'd learned to punish myself.

Willow was so often my savior, and even after what I'd done that horrible night, she continued with her excuses. Right up until the day I left, she found ways to bend the story so that I wasn't at fault, wasn't negligent, but the truth was staring me right in the eyes. "You have to stop with the stories, Willow. Stop defending me."

"I'll always defend you. That's what sisters do."

"That doesn't make it right. It doesn't take away what I did. You trying to avert blame . . . it's not helpful."

"You didn't mean to hurt anybody." She shakes her head. "When will you stop punishing yourself? Haven't you suffered long enough?"

When I speak, my voice feels shaky. "Respectfully, you have no idea . . . you have no idea how you would've dealt with this . . . how you would've been able to process . . ."

I only stop because Willow's eyes fill up with tears, and I *feel* her pain. She reaches for me, but I back away, and so she slowly gets up and makes her way back inside.

How can I forgive her when I haven't yet been able to forgive myself?

CHAPTER 18

I'm startled awake, surprised to find I've fallen asleep outside. There's someone leaning over me, and when my eyes focus, I see it's Elle, sipping from what's left in my glass.

Sitting up, I grab the drink from her hands. "Whoa, what do you think you're doing?"

"Hmm . . . one more sip."

"Not one more sip," I say.

"You're no fun, Avery."

"I'm not supposed to be fun, Elle."

"What's one sip? Kids in Europe drink gallons of wine with their parents."

"Go fetch your map. You'll see we're a few miles from Paris."

"Well, someone needs to change that stupid law."

"Wait," I begin. "How'd you get here? You didn't walk back by yourself, did you?"

"No. Luke walked me."

She plops down beside me, closer than usual. A lot closer. Our shoulders touch.

"Avery," she begins. "I'm in trouble. Serious trouble."

A rush of worry courses through me, and I close my eyes. "Please don't say that."

She starts and stops the next sentence multiple times. Elle, normally cool and confident, is nervous. And *her* nervousness makes *me* nervous.

"I have to ask you something."

"Does this involve the police?" I'm listening for sirens, waiting for the flash of red and blue.

"How do you feel about my staying here and skipping New York?"

Her head is now fully resting on my shoulder when I lean over, checking her eyes. A million dreadful thoughts have spun through my brain, but none could have predicted this. "I'm not following."

"Something happened tonight."

I sit up straighter. "Did somebody touch you? Did they hurt you?" My eyes do a once-over, searching for signs she's been compromised, and the need to protect her kicks in.

"No, nothing like that." A crack of relief splices the panic, though I'm still on edge. Elle rarely gets jittery—she's flame and fury in one tall wick, and it's hard to miss the way in which she twists her fingers, ambling around her next thought. "Maybe Daddy can delay my flight a few days?"

"Why would he want to do that?" This revelation is nothing short of shocking. Elle, who fought me like a bull to not come here, now wants to extend her trip?

"Can you just ask him?"

"You want to stay here? With me?"

"I know," she says, hiding her face in her hands. "I think I've gone mad. How could I want to stay here? With *you*. Without acai bowls or Sephora."

Her insults barely make a dent, or perhaps it's my pulse returning to a steadier pace. Then it clicks. This is about Luke. Nothing makes the mind crazier than good old-fashioned love. Elle has a five-minute crush, and the universe is forced into a reverse spin.

I'm privately amused, and stunned, when I tell her it's not up to me, but her father.

"I know, but can you put in that good word again?"

"How many nights are we talking about?"

"A few. I don't know. How long are you staying?"

The last part she whispers, but I hear it, raising my eyebrows before chuckling. "You hate it here," I remind her. "You said the people were . . . what'd you call them . . . not your 'tribe.'"

"They aren't. Most of them anyway. But Luke said I could help out on the farm—"

"Luke said . . . You've known this boy all of twelve minutes."

"You said it yourself," she argues. "The Manleys are family."

I soon come to learn that they'd already gone as far as to run this proposition by Cole, and wouldn't you know, he thought it was a great idea, seemingly because he had no idea of the circumstance that brought Elle to the farm in the first place.

"Lots of kids volunteer on the farm," she says.

"You're hardly the type . . ." And then I stop. This makes no sense. She makes no sense. But then I imagine Elle experiencing the farm as I once had. "What about your grandparents? They're expecting you. Won't they be disappointed?"

"Come on, Avery." She sits back, and I can feel her mood shifting. "New York is fun and all, way cooler than this place, if you know what I mean—"

"You've made that abundantly clear."

"But . . . the grandparents can be a bit of a drag and . . . What does it matter? I don't want to go."

"You couldn't wait to get to New York. You talked about it nonstop. For ten straight hours."

She smiles, and I see the faint spray of freckles across her cheeks. "Funny how things can change . . . but it's silly for me to pack up and leave again. Don't you think?"

"You're not exactly packing up."

"Come on, Avery, work with me here."

"I'm trying, Elle, but you're talking in circles."

"Fine"—her voice rises—"you want me to say it? I don't want to go. They said these things . . . like, stupid things . . . really stupid things . . . whatever."

"Who? Your grandparents?"

"Please just convince Daddy to let me stay. He trusts you." She quickly adds. "I guess."

And while I soak in the idea of Jude trusting me, I can't let her off the hook. This matters. "What kind of things, Elle?"

She licks her lips nervously and twirls the ends of her hair.

"Nothing."

My arm drapes along the back of the cushion, my fingers teetering close to her shoulders. "You know you can tell me anything."

She looks everywhere but at me.

"No, Avery. This isn't going to be our moment."

But I don't let the rebuff deter me. "Tell me what they said."

There's no way she can ignore my request or concern, so she shuffles in her seat until the back of her head rests against my palm.

She sighs. "It's no big deal. Just stuff." And then she adds, "Like how I can be difficult. And Dad's already been through so much since Mallory died. They think I make life harder for him."

Hearing this is not entirely surprising, but far worse for Elle as the recipient. My fingers lightly press against her skin. She stares at her fingernails when she continues. "They didn't say it to me. I heard them talking." She looks up from the colorful tips. "But what's the difference? They said it. That's what they think of me."

"I'm confused, though. You were ready to go there . . . What changed?"

I'm gently stroking her shoulders. They're stiff and filled with hurt. "Do you really want me to spell it out for you?"

She means Luke, so I play along, though it still couldn't have felt good to hear her grandparents talk about her. "I'm sorry you had to hear that."

"Yeah. Me too."

"But you know, you have been giving your father a hard time, and maybe you took what they were saying out of context? Maybe they're worried. About you. And about their son." But then she backs away, and my hand drops.

"Can't you just talk to him?"

Pleading wasn't in Elle's repertoire, though her will and her losses were chipping away at me. It was a ridiculous notion, Elle wanting to stay in Crystal, helping on the farm (laughable), but I sensed a change in her, as though she needed someone, needed us. And I wanted to be there for her. To prove to myself, to Jude, that I could. "Let me see what I can do."

Her face brightens as our eyes meet. "So *you're* okay with me staying?"

The idea sparked something in me; I wasn't sure what. Maybe it was Elle and me connecting on some deeper level. Maybe it was holding on to this thread with Jude. "Let me talk to your father. And Willow. My dad's coming home this week, and I can't have you getting into trouble or disturbing him."

"OMG, Avery, I promise. I swear." She presses her palms together to prove her point. "You won't even know I'm around."

"That's not exactly what I have in mind either, Elle. To you this might be just a farm, but to us it's a business. There are rules to follow, and you'll be expected to work."

"I know. I know. But think of it as a way for me to *learn* from my mistakes." This is when her flair for the dramatic kicks in. "Be more *responsible*."

"You're going to get dirty." I point at her fancy, done-up nails. "Those are going to have to go."

She hesitates but for only a second. "Done. Gone. Off with the nails."

"You can't wear fancy outfits. You have to be dressed to get messy."

"Target wardrobe, check."

"No insults."

"Target is the greatest store on earth."

She must really like this boy, because I see, in her face, remnants of the girl I used to be. Eager and willing to jump.

So when Jude and I get on the phone again, I find myself faced with a strange turn of events.

"This isn't what I expected," he says when I explain what Elle's up to. "And so out of character for her. A job. On a farm? Does she have any idea what it involves?"

"No. Maybe that's a good thing."

"I don't know, Avery. She should spend time with her grandparents. This thing with us . . . She requires supervision . . . stability . . . and you don't even know how long you're staying. How much time are we talking?"

I'd been thinking about this. Delilah already said to take as much time as I needed. Staying through the summer wasn't an impossibility—it was something I was strongly considering. I explain this to Jude. "And with my dad coming home and doing rehab . . . I think they need me here."

He's quiet, and I don't know if it's because he's upset by this or not. I know everything he's saying is valid, but I've already begun warming to the idea. "She'll be supervised. My sister. And Cole. He's the foreman. He'll whip her right into shape." And once I've made this decision, there's no turning back. "This isn't like Miami, Jude. There's no privilege or entitlement, at least not the kind she's used to. She'll be expected to get up with the sun and get down with the dirt, and sometimes worse. Just like everyone else. Think of it as boot camp."

"Now that I'd like to see," he says, his tone less doubtful, slowly coming around. "What about you, Avery? Is this what you want?"

I'd already been dishonest about so much. It clearly wasn't working to my advantage. "I think Crystal could be good for her. An actual job with responsibility and accountability . . . here in the mountains . . . It could be the best thing."

"You didn't answer my question. What about you?"

I'm worried that I won't be able to protect her, that I'll disappoint him and myself, but there's an equally scared part of me that doesn't want her to go. "Some of my best memories were on this land. I learned so many things . . . mostly about life. The idea of her being here . . . well, it gives me hope."

"I don't want to complicate things," he adds.

"I know. I don't want that either, but maybe it'll make things . . ." I stop myself from saying *better*, because there's no way of telling if this will be a drastic mistake or not. And although I can't believe I'm agreeing to any of this, somehow it feels right rolling off my tongue. "Being here will be good for her. For all of us. I'll make sure of it."

He's thinking this through, and I can see across the miles how his forehead creases with worry, how he tries to smooth it away. "She mentioned that you two are getting along nicely. She saw her first firefly." This makes me smile.

"I suppose no almost-sixteen-year-old wants to hang out with their grandparents all summer," he says. "Maybe you're right. Maybe some hard labor will be good for her . . . and being around nature will ground her."

"Will they be very disappointed?" I ask, not wanting to be the cause of a family squabble.

"Probably. But they'll get over it, and they'll have Milo and Henry to keep them entertained. But she needs to work on her project. Would you be able to stay on top of her?"

"Sure, that won't be a problem. Look, it's not as though Elle and I are strangers. We've had some"—I pause—"meaningful moments. She promised she'd stay out of trouble. I think she just might surprise us all."

"She'll need clothes," he says. "And her computer."

"Is that a yes?"

"It's not a no. But one screwup, and she's coming home."

At this, my heart bounces. Having Jude entrust me is one thing, but Elle's presence means she's my responsibility, and that comes with a whole other set of worries.

"I'll have everything shipped to Crystal when I get back. And Avery, I don't know if I've ever had a stranger breakup, but thanks for doing this."

CHAPTER 19

Time, I've learned, is a malleable concept. Time passes. Time flies. Time heals. Memories lie dormant and grab you when you least expect it. That's what being here does. And now that I've made the decision to stay, with Elle, I'm brought back to a time when the house was full and noisy with purpose. And I think it might be just what I need.

Over breakfast, on her first day, I explain the rules. She's inhaling a plate of avocado toast, but she nods when I state the obvious, "No mouthing off. Pay attention and be cautious; accidents can happen. Be respectful." And then, "No drinking, no pot smoking or pot gummies, and no more pranks involving kidnapping."

"That was funny," she says. "Admit it."

I remind her it wasn't.

That's when she narrows her eyes at me. "Your generation so easily forgets what it's like to be my age."

She couldn't be more wrong. I would've done just about anything to forget how happy I was at her age, the reminder of how adventurous I once was, and how quickly it all changed.

Willow joins us at the table, popping sliced bananas in her mouth. "You ready for shoveling shit and milking cows?" she says to Elle.

This gets Elle's attention, and she gives her best smile. "I can't wait. And speaking of work, what's my salary?"

Willow laughs. "Your salary?"

Without a trace of her usual humor, Elle replies, "I'm not shoveling shit for free, Willow."

We hadn't discussed pay, though all the kids who volunteered over the summer were given a small stipend. Willow decides to let Elle stew a little longer, doing a once-over at Elle's Target short shorts and tank top. "Let's see how the first week goes," Willow says, mixing her tea, the one she swears preserves memory. "You should wear those cute overalls we bought. They're perfect for work, and you'd actually look adorbs."

"Are you complimenting me, Willa?" Elle asks, flashing a smile.

"I think I am, Ella."

Together, they giggle, and the casual way in which Willow interacts with Elle fascinates me. Affection seems to come so easily to my sister. Not to mention her general friendliness, how she puts people at ease. I've never been wired like that. It's why I followed her everywhere when we were growing up, relying on her willing personality that made everyone a friend.

The three of us clunk down the stairs of the house and make our way on the dirt path toward the heart of Beckett Farm. The day is the kind worth bragging about: clear skies, lots of sunshine, and a mild breeze. Our land is like any other farm in the area, sweeping fields for the animals to graze, lines of crops, a nursery with fruits and vegetables, and a distressed, rusty-red barn. There are chicken coops, pigpens, and a newly renovated horse stable. It feels good to be back, strolling the fields that had raised us, our childhood knotted in the hills.

I watch Elle closely as she explores the property under a canopy of blue. It isn't the land she's used to, not the concrete jungle or the sophisticated swell of Miami, but there's something special about being here that can't be captured in mere words. The vastness of the land always excites me, as though I'm seeing it for the first time, too.

Willow wishes Elle luck as she breaks away from our trio and heads toward her office in the barn. In handling the business side of the farm, Willow's days are comprised of negotiating with suppliers and distributors, maintaining balance sheets, and handling the marketing. My sister's a force, and in large part, she's the reason the farm has been successful. The arrangement has also kept her close to our father as they share the day-to-day tasks.

Elle and I continue our stroll to the stables, where the volunteers have planned to meet. We pass the farmhands sprinkled around the fields, busying themselves with everything from weed management to picking fruit and caring for the animals. Bales of hay are stacked along the perimeter of the property, though I'll never look at them the same way again. I point out each individual crop and vegetable and where the cattle graze, the horses gallop, and the chickens are hatched. Her expression doesn't resemble any of the Elles I know. This one is of sheer terror. It crosses my mind that she doesn't understand what her impulsiveness has gotten her into, and I wait for her to reconsider. But she doesn't.

Halfway through our tour, Luke meets us, and the excursion becomes much more appealing with a handsome young boy leading the way. I can see Elle relax, smiling at Luke's tutorial, beginning to enjoy herself.

I hadn't realized how I missed the sprawling fields. The fragrance of fresh-cut grass, the sun patting the grounds, how free and young and alive it makes me feel.

But then I stop dead in my tracks when I see what's become of the flower garden.

Elle and Luke skip ahead, and I'm left to stare at the stretch of dirt and weeds, years of love and labor all but destroyed.

Furious, I catch up to them, and we walk the short distance to the stables, where the others are gathered. Elle asks me what's wrong, but I make light of it, surprised she noticed. She joins the group and appears to fit right in with the other kids. And when we say goodbye, I feel a pang, as though I've dropped my child at kindergarten. "Have a good day," I tell her. "Make me proud! Shovel hard, kid."

As soon as my legs will carry me, I am banging through the barn until I reach Willow's office. I barge in without knocking and find her behind the massive wooden desk that makes her look like she's straight out of Alice's wonderland. She's rifling through papers, poring through a stack of invoices, when I interrupt. "What did you do to my garden?"

She doesn't look up. She just keeps shuffling the papers.

"Willow, I know you hear me. What happened to it?"

When she raises her head, I notice her irritation at once.

"You want to know what happened to the garden?" she asks, trying to maintain her composure.

"That's what I said."

She sits back in the chair, studying me, with sounds of goats bleating in the pasture.

"You know something, Avery?" she responds in that tone she uses when she's arguing with a difficult client. "I've tried, I've really tried, but you haven't made this easy—"

"What happened to my garden?" I ask again.

She stands up and walks toward me. "What did you expect me to do?"

"I expected you to take care of it! Not let it . . . die."

"You left. You didn't think twice about this place, that garden, *your* garden. And now you waltz back in here, expecting everything to be as you left it? It's not. How could it? We had to go on. We had to make do without you. You think that was easy? You think we didn't have a hard time?" She pauses. "But you didn't care, did you? It's always about you, Avery. Poor Avery. I hate more than anyone what happened to you, but it's exhausting being blamed for everything."

My sister has never spoken to me this way before.

"There's nothing there but a pile of dirt," I scream. "And weeds. You know what that garden meant to me. Oliver and I planted every seed together. We watched them grow . . . for years. It was for Quinn. Damn you, Willow. Haven't you done enough?"

"Haven't I done enough?" She narrows her eyes, her voice taking on an eerie vengeance. "I think I have. *Done enough*. There's nothing I *haven't* done for you." She moves in closer, and I can see the whites of her eyes. Every line on her taut skin. "You want to come in here and argue over a garden that you abandoned, then go right ahead. You did this, Avery. Not me."

I back away, rage carrying me out of her office, the screen door slamming behind me. I stomp my feet, every step a punishment, and I don't stop until I reach the torn-up garden. Dropping to my knees, I sink to the ground, my fingers burying themselves in the dirt. In the absence of sunflowers and roses and rhododendron, I punch the barren earth, grabbing fistfuls in my hands and tossing them in the air.

I don't know how much time passes, but she eventually finds me there, Willow, and she sits beside me. She doesn't speak, just presses a hand against my shoulder. I fling her away, dirt landing on her white sneakers.

"I need to ask you something, Avery. Do you still talk to Oliver?"

I answer hastily. "No."

"Have you seen him since you left? In Florida? Did he . . . did he visit you?"

I shake my head no, and I sense she doesn't believe me.

"You swear?" she asks.

"I swear."

"Good. That's good."

But nothing about it feels good.

"You know," she continues, "you can go on and push me away, push everyone away, be angry, blame, throw dirt, but the people who love you won't give up. They'll be mad, maybe disappointed, but they'll stay. And they'll fight."

"I don't need you to fight for me," I say, shaking, dirt mixing with the streaks of tears falling down my face. "I just want you to leave me alone."

She waits for me to say more, catch my breath, and when I do neither, she says, "I just can't do that."

CHAPTER 20

That first night, Elle had literally crawled into the house, dirt caked to her body, sore and unrecognizable. I'd prepared her a bath with Willow's mineral salts while she described the hard labor, the stench, and Luke. "He's cute," she'd said, the compliment buried in exhaustion. "Don't you think?" She asked as though my opinion mattered. I agreed, and she didn't say more, though I believed in time she would.

We're sitting there in the bathroom on her third day when she says, "I don't know if I can do this." I've come to look forward to these evenings, with me perched on the toilet seat while Elle soaks beside me in the tub. Here, she was mostly calm, less temperamental. She didn't have to see my face when she talked either. She'd get in the tub so that I talked to the back of her head. I didn't mind, as long as we were communicating.

Her surrender doesn't come as a surprise. "Sure you can. You'll get used to it."

"Maybe I don't want to get used to it."

"It's only been a couple of days," I tell her. "By next week, you'll be in a groove, and you'll like it."

She laughs, but then it turns into a howl. "Don't be funny, Avery. It hurts. It's like torture, that place . . ."

"It's not that bad."

I hand her my phone like I've done the last three nights, and I listen to her repeat the same complaints to her father, and I assume he's offered her similar advice because after they hang up, she says, "You two sound like you're in cahoots."

Tonight, she tells me she really needs her own phone. "I need to communicate with people, Avery. This is, like, inhumane."

I try to explain to her that it's good for her to take a break from technology and that the animals and plants are better listeners.

What little strength she has, she uses to plead her case. "What if there's an emergency? What if I get flung from one of those horses? Or run over by a herd of sheep? Shouldn't I be reachable? What if I need you?"

She has never admitted to needing me before.

"You know I'm right," she continues. "You never know what could happen. Young girls get kidnapped, and horrible things happen to them. Wouldn't it be better for me to be tracked?"

"You're forgetting you made a joke about getting abducted." And I quickly remember her barricading herself in her room and this fixation she has on safety. "Elle, you're safe here."

"You can't promise me that. I bet every mother of a kidnapped girl said the same thing before some creepy man took her off into the woods and killed her."

I flinch at the images, though I catch her use of the term *mother*. Whether it's intentional or not, it's unexpected, and it stirs up all the emotions I'd been wading in. "I'll talk to Jude."

This seems to satisfy her. "My father's coming home tomorrow," I remind her.

While Elle was taming her inner farm animal, plans were being made to welcome my dad home. Cole and the guys installed a ramp at the front steps, and a railing was hitched to the wall in his bathroom. After the garden fiasco, my sister and I have barely spoken. She spends most nights at Jackson's, whom I haven't met, and we visit with Dad separately. On the rare occasion we're in the house at the same time, whether it's passing each other in the hallway or sitting at the same breakfast table, there's a rippling tension on the verge of erupting. Even Elle noticed.

"What's up with the two of you?" she had asked that very morning when Willow and I were continuing our silent treatment. "Ticktock. Ticktock. Someone's about to detonate."

And when neither of us answered, this insightful girl gave us the subtle reprimand, and reminder, we needed: "I would've done anything to have a sister."

Elle makes a splashing sound, and I get a whiff of eucalyptus. "You told me, like, ten times about your dad," she says.

I apologize. This thing with Willow has me on edge, and with Dad home, it'll be harder to pretend. "Did you see your clothes and computer came today?"

"Yes. And did you hear we're going fly-fishing?"

"Who?"

"Me. You. Willow."

I wasn't going anywhere with Willow, even if it was fly-fishing, something I love to do. But Elle didn't need to know that.

After dinner, I go for a walk. I love evening strolls when the sky turns into night, a spray of orange and purple. I bring my cell phone along and dial Jude. I know this isn't the break he had in mind, but we are connected, whether we like it or not. I begin the conversation by asking about Elle's phone. "She has a point about safety. Even if it's entirely self-serving. The farm's spacious. There's rarely crime in these parts, but I like knowing I can reach her, and she, me."

That's when Jude laughs. I've missed his laugh. "She's gotten to you. That's what she does. The Elle effect."

"Maybe." He's not wrong. Beneath the grouchy vitriol, there were sightings of a sensitive soul. I can't help but be reeled in. This odd arrangement has opened me to emotions I hadn't allowed myself to feel. Elle may be older than Quinn would be today, but I feel as though she's filling the void. I'd lost a daughter, but I was becoming someone's surrogate mother.

"I think I've given in on enough with her," he says. "I'm standing firm on the phone. She doesn't need it. Unplugging is good for her."

"You'll have to be the bearer of the bad news," I say. "Not a chance I want to be on the other end of that."

After he agrees, we switch over to FaceTime so that he can show me the fledgling vegetable garden. The plants are dry and wilted. "Have you had any rain down there?" I ask. "They need water, Jude. Regularly. And you should talk to them. They're used to me . . ." And I realize how silly that sounds, but he's not looking at me like I'm strange. He's looking at me like someone he loves, a stare that makes me shiver.

"What?" I say.

"I like watching you talk to the plants. And the flowers."

A flush spreads through my cheeks, I'm sure, and I wish it didn't feel so good. I wish our coming together were simpler, that I could have opened up, without risking his love.

"You know, Avery, this would be so much easier if I was angry at you. I understand not being ready for this commitment, but you haven't fully explained yourself. All this means is I'm confused."

I could tell him what I've done, the people I've loved and lost, how circumstances make it impossible for me to give myself to him completely. Then he'd have reason to hate me, push me away. He could justify this separation and more.

"I'm confused, too," I remind him.

There's an overlook with a small bench, and I take a seat, turning the phone so that he can experience the sky with me. "What do you think about me coming out there? I think I need to witness my daughter at work firsthand, and maybe we can see each other. Talk."

I swivel the phone back around to gauge his expression. There's a question there, but nothing gives him away more than his finger slowly rubbing his scar. That was his tell. When he was thinking about a patient, about Mallory, about us.

My eyes travel away from the screen and toward the range of mountains. "I would really love to see you. I would, but—"

"Is he still there?"

He doesn't let me finish. And when I return to him, there's accusation in his eyes.

Flustered, I respond. "Is who here?"

"The guy who broke your heart."

I hide the tremble in my voice. "I don't know what you're getting at."

"Don't you? Isn't that why you hold back so much? Why I know nothing about your life out there?"

"It's not that simple."

"But there's someone . . ."

"Jude . . ." I stop. He deserves the whole truth. He always has. Hurting him, withholding, was never part of the plan. But there's no easy way for me to respond to this, not when I've kept this secret for so long.

I'm staring at his lips, the blue of his collar hugging his neck, anything to avoid his eyes. "If relationships were easy, Avery, they probably wouldn't be worth saving."

"Do you really think it's a good idea to come out here?" I ask gingerly. Because if he does, I know I will have no choice but to tell him everything. There'd be no more hiding.

"I'm thinking about it."

It occurs to me, after we hang up and I'm contemplating his visit, that he said the same thing when he first told me he loved me. We were having dinner on Lincoln Road—Meat Market, one of his favorites—and the restaurant was noisy, packed with guests. They kept knocking into our table, and Jude was forced to shout when he asked me what I was in the mood for. I was feeling happy, flirtatious. I shouted, "You."

He smiled at me in that smooth Jude way. Effortless, but not overly confident.

Then he blurted, "I love you, Avery." And the words collided with David Gray and the laughter and noise. Everything froze, except my heart, which raced with heat.

I brushed it off, unprepared. "You can't love me! Not here. Not in this chaos."

"Isn't that love?" he asked. "Finding the calm in all the chaos?"

"You can't," I argued, and I could tell from his face that he thought I was being coy. He couldn't hear my heart pounding, and he couldn't see what I was holding back. All the things that might make him love me less.

"Well, I'm thinking about it," he said. "A lot."

And the restaurant didn't quiet down, but our table did. And there was chaos, sure, but there was Jude, eager and trusting, that effervescent calm, and I thought, *Tell him. Tell him right now. Tell him before he loves you longer and harder. Tell him before it's too late to go back. Too late to fix.* But I didn't. And here we are, this monumental thing still tearing us apart.

CHAPTER 21

On the morning my father's discharged from the hospital, it takes me and Cole, with my sister's play-by-play direction, to get him out of the car and into his own bed. I notice at once that his color has returned, the bruises healing; he appears to have more energy. With his room situated on the main floor, he doesn't have to worry about going up and down the stairs, and for the time being, because he doesn't know any better, he's thrilled to be home with his two girls under the same roof.

We surround him in his bed, fawning, making sure he's comfortable and unaware of our squabbling. Elle pops in, shyly introducing herself, and Dad says, "This skinny little thing is working on my farm?"

Elle shrinks into herself, turning bright red, no quick comeback.

"We need to fatten her up, girls." He's looking at me and Willow.

Cole starts to laugh, then changes his mind, so Willow intervenes. "Pop. Not everyone gets your sense of humor."

"Then we'll just have to break her in," he says, cracking a smile. "Make her feel part of the family."

Elle eventually flees from the room, and Dad hollers at the rest of us, "Who's taking care of my land while the likes of you are here having a party?" And relief washes through us that our father has returned home and back to himself.

As ordered, we file out of the room, Willow and Cole careful not to get too close. When Cole's out of sight, my sister rummages through the kitchen drawers, slamming them as hard as she can. "The vibes in this house are all off. You hate me. He hates me. I'm going to sage every last one of you."

I watch her, the gnawing guilt eating away at me. My feelings toward her are warranted, but this thing with Cole is different, and even though they're both happy now, I can't downplay my role in their rift.

Finding what she's looking for, she holds the sage in her hand before realizing she can't light it, not around me, so she waves it in the air, though without the embers, it's rendered useless. "Everything's wrong," she finally says, flinging the sage on the table. "All of it. Me. You. Cole. We're all so damaged. We just don't fit anymore."

She's right about some of that, and I feel to blame.

I was the one who'd pushed Cole away. I took his love for my sister and twisted it into knots. All my anger and madness, I couldn't unravel it. I wanted them to hurt like I had.

And now all I want to do is take it back.

I slip out the back door to be by myself. The disappointment I've caused, the ripple effect, weighs heavily on my shoulders, and I'm dying to talk to Oliver. He knew Cole. He understood Willow. But he knew me best. He'd make sense of what I've done.

Cole was out riding Dolly on the morning I decided to leave the farm. He saw me at the edge of the property, crying, foot on the gas. If only I hadn't hesitated, let him approach the car.

"You all right, Avery?" he asked, tugging on the horse's reins.

I didn't answer.

"Avery?" he asked again, Dolly's milky white tail swatting the air.

"I'm leaving, Cole. Get out of my way."

"Where you going?"

I turned, peering up at him, Dolly's rounded eyes questioning me, too. And I remembered what my sister had confessed to me. Cole had told her he loved her, and she'd been too scared to reciprocate.

That's when it spilled out of me. This ruthlessness toward Willow, unleashed on Cole. I told him he should leave, too. I told him my sister would never settle down. I said she was too focused on her career, the land. And then the kicker . . .

"There's a reason she didn't say it back, Cole. She doesn't love you. She'll never love you that way. Move on."

Cole peered into my eyes. A deep wound I'd never seen before. Perhaps it was my reflection; I couldn't be sure. But he pulled on the horse's reins and fled, and a spray of dirt sprung through the air as my tires screeched out of the drive.

I didn't look back.

And at the time, I didn't know how monstrous I'd been. How my words were a weapon that could inflict pain and quash dreams.

But I know now.

I hide in my room for much of the day, thinking about what I've done. I leave only to check on my father, and when he asks what's wrong—"It's there all over your face, honey"—I wave him off.

Later that night, I tell Oliver about Cole and Willow's estrangement, and he listens without an opinion.

"Please say something," I say. But he refuses. "Should I tell her? Or will this just make things worse?" He knows that when I get like this, I need to talk and talk, verbally process the situation. Sometimes he'll whisper for me to relax, slow down, unwilling to advise. In hindsight, I appreciate that about him. He wants me to figure things out on my own.

Before our goodbye, he says gently, "I told you it was going to be hard to go back."

And I lose it. Tears spring from my eyes, and I remember us spooning together at the cabin, Ollie rocking me, singing "Honey Bee." One minute his hands were warm and tender, and the next we were in the hospital. Baby Quinn entered the world, so soundless, so small. Ollie wasn't singing anymore. He was whispering, pleading, *It's going to be okay.* He was too distraught in the moment for blame. That came after.

CHAPTER 22

Those first mornings when Elle and Willow left for work and I was alone with my father were peaceful and without interruption. I'd sit with him until the physical therapist arrived, making sure he drank the fruity concoctions Willow left by his bed. We'd talk about the farm, mostly, the supply and conditions, and then when he was in therapy, I'd busy myself with cleaning the house and preparing lunch. Dad was a willing patient, eager to gain his strength back, and he made sure to practice his exercises as the therapist suggested.

On most days, we'd go for walks, me pushing him in his wheelchair while he pointed out problems or lodged complaints. He'd holler at the workers, and I'd try to calm him down, but he was nothing if not passionate about being the boss.

Today we're getting ready for our afternoon stroll when I notice the picture of him and my mother facedown on the end table. I set it upright, and he turns it back down.

"What's going on, Pop?"

"Your sister didn't tell you?"

His somber tone can only mean one thing. It must be the anniversary of the day our mother died. My father wasn't the kind to dwell or to give in to displays of emotion, so the date wasn't one etched in memory. Dad was tight-lipped about loss. The closest he ever came to describing any struggle was when he compared grief to planting flowers without light, crops without sufficient water. Deprivation, he called it.

Pop prided himself on his resiliency and providing a stable foundation for his girls. And because I rarely asked about her, this woman who birthed me, these conversations were few and far between. We skipped around them like the seasons.

But Willow knew. She always remembered. And I'm worried I've disappointed him.

"I'm sorry, Pop."

My father's wheeling himself out the door with his free hand, working his way down the ramp. A thick wall of clouds hides the sun, and our stroll turns gloomy. Like his mood. "Nothing to be sorry about, honey."

Most of the time, we take in the view, comfortable in our silence, but today feels like it should be different. "How did you do it? How did you manage us and the farm without her?"

"It wasn't easy, Avery. It wasn't easy at all."

It probably never occurred to me that my father might be sad. That he might wander into his empty room at night and cry himself to sleep. Because I didn't see it, it didn't happen. And since I didn't feel it, he couldn't experience it either.

"But you did it."

He reaches for my hand. "I refused to give in. I fought. I took all that love for your mother and I put it into you and your sister. I put it into the farm and creating new life, and it provided a strong foundation. If there's anything I taught you girls, it's that roots grow strong when they're cared for. This is what your mother wanted. And I lived and loved you girls the only way I knew how."

"I always felt your love. I just feel lost sometimes. Like I'm being punished for what happened."

My father inches closer when he speaks. "I felt lost, too, honey. Maybe I should've shown you that it's okay to grieve. That it's okay to trust again. I'm not sure I was the best role model."

"You were a great father."

"Your sister deserves a lot of the credit."

Willow, by birth order, became the maternal fixture in my life. She was the one I went to when I skinned my knee riding my bike down a steep hill, the one who responded to the peach fuzz on my upper lip and the thin T-shirts that revealed I was on the verge of becoming a woman.

Dad left these delicate aspects of parenting to her. And she excelled at them. She was constant in her nurturing, while Dad was the stabilizer, doting and playful. He was famous for his piggyback rides and spooky ghost stories before bed. He taught us to be fearless and proud, feminine, yet tough.

"You taught me to be strong," I remind him.

"That's what you think that was?" he says. "That's just it, Avery. You never saw me suffer. You needed to see those tears, watch me pick myself up. And I'm ashamed I never really introduced you to your mother."

"But I never felt alone."

I'd crawled into Willow's bed almost every night. It could've been a bad dream or the sounds of the gusty winds outside the window. She was the one I chose over all the others. She was the only one I needed.

My dad continues, even though it's clearly difficult for him. "Being strong . . . it doesn't always mean being tough. It means letting those terrible feelings in, not pushing them away. It's letting yourself feel all of it." He takes in a sharp breath. "But this thing with your sister . . ."

I stop him. "Willow and I will figure things out. Just give us a little time."

"No one's cared for you more than her."

Hearing him say it like that doesn't make me feel good. I recognize how Willow gave up a lot for me, how she ensured I never missed out on anything, that I was always cared for. There was the time she missed a neighborhood party because I got poison ivy, and she sat with me while I bathed in oatmeal she'd infused with chamomile. And the time she and Cole were supposed to go for a picnic hike at Boone Fork Trail, but I'd lost my first tooth, and she made me a fairy party instead.

"Your sister never begrudged you, Avery. Not once. You had the boyfriend, the attention of the farmworkers, the little sister to all. But you single-handedly gave her a happiness no one and nothing else could. I told her you'd be starting a life with Oliver and moving on, and she'd need to do the same. But she was content. Stubborn, I guess."

My heart hurts for my sister in a way I've never felt before.

"Now she's moved on, and you, my little angel, you're the one who's not living. You're the one who's holding back."

We stop in front of the pasture, and I spy Elle brushing Seamus, the palomino. "So that's what this is about."

He tilts his head to the side, and the concern is hard to miss.

"What happened with her father? And why are you babysitting his daughter?"

"Don't worry about me, Pop. Today's your day to remember Mom."

"I remember her every day," he says.

"You seemed happy with him in Florida. I heard it in your voice when we spoke."

I dig my fingers inside the pockets of my sweatshirt. "Was I?" He narrows his eyes on mine. "Could I really be happy when he knew nothing about me?" And that's when I confess that I never told Jude about the fire.

"Oh, honey . . . why would you keep that from him?"

The sheep are bleating, but I'm certain he can hear the knocking of my heart. "You know why." I face my dear, sweet father when I utter my confession. "Once he finds out what I did . . . what I'm capable of . . . how could he ever love someone like me?"

He tries to get up from the chair, but I stop him, stooping down instead to meet his gaze. He cups my face in both hands, the bandage scratching my skin, and I sink into his familiar touch. That's when it starts to drizzle. And the rain mixes with my tears.

"You have to trust him."

"I know, but I don't want to hurt him either. And I don't want to hurt myself. I can't go through that again."

My father's face crumples, and he can't hide his sadness.

And just as quickly as the rain appeared, it disappears, replaced by the sun.

We turn back toward the house. I'm pushing, and my dad is silent until we reach the ramp. "See how quickly things change, Avery? You need to grab sunshine when you can. The real tragedy is living the rest of your life in the dark."

CHAPTER 23

Willow and I are washing and drying the dishes, and I'm thinking about what my father said. I'm imagining his loss, all the days he mourned in silence.

Being here among the rolling hills, I can feel my own grief slowly beginning to thaw out. I recognize what my sister gave up for me, the sacrifices she made. And I feel awful about Cole.

When we're almost done, she tells me that tomorrow's field-trip day, and they need all hands on deck. This is her way of telling me, not asking, that I'm expected to be there.

"I love field-trip day."

"Always the farm girl. Head in the clouds. Off on the yonder."

"What about Dad?" I ask.

"I booked back-to-back therapy, so he'll have a full day."

Of course she did.

"And one more thing. Jackson's coming for dinner. It's time for you to meet him, whether you want to or not."

I always enjoy field-trip days. A few times over the summer, a handful of local day camps would visit the farm for a day of on-site activities and immersion. The children learn about food sources, how to care for the calves and chicks, harvesting vegetables, and planting new seeds. It's a hands-on, interactive afternoon merging education with fun.

Most of the time, the kids are fascinated by the animals, though the occasional camper turns out to be skittish. Those were the kids I'd gravitate toward, believing it was up to me to show them the magic. The day was always filled with rewards, but none greater than watching an otherwise nervous child cradle a chick in her hands, brush the length of one of our ponies.

A few of us are standing by the "Welcome" sign when the old yellow school bus chugs up the dirt path and comes to a halt. I board, sharing greetings with the excited faces. I hadn't done a tour, not since the accident, and I begin discussing the land I love when my sister takes over, talking over me, correcting my mistakes, because, as she's quick to point out, a lot has changed in the last seven years.

The kids are rapt when Willow tells them what we have planned for them today. There's ooh-ing and aah-ing, and one boy shouts, "Pigs! I want to play with the pigs."

Elle and Luke are there, along with a handful of staff, and they welcome the children, breaking them up into groups. Watching Elle in this environment brightens my mood. Her skin is golden from hours in the sun, and I notice how she readily takes to the kids, enjoying herself.

When the groups meet up for lunch and other activities, I observe her and Luke. A delicate line connects them, like spider's silk, a secret language only they understand, and yet, they manage to be attentive to the kids, as well as terrific leaders. The playful, adventurous side of Elle's personality emerges on the farm. Once wary around the animals, she now takes over the feeding of the baby calves, ensuring the children hold the bottle the right way, and when it comes to counting corn, she's nothing if not excited (and competitive). She digs potatoes without worrying about dirt caking beneath her nails, and she stares in wide-eyed wonder when the chicks hatch in the incubator. When the kids make personalized beaded bracelets, Elle is attentive and patient, helping them thread the string through the narrow holes. She's a natural. And it suits her. Not even Elle is capable of faking this much happiness.

Willow keeps her distance from me, but I hear her muttering under her breath to anyone who will listen, "I'll tell you, the world would be a lot better place if we all lived on farms."

The afternoon is fun-filled, and we share a good laugh when one of the baby pigs escapes the pen and forty of us are led on a wild-goose chase through the fields, Sammy squealing in delight. I decide Elle belongs here in some ways. That fate made it possible.

But then it comes time to milk the cows, the old-fashioned way, not with the automatic milker, and the kids are raising their hands to volunteer. I notice how Elle slinks back, wanting nothing to do with udders, but then she changes her mind and stands up, Luke patting her on the back for encouragement. The kids screech and clap, and my sister and I join Elle's side, Willow securing Clark's head while I demonstrate with my gloved hands the proper way to clean and lubricate the teats. Elle is clearly freaked out. She's inching backward, looking for an out. I'm guiding her, explaining how to pull downward from the base of the teat, Willow echoing the same, when Clark jerks backward, Elle squeezes, and the liquid shoots her in the face.

This happens often on a farm, but you can't tell that to a teenage girl in front of an audience, including the boy she's infatuated with. Elle is horrified. The kids are giggling uncontrollably, and milk is dripping down her face and neck. Luke jumps up, but she shoos him away, escaping to the back of the barn. I follow behind her, leading her toward a faucet where she can wash up.

"You did that on purpose!" she shouts at me, her eyes cold and accusing.

Now I'm horrified. "You think I'd do that to you? You think I'm that awful?"

She continues glaring at me, thinking about it. Undecided. Wavering. I grab some rags from a shelf and hand them to her. She's damp and sticky, and the flies are already buzzing around her.

"I would never do something like that to you."

Luke finds us, and he tries to console her, make light of it. But she's terribly embarrassed, a pink hue creeping down her neck. She can barely look at him. I overhear her tell him to leave her alone, to get away. He tries telling her it's okay, that it happens all the time, and I admire his bravery, but Elle is horribly ashamed. And her reaction hits so close to home, I shiver.

The remainder of the day continues without incident, but I'm carefully watching Elle. She's withdrawn and gloomy, and when we set off to the fields, collecting onions and broccoli and squash, her enthusiasm has all but disappeared, humiliation spoiling the earlier joy.

And Luke. He tried. Oh, how the boy tried, but the damage was done. He had witnessed an imperfection, and she couldn't take it back.

When I try to confront her, she snaps at me, so I back down. How could I advise her on controlling her emotions when I couldn't control my own? I retreated, closed people out, shame coloring all of me, instead of a small part.

This mirror she unknowingly held up to me was stirring up a range of feelings, a funnel cloud that was about to be unleashed. The uneasiness centered on more than Ollie and Quinn. Home had a way of emphasizing the other things I hadn't wanted to see, and hours later, after the kids had boarded the bus, loaded with their brown paper bags filled with fruits and vegetables and memories, I wished I could go back and change the past, except the part where I climbed into my sister's bed and we giggled until our cheeks hurt, falling asleep wrapped in each other's arms.

I'm toweling myself off after a long, hot shower, holding on to the memory, wiping off the regret. Elle's in her room, door slammed shut, and I worry what tonight's mood will bring, so I take my time getting dressed. Making my way downstairs, I spot my sister in the kitchen, the table set for five. I slip by, heading into my father's room, pleased he'll be joining us. He's resting, propped against a stack of pillows, his right hand elevated, and I take a seat on the bed beside him.

"How you feeling, Pop?"

He details his day, the hours of exercises with the therapist. "The old body's tired."

"Willow's cooked something special for you."

He asks about field-trip day, and I share the best parts, then decide to tell him the rest. "We had a little situation."

He chuckles because it's funny. "Poor girl." But then he sees that I'm not laughing.

"It happens to everyone, honey. A rite of passage out here."

"I know. I just . . . forget it."

"What's on your mind, little lamb?" He hasn't called me the nickname since I was much younger, and it fills me with melancholy.

"I'm not sure. Being home, having Elle here . . . I'm seeing how I could've done things differently. And I'm not sure how to fix it."

"You're here. That's a start."

I find his eyes, and there's an ocean of love inside. I'm his daughter, and it had to tear him up to see me suffer as I did.

"When I left," I begin, "what happened between Cole and Willow?"

His eyes narrow, confused. "What does this have to do with anything?"

I ask again, and he says he's not really sure. "We were all so torn up about you, I'm not sure any of us were thinking . . . What's this about?"

My eyes travel to the plaid quilt. He reaches for my chin and forces me to look at him.

"Avery, honey."

"Why didn't they . . ." I stop, gulping down the lump in my throat. "They loved each other . . . What happened?"

His hand comes down on mine. "I'm not sure. You girls . . . it's hard to keep up . . . but does it really matter? Your sister's happier than she's ever been. And Cole has Skye."

The clanging of pots and pans interrupts.

"She never said anything to you? Or Cole?"

"It was a long time ago," he says. "I guess we sort of went on . . . Cole took care of things around the house, checked on us, but something between the two of them had changed. They didn't tell me, and I didn't ask."

Sadness swells inside me. "I think I did something . . . I think . . ." And I don't say it aloud. I don't have to.

"You know, Avery, whatever it is, sometimes we make mistakes. We act out in anger. Rebel out of hurt. And we believe we're doing it for the right reasons. Then we realize how we've hurt people."

He could be referring to so many things, I can't decide which one. Lying to Jude. Hurting Cole. Escaping to Miami. Cutting Willow out of my life. I made decisions to protect myself, to protect others, and I caused hurt and had been hurt. Does it matter how well intentioned one is when there is shrapnel everywhere?

"Mistakes don't make you a bad person, Avery. They make you complex and human. Own them. Or the only person you hurt is you."

Swallowing the emotions, I thank him, his wisdom tucked close to my chest, and we get him out of bed and into his wheelchair.

I'm surprised to find Elle in the living room, working on her Napoleon project, and when I approach, pulling out the chair beside her, she growls, "Do you mind giving me a little space, Avery?" So I leave her to her mood. Which is fine, because Jackson arrives, and the energy in the house lifts.

A handsome bald man, Jackson hugs my sister as though he hasn't seen her in months. Then he makes his way to my father, who's beaming at him with a full smile. Their closeness reminds me of how Dad would once greet Oliver, a big bear hug and some private joke none of us understood. Soon Jackson's hazel eyes train on me. He's unsure. His greeting is well-intentioned but reserved, and I understand at once his loyalty to Willow.

I introduce him to Elle, who remains puss-faced, her shoulders slumped, making no real effort. And I soon learn that Jackson, despite the line in the sand, is forgiving and kind. He's animated, commanding the table with a sharp sense of humor, retelling stories about all the people who've opened (literal) doors to him: the man who collected gnomes, the lady who recited Shakespeare every time he came up her walk, and the husband and wife who received packages from a place called "Feeling Naughty" at least three times a week.

Willow laughs as though she's never heard these tales before. I see her happiness—more than ever before—and while I feel a rush of envy, a feral, unwarranted resentment of what she has and I have lost, I feel less bad about what I did. My leaving, even in that cruel, senseless way, gave her something of her own, someone to love her, someone to take care of her. It was finally her turn. And I can't take my eyes off them. Jackson, muscled, all boy, gushing over my sister. He hangs on to her every word, scooting his chair so that they're touching, his eyes never leaving her face. He is enamored with Willow, as though she's a sunset he just can't miss.

I do my best to engage in conversation, asking details about his proposal, their plans for an engagement party and wedding. That's when Jackson starts to welcome me in. "Will, hon, I know you said you didn't want an engagement party, but now that Avery's here, we can throw one hell of a bash."

My sister catches my eyes in hers, and I know without her saying it that she refused to have a party without me, and my heart sinks. It leaves me to wonder if there's a way for us to coexist, bring back some of that closeness.

We all listen as Jackson describes this epic party on the farm, and I begin to relax around him. Elle, too. His positive energy is a burst of fresh air, and because we'd endured enough pain to stretch across the Blue Ridge, he is levity and light streaming through the clouds. But what endears me most to Jackson is his thoughtfulness. He knows all about my past, though never lets on, and I smile knowing my sister has found someone so accepting.

My father announces he's done, exhaustion settling in, and Jackson gets up. "Let me help you into bed, old man." I stand, too, kissing my father good night. His whiskers scratch my cheek. "We'll have to take care of that tomorrow."

"You kids enjoy each other," he says. "I'll see you in the morning."

"Good night, Pop," Willow says.

"Good night, Mr. Beckett," says Elle.

When Jackson returns, he asks Elle about herself.

"Go on," I encourage her.

"There's not much to tell," she says. "Aren't all teenagers boring?"

"There's nothing boring about you," I tease.

"You know what I mean," she says. "I don't have any of that weird drama or those secrets you all seem to have."

"She's being modest," I deflect. "She's had her share of drama." I describe to them our encounter with the officer on our drive up. And how she's a gifted actress in her school's theater program. And a wonderful big sister.

The table breaks into laughter, Jackson commending Elle's moxie. "We're going to be great friends, young lady." He lifts a glass of wine in her direction, relaying the time he got pulled over without his wallet and gave the officer his twin brother's name. "The citation was issued to Kevin. Boy, was he pissed." We're all chuckling, even Elle, and Willow beams at her guy. Eventually, Jackson asks for some clarification on my relationship with Jude. "But you're broken up, right?" I nod, and the laughter wanes, Elle searching the table for something that's not there.

"We're taking a break." The admission comes out stiff because I don't want to believe it myself.

"She's the one keeping secrets." Elle's staring, pointing in my direction. Her blank expression is hard to read. "She basically left him at the altar."

And like that, the night splits in two.

I try to shrug it off. "That's not what happened, Elle." I say this more to Jackson for some reason, as though his approval matters.

Elle reaches for a partially empty glass of wine when my hand comes out to block her. "It's only a sip, Avery."

"I said no."

"There." She points again. "Exactly that. No. She didn't leave my dad at the altar. She just jilted him when he proposed at Vizcaya. Have you ever heard of Vizcaya, Jackson? It's like the most romantic place on earth."

I don't know what shocks me more. Her nerve, or the way she describes the gardens. Most often, she complained about spending time there.

"But it's fine," she says, leaning back in her chair, "now they're taking that break, and maybe Daddy will realize that she's . . ." And her voice trails off, and three sets of eyes wait for the sparks to fly from her mouth. I imagine several things rolling from her tongue: *Avery's an impostor. A phony. Unqualified to be a stepparent.* The list goes on.

Willow intervenes. "You know, Elle, that's not a very polite way of thanking Avery for letting you stay here so you can crush on Luke Manley."

Elle's cheeks flame, but she backs down, and it occurs to me how Willow handles Elle in ways I can't, ways perhaps I don't allow myself.

"Ah," Jackson pivots. "So there's a boy in the picture."

"There's always a boy when it comes to adolescent girls," Willow says.

"This is what middle-aged people discuss at their dinner parties?" Elle begins teetering on full-blown fury. "Teenagers and their, like, sex lives?"

I reach for my glass of wine. Was Elle already thinking about sex? With Luke?

And as if reading my mind, she tells me to chill. "We're not even close to having sex." Which helps the smooth liquid go down, though I'm wondering how much of this I'll need to report back to Jude. She kicks me under the table, reminding me I don't have to bother her father with all this. "He's a very busy man, Avery. He doesn't need to hear every little detail . . . especially from someone like you."

I'm too offended to respond.

"We've been working on her manners," Willow chimes in.

Jackson turns to Elle. "Avery can't be all that terrible if your father asked her to marry him."

This quiets Elle. No snarky comeback. No eye roll. I'm liking this Jackson more and more, quietly grateful for his support. But his simple statement of truth reminds me of what I lost, of what my silence has destroyed. And it's like losing Jude all over again.

And soon I realize that I empathize with Elle. At times, when she isn't tossing grenades at us, she's like having another sister around. It's easy to blend conversations—to weave through adolescent crushes and modern issues. But then, as quickly as we let her in, she'll snap, a lever pulled, and our inclusivity backfires. At times, it's exhausting keeping up with her temperaments. But not now. Now she appears defeated.

"Elle's father is a terrific man," I say. "My saying no to him had nothing to do with who he is as a person." I pause. "I love Jude." This I say as I'm staring into Elle's eyes, and the intensity forces her gaze to the scattered plates on the table, the half-eaten food. "I haven't loved anyone like that in a long time."

And maybe it's the wine, or the depth of that love I'm feeling and have now lost, because of my silence, but I keep talking. "Something terrible happened to me, Elle. Here. In Crystal."

My sister reaches for my hand, and I let her. "You don't owe anyone—"

"But I do, Willow. I owe her. And I certainly owe her father."

Whether it's for me or for Elle, I'm not sure, but this part of me I've kept from the world has been clawing to come out, spreading through my veins like venom. My sister is concerned, rightfully so, and I try to keep it as vague as possible.

"There was a boy. We loved each other. I thought we had all our lives to be together. But a tragedy struck, and we couldn't be together anymore. I lost him. I lost love. And I . . ." I'm inches from telling her the rest, but I can't muster the courage. "Just know that relationships are far more complicated than they appear. And sometimes you can love someone and find it difficult to give love. I'm not making excuses. I'm just trying to figure it all out."

Elle shifts in her seat. "Heavy shit."

"Don't do that," I say.

"Do what?"

"That. That blasé . . . uncaring . . . apathetic . . ."

"Wow. You couldn't just pick one insult?"

Maybe my reaction is off-putting, but there's a nonchalance to Elle's tone that hurts. And I've been so afraid to stand up to her, wanting her approval so badly, but it's only hurting us more. "If you want to be treated like an adult and a part of grown-up conversations, you need to start acting like one."

Abruptly, she gets up from the table, knocking her chair to the ground. "I don't know who you think you are, Avery, but you're not my mother, and you can't tell me what to do . . . or how to be . . ."

She crosses the room, fingers clenched in a fist, while Willow and Jackson stare, their mouths agape. Her eyes narrow, and her lip trembles. "The more I think about it, I'm glad you said no to my dad, because I would never want you as a stepmother."

This. This cuts me to the very core. A knife twisting. She storms out of the room, oblivious to the destruction she left in her wake, and I am frozen in place. A door slams, and I jump. Feelings are closing in on me. Smothering. This is what had kept me closed off. And now my worst fears are coming true.

Willow speaks first. "That girl is filled with a lot of anger."

But I disagree, because I know what's inside her, and I know how it feels. "That's not it at all," I say. "What you're seeing is a girl filled with a lot of pain."

CHAPTER 24

Elle left the house before dawn. I know this because I heard her when she thought I was asleep, heard her washing her face and tiptoeing not-so-lightly down the stairs. I didn't sleep well, tossing and turning, our dinner conversation spooling around my head.

I wrestle myself out of bed. Admittedly, I avoided a confrontation, waiting for her to slip out the door before I heard a voice that could only be Luke's. The girl perplexes me, drawing me in and casting me far. I want her affection, and I'm also afraid of it.

Checking in on my father, I find he's already awake and dressed, shaving with his good hand. I kiss him on the forehead, getting a whiff of menthol, and when I try to take over, he pulls back, letting me know he's able. I grab my things and launch my own early start. It's the mystical hour between light and dark, rife with possibility, and I relish the quiet pause before the world awakens. I'm making my way toward the garden, to fix what Willow neglected, when I spot Elle frolicking around the sheep. Wiped clean of last night's ugliness, she's in her element, that girl, chatting aimlessly with her new friends. Her long hair, parted down the middle, falls over her sun-kissed shoulders, and there's a bright smile fastened to her face. Here, among the wild, is where she thrives.

That's when I spot Luke walking toward her, carrying bales of hay. *Oh no you don't.* Together, they tear them apart, spreading the hay evenly across the dirt. I'm whispering under my breath, "Don't you get any ideas, Luke Manley." The sun's making her appearance, fiery orange spraying the sky, and I have a clear view of them making their way toward one of the dogwoods that line the property. This one is brimming with pale-pink flowers.

Shovel in hand, I'm digging up the weeds that have taken over, though my eyes dart back and forth to Elle and Luke as they move closer toward the tree, finding a spot beneath its limbs. Elle tries to contain her happiness—an expression I recognize—while Luke searches the branches. When he finds what he's looking for, he tugs the biggest and brightest blossom from off the stem and hands it to her. She takes it, admiring its beauty, and I imagine he's telling her she's as pretty. Prettier. Because I'm sure her cheeks turn bright red.

And this makes Elle nervous. I can see the uneasiness in her stance, the way she hangs her head, afraid to meet his gaze. At this point, I dig my shovel into the ground and just stare, relieved they moved away from the hay. Luke is talking, trying to catch her eyes in his, and I'm chanting under my breath, "Look at him, Elle. Smile. Thank him for the flower." And I'm remembering what it's like to fall in love, to have nothing but time ahead of you. To let it all in until it physically hurts. Yet, Elle fidgets. The girl who can tame with her eyes and command with her fingertips is suddenly shy and unsure.

And Luke's the opposite. He's leaning in. He's going to kiss her, and I'm ridiculously excited, and nervous, about this. Should I stop him? What would her mother, Mallory, have done? I look away to give them some privacy, though I'm not particularly good at discretion, so I return to their willowy figures. Their breezy innocence makes them look as though they're straight out of a movie. Mallory would watch, wouldn't she? That moment when her daughter realizes her heart is no longer hers?

My phone vibrates, plucking me from their moment. Jude is FaceTiming me.

I smile. Happy to see him.

"Why are you up so early?" I ask.

But then Luke kisses Elle.

"Hold on a sec." This requires my complete attention, and I turn the phone around so that I can unabashedly stare.

"What's going on, Avery?"

My voice takes on a whisper, as though the kids can hear. "Give me a second." But Elle pulls back, barely reaching his lips. She fumbles, and Luke's expression is unmistakably hurt.

I gather by the way in which Elle's face goes slack and how she looks around that there is an exchange of tense unpleasantries. Luke is wringing his hands, his head shaking back and forth, when Jude interrupts, asking about the garden. "I think I may have overwatered it."

"You're gardening?" I say, pleased, giving him my attention. "So am I."

The synchronicity of the moment makes me smile, and he shows me the water-soaked stems. I instruct him to lay off the water. "Give them a few days to dry out." And I wonder if this was merely an excuse to call me. But then Elle is heading in my direction, and I ask if I can call him back.

Elle's shoulders slump forward, and Luke stands deflated beneath the tree. She looks as though she's about to cry.

I pretend to be knee-deep in my project when she appears, startled to find me there.

"Avery?"

I look up and see the tears streaming down her cheeks.

"Elle. What is it?"

She's only a few yards away; her steps are unhurried, one shaky foot in front of the other. She stares at the ground, and I think she might walk past me toward the house, but she stops directly in front of me so that my arms can take her in.

Elle and I have never really found a way to fit, but today we do. "Whatever it is," I whisper, "it's going to be okay."

This sends her into full-blown sobbing, her thin frame trembling as I squeeze her harder. She is Elle. Mercurial, contradictory Elle, but I hold her against me, remembering a little girl I couldn't save. I'm terrified to get this wrong, and I let her cry, refusing to release my grip. I'm ready for whatever it is she wants to share. I'm ready to curse Luke out, to defend her, do battle, no matter what we're up against, when she says, "I've never kissed a boy."

I don't move. I let her continue.

"Luke tried to kiss me, and I messed it all up."

She pulls back, so I can see her pinched, damp face, and I'm shocked, quite honestly, that this is cause for a hysterical outburst by one of the toughest teens I know.

"That's all?" And before the words slip off my tongue, I try to reel them back. *Shoot.* And there couldn't be a worse possible response for a crying young girl. Obviously, that isn't all.

"Okay," she says, wiping her nose with the back of her hand. "That's not what I expected you to say."

I brush her hair off her face. "That came out wrong." The farm's coming alive around us, Cole and his men scattering across the fields. The squealing sounds of fowl, the buzzing of the tractors, but I only hear Elle's disappointment.

She drops herself to the ground, paying no mind to the dirt. Her back is to Luke, so she doesn't see him sitting there under the tree, dejected, before hopping to his feet and sulkily stalking off. The scene reminds me of how I'd rejected her father—out of fear and out of shame.

"Why do I always screw things up?" she asks, kicking the dirt that I'd just set into neat piles.

"That's not true."

"Of course you're going to disagree with me."

And instead of arguing, I aim to be more helpful.

"You didn't blow it," I assure her.

"How would you know?"

I could say, *Because I rejected your father, and here I am spending the summer with you,* though Jude and I were far from being back on track. So I choose a different tactic. "Relationships are complicated and messy, Elle. They're not always so black and white. They're hard to come together and easy to tear apart. This'll blow over. But can I make a suggestion?"

She eyes me warily.

"Talk to him. Tell him the truth." This hits home, all the parts of myself I'd held back from her father, from Willow. The only word that comes to mind is *hypocrite.* But it's so much easier to give the advice than to take it. "He makes you nervous?"

"Sort of."

"And that makes you afraid? You want to take things slow?"

"Maybe."

"That's not a bad thing, Elle. You're still young. You should be afraid of relationships. It's okay to be cautious."

That was putting it mildly. Falling in love had whittled me down to nothing. I let this sink in while she wipes her nose with her shirt. "If you're so good with relationships, why'd you mess up yours and my dad's?"

She wasn't wrong. "Fair . . . but you can learn from my mistakes, and maybe I can help."

She's finished wiping her nose and reaches for one of the nearby shovels, picking it up and pounding it into the ground.

I think back to that first kiss, my whole body shivering with anticipation. "I have an idea." I wait for her to argue, but she lets me continue. "This dirt . . . it used to be my garden. It meant everything to me because I'd planted the flowers with someone I really loved. The boy I was telling you about."

"How come you can't be together?" she asks.

I drop my hands into the pile and watch as the dirt and rocks slip through my fingers. "We can't . . . It's just not possible . . . But I was thinking, maybe you and I can revive the garden. We can do it together . . . choose the flowers . . . plant the seeds . . . watch something we care about grow. I know it sounds silly, like some stupid bonding moment you'll just make fun of me over, but you and I have been through a lot, and if there's one thing I'm sure of, nature is an exceptionally good healer. We can do it together."

She takes her time in answering, but I can see she's considering what I've offered. She scans the property that has become her friend, and I know she feels it, too. I know she feels the pull.

"Bonding over a day of shopping would be so much more fun," she says.

And before I can get upset, she laughs. "I'm kidding. Sort of."

"So you'll do it?"

She nods. "But what about Luke?"

"Here's what we're going to do about Luke. You're going to get your cute bottom off my precious soil, and you're going to go find him. Then you're going to talk to him, tell him how you feel. Let him see who you are."

"I'm scared."

"I know," I say. "I'm scared, too. But think of it this way, we're scared because we care. Imagine not caring at all."

She doesn't argue. She doesn't lob a quick comeback. She actually considers what I've offered, wiping her eyes and standing up.

"Rouge Coco?" she asks.

I take her in. "You definitely don't need it."

She turns and runs off, making her way to find Luke, and I get back to work, digging up the weeds, tending to the barren soil. I think about this young girl carrying around barrels of repressed emotions. She intrigues me and terrifies me, and the closer we become, the more our similarities brim to the surface. These are the thoughts that swirl around my head as I stab the shovel into the dirt, digging up the tangled roots and tossing them into the nearby wheelbarrow.

When I'm just about finished for the day, Cole approaches. He's wearing his cowboy hat, the one that hides his eyes, and he removes it, so I can see their blue. Cole may appear intimidating in size, but around these parts, they refer to him as the Gentle Giant. Big like a bear, with a huge, soft heart. And I know what I must do.

I begin by telling him how nice Skye seems and how I'm happy that he's happy.

"You gave me the push I needed. I think I would've chased after your sister forever. You did me a favor."

I shake my head. "No, Cole, I was wrong."

He waits for me to say more.

"She went to your house that night . . . to tell you how she felt." I can't look at him. "I should've never said what I said."

He's shaking his head, his eyes blinking something away. "She needed to borrow a lemon for some tea she was making—"

"No. She was going to tell you she loved you back. She always loved you . . . She was just scared . . . and then she saw Skye . . . and it was too late."

"You told me she'd never love me . . . the way I loved her . . . You told me to move on." Now he's getting angry. "And I did. Because I believed you." The sun catches the waves of his hair, and I feel every bit of awful inside.

My weak attempt at fixing this is falling flat. "You found Skye. She found Jackson. Everyone's happy."

His hands cover his face, and he's unsure of what to do with this.

"You are happy, aren't you, Cole?"

His eyes reach mine. "I'll never love anyone the way I loved your sister. It's just the way it is. Like you and Ollie. There's always the one that got away. They hold your heart in a different way than anyone else."

I don't have time to absorb those words, almost identical to Willow's, before he continues. "You need to tell her."

I let it sink in. "I know. I will. We have other problems to deal with first. But I'm sorry. I really am. I should've never said what I said."

Neither of us hears her approach.

"Should've never said what?"

Cole and I exchange looks, and he answers Willow because I can't. "It's nothing."

But my sister doesn't back down. "You're lying, Cole Manley. You think I don't know when you lie?"

"Leave it alone," he says, finally gazing in her direction, all the love spilling out of him. Willow sees it, too. And the three of us stand there in the garden, so much destroyed, too much to fix. And because of that love, Willow lets it go, but I know it won't be for long.

CHAPTER 25

"Avery!"

It's nearly dawn, and I've been in a deep sleep. The lights come on, and as my eyes adjust to the brightness, there's my sister smack in my face.

"Go away," I tell her, sinking beneath the sheets.

"It's time to get up, Sleeping Beauty," she says, pulling the covers back, her tone implying I don't have a choice. "Elle's getting dressed. Begrudgingly, I might add, but uppity-up—we're going to the river."

I turn my back to her, coming face-to-face with Oliver's words, realizing it's been days since we've spoken and wondering whether that means anything. But Willow's too quick. "No excuses. Dad's taken care of. Cole's here for any emergencies."

My sister rarely takes no for an answer, and I was hoping she'd forgotten about these plans.

"Look, Avery. Things have been tense around here. We need some old-fashioned fun. Just the three of us. Me, you, and the monster across the hall."

"I hear you," Elle says, entering the room with her hair in a messy bun but fully clothed. "And I have some ideas for that old-fashioned fun."

"Is that a thingy on the back of your head?" I ask.

She laughs as she plops beside me on the bed. "Come on, Avery." And her willingness astonishes me, as though we're somehow all on the same team.

Leave it to Willow, a pseudo camp counselor, to come up with a way to unify us. As far back as I can remember, the four of us would go down to the Watauga River, she and Cole, Oliver and I. We'd pack lunches and dock at our favorite spot beneath a shady tree. Our troubles were far behind; we were just innocent kids, relishing the moment. But we aren't the same people, and I don't want to be in a position where she asks me what Cole and I were talking about. "I can't."

"Sure you can," Willow says.

I don't want to be on the river, and I tell her so.

"I expect both of you downstairs in twenty minutes. Six thirty, sharp." And she taps on her watch like a drill sergeant.

Elle and I glance at each other, neither of us arguing. And when my sister leaves the room, her compact body making loud, stomping steps, we can't help but giggle.

"Guess we're going fly-fishing," Elle says.

At precisely 6:32 a.m., Elle, Willow, and I are packed in Willow's truck as she steers us off the farm and toward the river. The town is still, a gray film coating the sky in sleep. We're sipping coffee and munching day-old muffins as the sun begins to rise, and the curvy mountain road leads us past rows of fields with their freshly plowed lawns. American flags wave proudly in the wind, and Crystal slowly comes to life.

Watauga River stretches over seventy miles through parts of western North Carolina and eastern Tennessee, and we catch glimpses of her tranquil waters through the trees. Before long, Willow takes a sharp right, veering downhill, and the dam comes into view. As we wind the corner to the riverside shop where Duncan Powell runs the area's fishing outfit, I feel the memories closing in.

Duncan, slight, with bleached-blond hair and a bandanna around his forehead, is happy to see us. "Willow and Avery Beckett. Ain't you a sight for these sore eyes."

"Duncan." I smile, introducing him to Elle.

Willow moves in for a hug, but I keep my distance.

"I thought that was your name I saw in the book," he begins, hesitant. "How've you been?" I recognize the delicate tone, the kind that's meant for me. I imagine this is a difficult subject for locals to broach.

"I'm good," I say, offering a weak smile.

"The usual?" he asks before taking it back. "I've got the perfect boat for you, ladies. I'll have one of the guys meet you out back."

We fill out forms, and he hands us each a pair of waders, the shapeless rubber overalls that reek of mildew. Elle backs away. "You've got to be kidding."

Willow laughs. "They can give you a cootie shot if you want."

And Elle gives her a look. "Ha, funny."

"The scent that never goes away," I quip, stepping inside the dark, damp tunnels, pulling them up over my leggings. Elle and Willow follow as Duncan busies himself with a tangled fishing line, an uncomfortable silence filling the air. He's different. They all are. Before, he would enlist us in conversation, catch up on the town gossip. He and Oliver had once been friends. Now, people just avoid talking. Who wants to discuss one of the sadder tragedies the town had ever faced?

A group of guests interrupts the quiet, and I'm amused that I've left Miami, only to be greeted by two couples from Aventura. I know this because they're wearing Turnberry golf caps, the well-known South Florida resort, and because they've signed in before us and scribbled their hometown.

Duncan comes back up around, tightening the straps of the waders one by one while I work on Willow's and she works on Elle's, who whispers, "What have you gotten me into?"

"The river's stocked with trout," Duncan says. "Rainbow . . . Brook . . . Brown . . ." Then he hands us poles and a bag of flies. "Everything else is in the boat."

When we get outside and walk the few yards toward the loading zone, the river comes into view, and I'm thinking this isn't a mistake after all. Despite the difficulties in being back, the tranquil, flowing water reminds me of how uncomplicated life used to be.

I spot the two Florida couples by their boats, their chuckling dancing through the air. The women are older, similar pink lips and wide hips. With each step, their waders and boots make a loud squishing sound. The tanned older gentleman, the one who resembles George Hamilton, calls himself Frank. He's smiling widely at his guide, Otis Fielding, Duncan's partner, as he introduces his wife, Estelle. Then he gestures to his friend, tall and thick, with a shiny bald head. "And this here's Herb, and the other beauty over there is Margo." She's excited to tell the entire river how they won the trip to the Carolinas through a raffle at Porta Vita, their condominium, with a weeklong stay at a luxurious mountain cabin and a day trip to the local wineries, concluding with an afternoon at Westglow Spa. She never mentions the fly-fishing. In fact, upon closer inspection, she and Estelle look downright unenthusiastic about today's activity.

We scoot beside them, making our way onto the floater that's been loaded into the river.

Four sets of eyes train in our direction before Estelle lobs one.

"I don't really like fish," she says.

Margo nods her head in agreement.

"And flies. I don't get it. Who wants to touch flies?"

Willow steps in. "They're not real flies."

"What do you mean, they're not real flies?" Estelle jabs Frank. "I thought we're fly-fishing."

A rustling in the nearby trees turns the group's heads, and Margo is thrown into a mild panic. "Did you hear that? What if it's a bear?"

Positioning herself behind Herb, she fiddles with her iPhone, and soon Diana Ross fills the air, because Margo, like most visitors to these parts, has been advised to make her presence known if approached by a bear. She sings along at the top of her lungs, palms clapping wildly in the air, and when she realizes she has an audience—Elle is literally laughing out loud—she retreats, dropping her hands to her sides. "Fine. Make fun of me all you want," she half jokes. "You won't be laughing when you're the bear's breakfast."

Willow grabs the oars and steps on the boat, positioning herself on the cushion toward the front. Elle follows, taking the seat behind her, while I push us off and hop in the back. These were our usual seats, Willow paddling effortlessly, her stroke mostly even and gentle. Flumes of water shoot from the dam, and we're soon passing through a light mist, away from shore, away from the loud, shrill voices.

"Did you hear that woman?" Elle laughs.

"I think the whole county heard that woman," Willow says.

The river is clear and flat, and the sycamores and oaks surround us on both sides. The current pulls us forward, the forest propping us in its hands. A stillness prevails, a quiet rhythm that fills the parts in me that had been asleep. It doesn't take me long to feel centered and at peace.

Elle notices it, too. She's all but gobbled up in her waders, but she owns the baggy rubber look, making it seem chic. "It's pretty," she says, reaching over to touch the water. "And cold."

As the current picks up, Willow drops the paddles, and we are carried down the first rapid. I toss my head back and breathe in the fresh air while the sun begins to climb over the treetops. And when we begin to idle, Willow finds a clearing and drops the anchor. The surrounding water is so clear you can see through to the moss-covered stones at the bottom. I close my eyes and take it all in. The lapping of the river against the boat, the rustling of the trees, the fresh smell of pine.

Most fishermen will tell you that the key to success is patience. But I don't have time to savor the moment, not when my sister is on her feet, barking out orders. Willow's always been militant when it comes to our excursions, and today's no exception. She's hollering: *Hold the rod this way, cast like this, here's how to tell when a fish is biting. Set! Set!* Elle's confused and keeps getting caught in the line. "Whose idea was this?" she mumbles while I remember Oliver being the kinder, gentler teacher, coming up behind me, his hands over mine, as we reeled in a slippery fish.

Oliver used to say my sister's loud voice scared the fish away. It almost makes me laugh as I hear her now, Elle frustrated and annoyed. Oliver was the one who understood the art of the sport, the need for quiet. He and his grandiose dream to open a fly-fishing outlet in these parts. I often picture him casting his line somewhere, the smooth way he'd handle the rod and reel. I reach for my own rod, knowing I'm expected to remember the technique after all these years.

"We could stay in the boat and cast our lines," Willow begins, "but it's always better to get in the water."

"Wait," Elle stops her. "I have to get in the water? Nobody told me anything about getting in the water. It's freezing."

Willow's already stepping off the boat and into the shallow river. I follow, and she explains to Elle that this is the reason we're wearing insulated bodysuits. "You won't feel a thing."

"Guys," she says, not making a move, the only one left in the boat. "I can't go in there."

"What do you mean, you can't?" I ask, standing with my pole in the water, which is only knee-high, waiting for her to join us.

She's got one hand on her hip and the other clenching the rod. "I've been a pretty good sport." By now, Willow's already launched her line into the water, narrowly missing Elle's head by an inch. "I've woken up at the crack of dawn to clean shit out of chicken coops, and let's not forget taking cow's milk straight in the eyeball . . . I've done what you all thought couldn't be done . . . got out of . . . *jumped* out of my comfort zone, but I draw the line at sharks."

My sister and I find each other's eyes, and it's impossible to hide our amusement.

"I'm glad you think it's funny," she snarls.

"Oh dear," Willow says, her lips repressing a smile. "There's nothing funny about that at all."

"Elle," I begin delicately, "we're on a river."

She stands, either confused or unconvinced.

"These rivers don't have sharks," I add.

"That's what everyone says, Avery. Then fucking *Jaws* rips you into pieces."

Willow laughs. She can't help herself. "O-M-G," she says, spelling it out. "Elle, what Avery means, specifically, is that sharks can't survive here. They're saltwater creatures. And we're over three hundred miles from the ocean."

Elle's face turns a deep red. Her blue eyes darting everywhere but to us. "Good one. You're just trying to get me to go in there. I'm not stupid."

Now I'm laughing. "I wouldn't lie to you about that, Elle. The water's completely safe. No sharks."

She drops the rod against the side of the boat and crosses her arms. "I'm fine right here."

Resigned to Elle's pigheadedness, my sister and I stand side by side, casting our lines, while Elle watches us from her seat. The currents slip by, and though I wish she'd join us, I'm happy she's near. The water has always been able to heal, and it's washing away a lot of the messiness of the last few days. Here, we're forced to be still. Patient.

Unlike regular fishing, your bait is your fly, and it rests atop the water. You have to pay close attention to know when the fish is biting. There's no forceful pull, just your bait dipping below the surface. When I spot the slight movement, I hear Oliver's instructions. "Set. Set." But it's

Willow shouting. And all I can do is tug at the line, jerk on the rod, a clumsy effort that causes the fish to escape.

"You'll get the next one," she says. And it's not long before there's a nibbling on her line, and I watch how she effortlessly plucks the fish from the water, suspending it in the air above us. Elle's shrieking because the fish is flapping close to her. She hides her face, and Willow's grabbing her net from her holster and dropping the feisty fish in.

"Rainbow trout," Willow proudly announces, taking the fish in her hand and holding it up for us to see. Elle peeks through her fingers as my sister removes the hook and holds up the colorful fish for us to admire. "You want to hold him?" she asks me. "You used to love throwing the fish back."

I used to be a lot of things, an enthusiastic fisherman one of them. I used to touch the fish and climb into the water with them, sinking my feet into the muddy bottom. Today I'm more restrained, at the water's edge, cautious. At least tossing the line in the water is a practice I can control.

"You can do it," I reply.

She tosses the fish into the glassy water, and we watch it scamper away. I wonder if the innocent creature knew how close he was to death. How did it feel to return to the water again? To go home?

"Hold on," Elle says. "After all that, you throw the thing back?"

"It's not about the catch," Willow explains. "It's never about the catch."

Turning my attention to Willow, all I'm thinking about is the catch.

But Elle interrupts. "Do you think that was the same fish?" she asks. "The one Avery let get away? Like, why would it ever go near the bait, knowing—"

"I didn't *let* it get away . . ."

"Whatever, Avery. You did." She's arguing, but at least she's engaged.

Willow intervenes. "Okay, kids, simmer down. To answer your question, Elle, once they feel the hook, they get skittish. It's usually one and done. You get one shot."

This seems to appease Elle, but not me. And while I'm caught up in everything beautiful about the river, feeling nostalgic, missing mornings out here with my sister, with Oliver, a deep worry hovers around. I think about second chances, *having one shot*, and I have to ask, "Do you think the same applies to us?"

CHAPTER 26

Elle still refuses to get in the water, so Willow and I decide to join her and fish from the boat. This doesn't seem to make a difference; Elle just stares at her rod and complains that she's hot and hungry. My sister and I exchange knowing looks, so she pulls up the anchor, and we begin to paddle downriver. I know where she's headed and brace myself for the feelings.

Sawyer, as we've come to call it, is a little parcel of land—easy to miss—situated in the middle of the river. The small, secluded island, covered in trees and foliage, is mostly inhabited by locals who access the spot by rowboat or the hidden footbridge connected to the main road. The location makes it an untamed jungle, one where we'd had our fair share of adventures. My sister always said the property put a spell on anyone who came to visit. I know it put a spell on me.

As Sawyer comes into view, I notice the land is deserted, a lone wooden swing hanging from a tree, the empty gazebo, the weather-beaten hammock. Willow's explaining how this was the hangout when we were growing up, where we made all our best memories.

I envy Willow's happy memories.

Elle stands up to get a better look, her hand coming up over her eyes.

Willow docks the boat on the marshy shore, and the three of us get out. "Do you remember the night we brought the Ouija board here?" she asks.

Elle skips ahead, entranced by the little island. She drops herself in the hammock and slowly begins to sway.

How could I forget? It was one of those blistery cold nights, a full moon hovering in the sky. She and Cole were seventeen, Oliver and I just twelve, but they took us along, packing Cole's truck with blankets and sleeping bags, our plan to roast marshmallows under the stars, ask ridiculous questions of the board. But then Willow brought out the game. Everyone said she was crazy, but that was Willow's way. Séances and talking to spirits were all part of her unconventionality. And what began as a starry night, not a cloud in the sky—good teenaged fun—turned into something else.

"We were asking the Ouija board all these questions," Willow says, "and all of a sudden, the hammock started swinging side to side, the swing going up and down. All on their own."

I take a seat in the nearby swing. "Oliver started to cry," I say. "Cole said it was the wind, but it wasn't. If there was wind, we would have felt it; you'd have heard the trees rustling. There was dead quiet."

"And you'll never believe what happened next."

She's getting to the best part of the story, the spookiness that led us to pack our blankets and run off to the truck, but Elle, swaying in her squishy waders, makes no move to hear the rest. When she finally speaks, she doesn't ask what happened. She says, "Who's Oliver?"

Willow keeps talking. "Cole was wearing a cap on his head, and it just came flying off. Disappeared. Poof. No wind. Just gone." Elle doesn't flinch. She just asks another question. "But why were you and Cole out on a Saturday night with two twelve-year-olds in the first place? That's not very romantic."

"Oh, jeez, Elle, you're no fun," Willow says. "Dad was on a date."

This gets me to stop swinging and look up.

"He was on a date?" I ask.

Willow tries to avoid my question, too, but I won't let her.

"I never knew he went on dates."

Elle sits up. "This should be fun to watch."

"Are you kidding me, Willow?" I ask.

Willow never stammered, her words always perfectly timed.

"This is ridiculous," I say. "Why would you hide that from me? Why would *he* hide that from me?"

"He didn't tell me either, Avery. But I had my ways of figuring those things out."

"Did your Ouija board tell you?" Elle asks.

Willow eyeballs her.

"You still didn't answer," Elle persists. "Is Oliver the ex-boyfriend?"

"Dad was dating." I shake my head in disbelief. "And you never told me."

"What does it matter?" she asks.

I'm not sure why this bothers me so much. Back then, I thought Willow and I told each other everything.

"Is anyone going to answer me?" Elle whines.

"The point of the story," Willow says, growing impatient with her audience, "was that we channeled a spirit. I'm certain of it. I'm like a rod for those things. What else would explain windblown objects without any wind?"

"Willow, you sound like a complete nutcase," I interrupt. "I just can't believe you didn't tell me. Don't you think it might have benefited me to see Dad moving on? Having a life?"

This quiets my sister. Quiets all of us.

"This is so much better than any ghost story," Elle finally says.

At least she's off the subject of Oliver, but this thing with my sister weighs on me. We had never kept secrets from each other, especially one this big. Willow inches away, reaching for her backpack and the snacks she'd prepared.

"Nice try," I say.

"Come on, Avery. Did you really think he was celibate for the last thirty years?"

I honestly couldn't answer, which is more troublesome. "I'm sorry I never thought about his sex life."

"There we go again," says Elle. "You people talking about everyone else's sex lives."

We turn to her at the same time. "Shut it, Elle."

Willow passes out the sandwiches and fruit, and I just watch her going through the motions, our magical place turning out to be not so magical.

"It's not such a big deal, Avery," Willow says. "Kind of like you not telling me what you and Cole were talking about."

I shrug. "I knew you wouldn't let that go." And even though I was hungry moments ago, the sight of the cheese sandwich with apricot preserves she drops in front of me makes me queasy.

"Why do you care? He told you, it was nothing."

Elle is rapt, paying close attention, watching two sisters tangle in the woods like one of her reality TV shows.

"I sense things, Avery. You, of all people, know that. It's all over your face, and the very first thing I learned to read was you, little sis."

Elle catches my eye, and if I look deep enough in hers, I see a slow-building sympathy. I don't want to do this now. I don't want to ruin a perfectly imperfect day with this revelation. It could go one of two ways: Willow might laugh it off, admit it was the best thing that ever happened to her, or she could be furious. I break the stare and search the ground.

Willow has the sense to leave it alone in front of Elle, and she heads back toward the river with her pole.

I turn to Elle, who's now taken a seat in the gazebo, biting into her meal. I sit beside her. When she swallows, she says, "You're a little bit of a hypocrite, Avery. Giving advice about being honest and all that stuff."

"Does that mean you took my advice?"

"Does that mean you're trying to change the subject?"

"You never did tell me what happened with Luke."

"The secret between you and your sister is way more interesting."

"It's not a secret." Then I change my mind. "Fine. Maybe a little one."

"Tell her," she says. "What's the worst that can happen?"

I don't answer, which leaves us both to consider the consequences of honesty.

Her eyes are glistening, and I have a Willow-like intuition that's telling me Elle's about to say something important.

"I didn't go after him, Avery. I was too embarrassed. And now we're not talking . . . Now he must think I'm such a loser. *Him.* This farm boy thinks *I'm* the loser."

"You must really like him," I say gently, careful not to push.

She turns to me, young love strapped to her heart and pulling her in all sorts of directions. "What if I'm like that fish? One and done?"

And she sinks into me, and this time, she's the one who won't let go.

I reassure her it's going to be okay, even though I told her that once before. And I begin to understand more and more what it means to be a parent. It's hoping for the best while advising and consoling, knowing there are never guarantees. It's saying the same thing over and over again until it sticks. Never getting tired. Never giving up.

And it's never walking away.

CHAPTER 27

Willow joins us in the gazebo, and the three of us eat in silence until I decide to take advantage of the union.

"Elle," I begin, "I really would love it if you fished with us. I've seen you on the farm. I've seen how you handle the animals. You're a natural. I promise you, no sharks."

I can tell she's thinking about it, so I continue. "Willow and I have made some of our best memories here, and I want you to have the same." Then a thought pops into my head, and before I can make sense of it, I blurt it out: "I want *us* to make memories."

The frown loosens, and she balls up the tinfoil with the bread crust still in it.

"What's the point?"

I don't know if this is because she's just upset or because she's thinking about me and her father. "Come on, take a look at this place."

She slowly lifts her head and scans the property. The sounds of the rippling water curl around us. "Will you try?" I ask.

She looks over at me, her features forming a question mark.

"Are you crying?" she asks.

I knew I was getting emotional, but I hadn't felt the lone tear slip down my cheek. I see Elle. I also see a little girl. I want to show her my love, put it in her hands, but I don't know if there's enough to give, or if she'll accept it.

Elle stands up, and Willow and I follow. We gather the leftover food and trash and stuff it inside Willow's bag so that the animals won't get to it. Elle takes her time, contemplating her next move. She reaches the water's edge and drops to her knees, letting her fingers run through the cool water. Then she stands, taking a few steps in.

The waders prevent her from feeling the cold chill, and each step is made with caution. I take this as a sign to grab the poles and hand her one. We walk a few yards out while she inspects the water, searching for sharks. After a few moments, her body relaxes, and I explain how to hold the rod, which she does with ease. The cast is a little trickier. It's a seamless motion where air meets a rolling line. The entire sport is based on this rhythm, a weightlessness connecting the water and the senses. Getting it right means success or failure. Elle tries several times, coming up short, the line flailing, the fly nearing my face.

"That wasn't on purpose," she says.

"I know. If it were, you'd get me right between the eyes."

She doesn't agree or disagree. Willow grabs her pole and casts out a few feet from us. I'm still a little rusty. It's been some time since I mastered a line, but I do my best to make this a moment we'll both remember. "Try casting from your shoulder, less from your elbow and wrist."

I do the same, and my line lands beautifully in one of those deep pockets that attract fish.

Elle scuffles with the rod, kicking at the water. "I can't do this," she says. "I don't want to."

I tell her to be patient. "Like any sport, this takes practice."

She resists. "I don't remember signing up for this." But she keeps repeating the technique, and with each cast, she improves, her line showing promise. And though she tries to hide it, I see the satisfaction in her stance when she lands the perfect line. Effortless, as though she had been practicing her whole life.

It hasn't been an easy few weeks. It's no wonder Willow brought us here—to recharge and refresh, immerse ourselves in nature. Feelings, however real, could always be managed under a canopy of trees, along a crystal river. The fresh air was a release, a balm for whatever ached.

Elle gets the hang of it, and I feel a swell of pride that she persisted. Now on to catching a fish.

"This is taking forever," she says, the pleasure in the cast slipping away without a bite. She's losing focus, and I remind her she has to watch the fly or she'll lose the fish. I encourage her to re-cast, maybe wade through the water a little deeper, which is answered with a look of disgust.

But she's at ease, no silly jokes, no wise-ass complaints. And though I'd like very much to delve into a deeper conversation with her, peel away the layers, we remain in this comfortable place, my sister and I buoying her.

Elle's learning about trust today. About not giving up.

That's when I notice her fly dipping beneath the water and her eyes drifting toward the sky. "Set!" I call out. "Set, Elle!" And she's startled, but she pulls up, and by some stroke of great luck, she's pulled at just the right angle. There's a fish on the end of her line, a pretty large one, and her pole is bent and she's shrieking, and I come up beside her. "Reel it in. Reel it in." She follows my directions, and the fish is flapping and flapping. She keeps reeling and I'm shouting and Willow's yelling, and the fish flies through the air and slaps Elle right in the left cheek.

Her scream is loud, and she drops the pole, thinking she can run away, but forgets she's standing on a floor made of slick rocks, and when it happens, it happens in slow motion. One minute Elle is upright, trying to flee, and the next she's falling face-first into the shallow water.

Willow throws an F-bomb into the air as we close in on her. We know what this means. Elle will yell, blame us, her loud voice bouncing off the trees, echoing across Tennessee.

When she pops up, water shoots from her nose, and she peers around, ready to pounce. She's not yelling; she's not even racing to get out of the knee-high water. She's soaked through, hair flattened against her scalp. Droplets of water stick to her eyelashes, and her blue eyes sparkle.

She dips back under the water.

I drop my fingers for a temperature reading. It's pretty cold, for Elle standards.

"I think we're witnessing some form of miracle," my sister jokes.

Elle pops up again, this time grinning. "This feels amazing!" And with her waders filling with water, she removes the straps and wriggles her body free.

I look to my sister for some semblance of understanding.

"You know there are fish swimming around in there," Willow says.

Her skin is pink from the chill, but Elle smiles. I have her rod in my hand, the fish she caught long ago escaped.

"I dare you two to come in," she finally says.

I don't hesitate. I drop the rods into the nearby boat, slip out of my waders, and fall into the crisp water. Willow quickly follows. It's cold without the extra layers, but none of us appear to notice. The water drifts by, and we dig our heels into the bottom, and where it's slightly deeper, we float, arms stretched out, staring up at the blue sky. The river is a vein, giving us life, washing away the indifference. Soon we're splashing each other and laughing.

"I'll be really pissed if I see a shark in here," Elle says.

"I think you have a better chance of seeing a mermaid," Willow jokes.

The Floridians are rounding the bend, their two boats side by side. When they see us in the water, they ask if we need any help.

Elle laughs. Willow, too. And I just smile.

CHAPTER 28

The days blend into one another, a mostly steady rhythm, though I know this thing with Cole is bound to come to a head. Willow and Elle are busy on the farm, my sister now calling Elle *Little Mermaid*. It's an endearing memory, and I hold on to it tight. My father's improving daily, taking rides in his wheelchair while rehabbing his hand. As I had predicted, he has already become a southpaw.

Elle and I are on our way into town to pick out the flowers and soil to replenish the garden. The route is hilly and green, a contrast from our last drive through the arid flatlands of the South. This time, we are on a mission together, Elle sober and reflective.

We spend the first ten minutes arguing about my not letting her drive. Gone is the girl who giggled in the river days ago, who caught five fish and walked out of the water transformed.

"I have my restricted, you know. And last time I checked, you're *way* older than twenty-one."

I thank her for the reminder and tell her it's not happening. "This isn't Miami, Elle." Although she'd already mastered the Polaris, jetting around the farm and its rolling hills. "And this isn't the farm."

"It's the same difference," she says.

"It's really not," I say. "And it's not that I don't trust you. I don't trust the other drivers."

"You'd make a ridiculously nervous mother, you know that, Avery? Like the worst of the helicopters."

She has no way of knowing how her comment affects me, tapping into my deepest wounds. I take a moment to swallow it back. "Is that such a bad thing?"

"To be a neurotic nelly? Um, yeah. What's good about that?" She pulls down the visor and peers at herself in the mirror. Then I see her whip out Rouge Coco and apply it to her lips. "Mallory was pretty cool. Most of the time. Except when she became Inspector Hygiene." She smacks her lips together.

"What's that supposed to mean?" I ask.

"Nothing. And look what happened to her."

Neither of us responds to that sad fact, and the radio suddenly seems louder than before. We let reality sink in, Halsey singing in the background, and we know we can't prevent bad things from happening, no matter how hard we try.

We spend the next twenty minutes or so listening to Taylor Swift and Harry Styles before turning into the lot for Holly's Nursery & Garden Center. There Elle helps me pick out flowers, and we discuss which will thrive this time of year and which will require extra care. She seems to take an interest, so I let her be a part of the decision-making, and she fills our platform truck with Carolina lupine, azaleas, and swamp milkweed while I throw in the soil and fertilizer and a pair of new gloves for her. We stop in front of a section of garden accessories and pick out a few pieces to decorate the space. I choose a colorful blue butterfly; Elle decides on a large green toad. "He's so ugly he's cute," she says. And then we agree on a sign to personalize. "Beckett Garden," she says.

"Avery and Elle's Garden," I correct her.

We stop for lunch at the diner and scarf down burgers and fries while seated across from each other in a cherry-red vinyl booth. I tell her how much I enjoy spending time with her and that I'm looking forward to our digging in the dirt.

She accepts the compliment, though her mood is difficult to read. Elle and I have never spent this much time alone together. At home, there's always the distraction of Jude or her brothers. Here, we are not quite friends and not quite strangers, so our relationship skips around a range of bumps, landing somewhere in the middle.

When she brings up Luke again, she tells me that she took my earlier advice—shocking—and they talked. And she was honest. "A little honest, I guess. He was just worried I didn't want to kiss him. Like he thought he had bad breath or something. And by the way, his breath is never bad. Not like most boys." And once she opens the floodgates, she's off, sharing all the things she likes about him—his kind eyes, the way he holds the door for her, how funny he is, funnier than anyone she knows.

"I think you're pretty funny, Elle."

"Trust me, he's funnier. And it's never in a mean way. He's really polite, always using manners, and everyone likes being around him."

"That's the South for you," I remind her.

"Miami's not the true South. That's for sure."

As she talks endlessly about the boy between bites of her food, I decide I'd be happy to listen to her talk about anything, even bad breath, if it means she trusts me enough to confide in me. And when she brings up her assignment, she confesses, "I've been having a hard time deciding if Napoleon's a tyrant or a hero."

"Let's talk about it."

"That's just it. I overheard you and your dad the other day. When he said how sometimes people do things for the wrong reasons. They think it's for the best . . . and that's where I'm stuck."

I hadn't known she could hear us, though I'm glad she did. I want to talk her through it, hopeful I can help. "First, tell me why you chose Napoleon."

She looks up. "Too many choices . . . Churchill, Caesar, that Otto von Bismarck guy, and I, well, I suck at history. Too many names and dates and battles to keep up with. You're good at it, I guess. And the boys are obsessed with that story you told them about Napoleon and that stupid bowl . . . It's like a game of treasure hunt for them."

She recognizes the connection to me, my influence, however small. I know this because she quiets, playing with the fries, making shapes with them on her plate. She chose Napoleon because of a two-second story I relayed. And I know I shouldn't read into it, but I do. I wait for her to go on as though I'm seated at the edge of a cliff. Will she push me off or sit beside me and enjoy the view?

"Do you think I made the wrong choice?" she asks.

"I don't," I say, feeling this giddy expression warm my cheeks. "I'm glad you chose Napoleon."

"So," she continues, "I'm confused because in a lot of ways, he was a hero. I read how he saved the republic and promoted education. He supported the Jews, and there was that Napoleonic Code. But then he was kind of a jerk. He basically controlled the arts and the press, which doesn't do anybody any good. And there were wars that killed a lot of people, and he didn't really believe in democracy. So he's sort of both. Like that guy who stole from the rich to feed the poor."

"Robin Hood?"

"Yeah, him," she says.

I slide back in the booth, appraising her.

"What?" she asks.

"You."

"What about me?"

"I like the way you think."

She seems to have a hard time accepting what I say, and she reaches for her chocolate milkshake and takes a gulp.

"I have to choose," she says. "That's the point of the paper."

"You can't even let me compliment you."

"Come on, Avery. Don't get all weird on me."

I'm staring at her. She's the same girl as yesterday and the day before, yet she's different. And the stirring inside me is too powerful to ignore. "I'm really proud of you."

"Hero or tyrant?" she asks, taking another sip, a milk mustache covering her upper lip.

"It's okay for you to take it in."

She refuses to look at me, thrusting the milkshake in my direction. "Do you want some?"

I don't make a move.

"Taste it," she insists. "It's really good."

"I know you hear me. I know it's hard to let me . . . anyone . . . love you. I get that. But I'm going to keep telling you until you let it in."

And because I can see she's openly struggling with my attention, wanting to accept what I have to offer but also needing to reject it, I point out the mustache on her upper lip and tell her I don't really like sweets. Relenting, she sets the shake down.

"I quite like my mustache." She takes on an English accent when she says this.

"What kind of person doesn't like sweets?" she asks, relieved to have the focus off her. She grabs a straw from the metal dispenser and chews on its end. "That's unnatural."

"I never really acquired a taste for them."

"That's weird, Avery. You never crave a fat chocolate chip cookie or Nutella brownies? Everyone loves Nutella brownies."

"Not everyone." I smile, watching her lick her lips, the chocolate mustache still there. "Enjoy it while you can. When you get to be my age, it lands squarely on your butt."

She drops the straw in the glass, sitting back on the red plastic. "You can't even say *ass*."

"I don't need to say it. There are far better options."

"Like what?" She crosses her arms, amused. "Let me hear. Give me some examples."

"You want examples?"

She smiles. "Yes. I want examples."

"Okay. Let me think. There's *tush . . . bottom . . . rear.*" I pause, racking my brain, a thin smile making its way across my face. "*Rump. Buns.*"

Elle breaks out into a laugh. "Buns? Who talks like that?"

It's hard to keep a straight face. "The British?" And then I adopt the accent. "What's wrong with buns? They go with the mustache."

She waves her hands in the air. "Like, *everything!*"

I start singing in my English accent. "I like big buns and I cannot lie," and she fights it, but I can tell she finds my terrible voice entertaining.

We're interrupted by a nearby table of screaming children. One of the little girls takes my breath away. A mess of auburn hair, light eyes. She looks to be about the same age Quinn would be, and I watch as her big brothers torment her until she cries. Elle's watching, too, as they squirt water at her through straws and pull at her hair.

"I can't believe I'm actually saying this," she says, "but Milo and Henry just might be better behaved than those two."

"We were once small like that. And imperfect."

"Hard to believe," she remarks, reaching for the straw again. And then her voice changes. "Mallory used to tell me that I was the easiest of all of us."

Whatever the reason, her continuing to call her mother by her first name makes me uncomfortable. When I try to pin her eyes down, she's looking everywhere but at me. "Henry cried all the time, and Milo, he never slept. She'd say I was the best helper. I'd make Henry laugh with stupid faces, and I'd push Milo around in that buggy to make him tired. She used to get into my bed when she finally got the monsters to sleep. Curl around me."

She hesitates before continuing. All her lonely feelings culminating into this. "She smelled like flowers."

A profound sorrow sneaks up on me, and I want to take away her pain. "I know how much you miss her, Elle."

She sits there, unchanged, not agreeing or disagreeing, only a slight quiver in her lips. And I feel myself being pulled in. I didn't have a mother to miss, only Willow and the love and memories that came along with her.

"Do you miss your mom?" she asks.

"I never knew her."

She leans back against the booth. "But you miss her, right? Like birthdays, when she bakes you a cake and makes you pose for a gazillion pictures? And that serious voice when she wants to have a talk . . ." She slows down when she adds, "That one person who always knows the right thing to say . . ."

It's not difficult to figure out what's going on here. Elle's not talking about my mother; she's talking about hers. And the images that flash, the sepia-colored memories, remind me of Willow and the closeness we've lost. An achy burn settles in my throat. My sister, my pseudo-mother, the one who did all those things my own mother couldn't.

Elle wants to say more, but she hesitates. And I should find a way to console her, to turn the story around so that she sees the wound and can tend to it, though we both know it will never fully heal. The hurt is too great, and I have to tread lightly. She could turn on me in an instant. Blame me for exposing what she's tried to avoid.

Which means we are more alike than I care to admit. I had that person, I have that person, and I just might have let this rift go too far.

"I was six months old when my mother died, Elle. My only memories are those that have been shared with me."

"That's so fucking sad," she says.

And I forgive her for the curse word because there's no better way to capture that kind of loss. "You're lucky you have memories," I say to her. "And I guess I was lucky to have a big sister who filled in."

There's a tear sweeping down her cheek. She doesn't try to wipe it away, and I pretend not to see it. "I don't know what's worse," she says. "Maybe it's easier without all this stuff . . . her voice in my ear . . . her smell . . . Sometimes I wish I never—"

I cut her off. "Don't say it. Don't ever say it. Her love for you . . . it's irreplaceable. There's nothing more sacred." I reach across the table for her hand. "Don't wish it away."

She pulls back. "You can't really understand, Avery. Like you said, you don't have memories of your mother."

True. But I'm thinking about someone else.

Interrupting our moment is the sound of my phone ringing. Jude's FaceTiming, and Elle perks up, happy, like me, to see his smile.

He pans the phone at the garden, and it looks as though he's salvaged the plants. I fill him in on our plans and the garden we'll be creating.

"Let me talk to him," she says.

I hand her the phone. "I miss you, Daddy."

And I feel a lump in my throat, missing him, too.

They talk for a few minutes, and she says, "Okay, I'll tell her."

When Elle hands the phone back to me, I'm disappointed we didn't get to say goodbye, but then she says, "He's coming to visit."

The idea wraps around me, warming me, frightening me. The only way to move forward is with the truth. But then what?

"Do you miss him, Avery?" she asks, plucking me from my thoughts.

I miss him. I miss everything about him.

"If I tell you I miss him, will you use it against me?" I ask. "Will you threaten to set up a profile for him on Tinder like you did last summer?"

"That was funny. Admit it."

I didn't think so, and neither did Jude.

"You were trying to break us up."

"Why would I want to do that?"

"I don't know, Elle. When I asked you about it, you made me sound like I was overreacting. You told me to chill."

She remembers. "I'm sorry."

It's the best she can do; I understand that better now. My presence in her father's life means her mother's never coming back. Who wants some woman trying to take her place?

"So if I tell you I don't miss him, then I run the risk of being insensitive, someone who doesn't deserve your dad."

"You're right," she says. "You can't win with me." She reaches for her napkin, but I stop her. "The answer's yes, Elle. I miss him. I miss him a lot."

She looks at me squarely, with awareness and understanding that feel real. And that's when she decides she's not going to choose. "Why should I have to lump Napoleon into any category? What a stupid assignment anyway. He's done good. He's done bad. Isn't he just being human like the rest of us?"

CHAPTER 29

Jude's confirmed his plans to visit. He's staying at the Albemarle, a nearby bed-and-breakfast, and I know what's expected of me. He'll want to know *everything*. If there's one thing this separation has taught me, truth matters, and because I love him, I'll have to introduce myself to him. Not just a part. All of me.

The decision weighs on me, and I can't even talk to Oliver about it. We spoke right after the fly-fishing trip, and I could tell something was shifting between us. Normally, talking to him helped ease my troubles, but after he admonished me for not coming clean with Willow, I felt annoyed. He tried to smooth it over, bringing up memories of us, memories I forbade myself, like him touching me in my favorite places, and I worried he'd surprise me and return to Crystal. "Stay where you are," I told him. "It's better for all of us."

So in the days leading up to Jude's arrival, I've been thinking about Oliver a lot. I've been confusing the past with the present, wondering if Oliver will be the reason I'll lose Jude.

The only way to combat the uneasiness is to keep busy. Elle and I begin laying the groundwork on the garden. We've arranged for her to spend a couple of hours with me in the morning, then finish her afternoons on the farm. "It shouldn't take us more than a few days," I tell her. She doesn't argue. She seems to look forward to this project, as do I.

During these peaceful mornings, I watch her tend to the soil, carefully preparing it into a smooth finish. She pats the dirt tenderly, as if ensuring the seeds feel her love. We have to extract hundreds of roots and weeds and install an irrigation system, and she never complains. Working side by side, we're quiet, just enjoying the sounds of our shovels and the animals in the nearby fields. I love having this time with her.

My father, finally able to abandon the wheelchair, takes the steps to the garden with his cane, shouting orders. "You need a plan, girls! You can't just dump the seeds into the ground."

Elle and my father handle each other flawlessly. His practicality and her edgy innocence make them entertaining to be around. By the end of the week, she's calling him Grandpop, and with that title comes a whole slew of unsolicited advice. My father can turn any aspect of the farm into a teachable moment. "You listen here, Miss Elle, your garden's growth is a lot like life. First, you need a vision for it. A plan. What do you want it to look like? Then you need a strong foundation. That starts with rich, healthy soil. For you, that means education and good habits, prioritizing. Preparation is key."

Elle doesn't roll her eyes. She listens, soaking it all in.

"Your garden and dreams require an investment of time," he continues. "You'll have to be patient . . . learn to trust the process. And above all else, heed this advice. Much like life, your garden is going to face unforeseen conditions. Temperature. Wind. Soil. Water. You'll have to manage your expectations, accept that some things are beyond your control." We all know what he's getting at. A garden, and the hours spent tending to it, can be instantly destroyed by drought or hungry deer. No matter how well we prepare our little plot for success, fate can intervene at any turn. "Do you know how to respond to that?" he asks.

We've just finished surrounding the garden with chicken wire. Elle understands, her long hair pulled off her face, revealing her bright-blue eyes. She turns to my father. "You can't," she says. "You just have to keep going."

"Atta girl." He smiles. And then he turns in my direction to be sure I've heard.

A few mornings later, Willow walks with my father to her office in the barn, and I decide to join. It's a short stroll, and our father, freshly walking, manages to keep up.

My head feels foggy; I'd only slept on and off. Jude's arrival had me tossing and turning, and when I finally fell asleep, Elle's alarm went off. Listening as her steps, eager and purposeful, passed my room, I eventually crashed. The dream was vivid. Oliver showed up. Here. At the farm. In my room. He snuck under the covers, and I felt every inch of him against my skin. I woke up in a sweat, wanting him, feeling not a shred of guilt.

Now, the day is lazy and hot, Oliver buried under my skin, and I turn my attention to my sister and father. The afternoon is reminiscent of when Willow and I were kids. Our steps are in sync, and we're peacefully coexisting, though there's still a bridge for us to cross.

"What's better than an old man having his two girls by his side?"

We relish the attention and his happiness, but then he responds to what I assumed was a rhetorical question: "Having three ladies by his side!"

I had presumed he was referring to Elle, but then my sister chimes in, slinging her backpack from one shoulder to the other. "Careful, Pop. This one only just learned about your many conquests."

"Avery, honey," my father turns to me. "Remember 'God Bless America' Patrick, from the hospital?" he asks, not waiting for me to answer. "I have a date with his sister, Jan."

"So there really were other women." I say this more to myself than to them.

"Oh, Avery." He smiles, offering me a sympathetic nod.

"C'mon, Dad," Willow says. "She can handle it. There were *women*," she repeats, "*a lot* of women."

My father laughs. "You make me sound like some heartless playboy, Willow."

"You kinda were, if I recall. I saw those women lined up at our door."

With a wave of the hand, he deflects. "It wasn't like that. The ladies in town just took pity on me." But then he thinks about it. "I guess there were quite a few of them. And casseroles and fresh-baked pies."

Hearing it come out of my father's mouth feels different than it did from my sister's. *Quite a few of them.* We don't always want to see our parents in that way. I search my sister's eyes for guidance.

"I told you!" she says to him. "You were young and handsome. Of course the widow brigade was knocking down your door."

"Maybe. But you girls were young. Most of my energy was spent on you."

"Did you hear that, A?" My sister elbows me. "*Most* of his energy."

But I'm off somewhere, and Willow sees it.

"What's the matter, Avery? Aren't you happy for him?"

"I'm always happy for him."

"Then what's wrong?"

I look at them both when I speak. "Jude's coming."

My sister smiles. "That's good, right?"

I'm not sure, so I don't respond. "I'm going to tell him what I've done."

They're listening, waiting for me to go on.

"I don't know if it will fix all of it, but I'm going to try . . ." And I pause for a second to shake Oliver out of my head. My voice wobbles when I say, "I don't want to be the woman who hurts people."

My sister moves in closer, the chill between us beginning to thaw. "Listen here, Avery Beckett. You don't hurt people. You love. And the world turned on you, so you gave it right back. But it's in there. I've seen it. I've seen you with Elle. You think it's me making the difference with her, but it's you. You're the one she wants around. You're the one she wants to confide in. I know you're scared, but don't tell me you hurt people. Not when I know what's in your heart."

I'm biting back tears, wanting to take it all in, even though she's wrong about my hurting people. She doesn't know it yet, but she will.

"I want to be the one to tell him. No slipups. If there's any chance I have with him, this is it."

"Honey," my father begins, wrapping an arm around me. "You know we support you in this. We won't say a word."

Willow's thinking; I can tell by the lines in her forehead. There's nothing that gives her more excitement than the pages of a love story. She reminds me, again, how Jude loved me enough to want to spend his life with me.

My father's lessons float through my mind. *A garden is a metaphor for life, Avery. Have a vision for it. What do you want in it? Who? How will you make it happen?*

Breaking up the moment, Cole passes by, riding Dolly toward the stable, and I catch his gaze lingering on Willow, who's in a short sundress, bending over to tie her shoe.

But then Dolly neighs, a loud, piercing wail, and she rears, standing on her hind legs. Cole turns his attention toward the unwieldy animal, struggling to calm her down, but he's been distracted, and he loses his grip and is thrown violently from the horse. Dolly takes off across the field while my sister hops over the wooden rail, running toward Cole, shouting his name, and I do what I've always done, I follow behind her. When we reach his side, Cole is still, too still. Willow drops to her knees, touching him, asking him where it hurts, but he's unresponsive.

My father's shouting, "Don't move him," and a crowd of workers gathers around.

Cole flutters his eyes. "Willow." He says it so softly. Then says it again.

Willow moves in closer, squeezing his hand.

He's wincing from the pain, opening and closing his eyes. "You trying to kill me?" he groans.

Tears form in Willow's eyes. "Why would I want to kill you?"

And maybe it's the adrenaline, the fear of losing someone she loves, but she continues with her crazy talk. "I love you, Cole Manley. I've always loved you. Don't you go closing those eyes of yours on me." Cole is barely moving, his lids painted shut. "I'm not going to lose you . . . I never wanted to lose you."

Silence descends around us.

My sister's confession seems to bring Cole to life. His eyes slowly open; his lips part to speak. "Avery . . . she told me . . . I shouldn't have listened . . . I should've . . . I loved you, too . . ."

His eyes become clearer; he slowly begins to wiggle his fingers, move his legs. Someone asks about his head, if he has any pain or dizziness. And his answer is, "It all worked out as it should." I back away, unable to face my sister's scowl. "What the hell is he talking about, Avery?"

Cole, with the help of my father, sits up, squinting at the bright sky.

My father pats him on the back. "Got the wind knocked outta ya, son. You'll be all right."

This calms everyone down, but not Willow.

She turns back to Cole, hands on hips. "What did Avery say to you?"

Skye comes running over, just in time for Cole to hobble to his feet, leaving the things that were said to hang in the air. Someone's retrieved Dolly. Her ankle's swollen to twice its size. Probably a bee sting or some other kind of bite. And when everyone disperses, and Willow and Cole appraise each other with a regret draped in long ago, Willow pulls me through the tomato field and up to the barn.

We stand, my sister and I, nowhere for me to hide.

"It was you," she begins, pointing at me wildly.

"Let me explain."

"There's nothing to explain. You . . . You." She's circling me like a coyote about to pounce. "I take it all back. You do hurt people. You took something that wasn't yours and wrecked it. How could you?"

This is worse than I'd imagined. I apologize. I beg. I try useless explanations. "I was angry. I was hurt. The world turned on me. You said it yourself. And wasn't it partially true? You were stringing him along for years! How was I supposed to know you'd figure it all out a couple of weeks later?"

"Jesus H. Christ, Avery." I'm afraid to hear what's about to come out of her mouth. She paces back and forth, unable to look at me. Then she gets in my face. "You're lucky, you know that? You're lucky I love Jackson with every ounce of my being, else I'd . . ."

"What?"

"Else I'd . . ." She's clearly trying to come up with something, but she can't think of anything. So unlike her. And that's when I see the corners of her lips turn up, the beginning of a smile.

And I feel a laugh coming on. The kind the two of us used to share when we were little, having no particular reason.

"I'm sorry," I begin, trying to hold it in. "I was giving the world a piece of my mind that day."

And she can't help herself; she's bent over in tears, her laughs sounding as loud as our mother's must have been. "Oh, Avery. It's fine. Except now the entire farm thinks I'm in love with him. I do love him, but not like that. Not anymore."

"So you're not mad?"

She stops to catch her breath. "I said Cole was the one that got away. That doesn't mean it would've worked if I caught him. Everything happened the way it was meant to happen."

The relief I feel is endless.

"It'll happen that way for you, too. Just tell Jude you love him, else I swear to you, I will. Don't do what I did. Don't go asking for a lemon. Ask for the tree. The roots. The stems. All of it."

CHAPTER 30

Jude's arrived, and I'm driving the winding streets toward his B and B. Elle's working, so he and I have the day to spend together before he picks her up for their dinner. I'm thinking about Willow and Cole's love for each other and all the different ways there are to love. I'm also going over what I plan to say to Jude and how I'm going to say it. I'm nervous and unsure, so I take my time.

When a John Mayer song comes on the radio, the melody takes me back to a night early in our relationship, when I knew Jude was someone I could let in, even if it was halfway.

It was late, long after Mayer's concert had ended, and we were seated at an outdoor café on Ocean Drive not far from my apartment. The street was bustling with tourists and locals and youthful bodies, but Jude's eyes were focused entirely on me.

His stare was playful and thrilling, and I loved what it did to my body. I'd forgotten how nice it felt to be wanted, before it had the power to scare me. Diverting my eyes to the scar on his forehead, I asked, "What happened?"

"Seventh grade. The fire alarm went off, and instead of filing out of the classroom in an orderly fashion, I panicked and zigzagged into Karen Breitbart's backpack. Landed headfirst against the corner of her desk. Twenty stitches. My badge of courage."

I remember reaching down to touch my leg, realizing how fire connected us, and a line of goose bumps trickled down my bare arms. The scar was noticeable, circling around my ankle and just up my calf. I'd reach for it out of habit, when I missed Crystal, when I thought about the past. In its tenderness I could channel the pain, imagine a different ending, and never forget.

My fingers moved to his forehead, where they traced the thin line, the thick texture. He closed his eyes. "I like your hands."

No one had ever complimented my callused palms or unpolished nails, so I kept rubbing the scar when I asked, "Do you believe there's only one person for each of us?"

He let out a deep sigh. "I hope not."

"I'm sorry," I said. "That's not what I meant."

"It's okay. It's a fair question, though I'm not sure I can be objective, considering my situation. Maybe it's just an ideal for the younger generations. The alternative unimaginable. People like me, I guess we fall into a different category. Don't we deserve a second chance?"

A brisk wind came close, dancing along my skin.

"I think you do. Yes." *But maybe not me.*

When I pull up to the bed-and-breakfast, he's waiting outside. Handsome Jude, dressed in jeans and a black polo. His hair's a little longer, his eyes brighter, and my heart skips.

We don't immediately embrace, instead offering our cheeks for a stilted kiss. But when that proves empty and unpromising, he pulls me into his arms, and I don't have time to think about it—I let him swallow me, and every inch of my body remembers every inch of his, and it's telling me not to let him go. To tell him. Everything.

We drive through Crystal, en route to Blowing Rock, and though I'm still jittery, I point out all the sights along the Blue Ridge Parkway. This time of year, the scenic road is packed with visitors and lush foliage, and we soak in the gorgeous scenery. The conversation shifts from Elle to the boys, to Jude's patients, to Cole's fall—all the subjects except for us.

"That's scary," he says. "That could've had a very different ending."

He wasn't wrong. I had thought about that quite a bit. Cole and my father were both lucky to be alive. It's why I was resolved to do this.

Blowing Rock is a small town nestled in the mountains, with spacious homes and spectacular vistas. The area's composed of hiking paths and trout-filled lakes, and the town center meets on Main Street, with an eclectic mix of shops, cafés, galleries, and a bustling park.

We get out at the far end and stroll the crowded sidewalk, stopping to stare into store windows, checking out the latest street art. At the corner of Main and Maple, we happen across a group of sprawling trees, their long branches sweeping the sky. When we get closer, I notice white plastic leaves hanging from the stems. They're tags, and inside each of them is a handwritten prayer.

"What is this?" Jude asks, staring up at the bouquet of messages.

A sign sits on a nearby table, "The Prayer Tree." Following the path of limbs and branches, I instantly feel a kinship and spot a framed news article pinned to the torso of one of the trees. The piece tells the story of Sherri Furman, the owner of Take Heart, the lavender shop that was once situated on this corner. One ordinary day, Sherri received a call to place a bowl of wooden hearts and pens outside the shop, beside a nearby tree. She left no sign or instructions. To her surprise and delight, passersby began jotting down their wishes, prayers, and dreams and hanging them on the branches. As word about the sacred tree spread through the town, Furman eventually provided paper and plastic tags for visitors to share their thoughts. I pause when I reach the last paragraph. On a scorching June afternoon, an electrical malfunction ignited a fire at Take Heart sending the building up in flames, but the adjacent trees and thousands of wishes remained unscathed.

Gazing up at the vines and the thousands of wishes, I'm struck by what has the power to survive and what must perish. I'm astounded by the tree's quiet strength and the willingness of those able to share their vulnerability.

When I look over at Jude, a woman's smiling up at him. They're standing in front of the supply table, and she's handing him a card and a pen. She's pretty and curvy, blond, without a stitch of makeup. And she's clearly taken by him.

I watch Jude's reaction. He smiles, enjoying the attention from someone so fresh and youthful. A feeling crawls up inside of me I don't recognize. By nature, I'm not a jealous person, never had a reason to be, but when I watch Jude and this girl laughing at something she said, I break a little inside. And while I know better than anyone that I have no claim to him, I can't deny what I'm feeling, what he brings forth in me.

Jude glances over his shoulder and catches me staring. He holds my eyes in his, and the pull is more powerful than I remember.

The girl sees me there, and her smile fades. Jude grabs another pen and card and heads my way. He doesn't mention the young woman or what passed between us, and we take a seat on one of the benches and fill out our prayers. As I write, he peers over my shoulder, but I shoo him away. "If I show you my wish, it won't come true."

He laughs. "You know you have to hang it on the tree. And once it's up there, anyone who walks by gets to read it."

"Maybe I want to hold on to mine," I say.

He doesn't ask me why I'd want to do that. He scribbles on his card, stuffs it in the plastic cover, and chooses the tallest spot on the tree to hang it. I don't know what he wrote, I may never know, but I love that he's willing to dream.

I think about what I've scribbled on my card, folding it over. The paper feels hot in my hands, and I'm clutching on to the idea that we can survive. Willow's voice filters through my ear, and I ask myself if I can do this. With him. And I know that I want to.

Just tell him.

"What's wrong?" he asks when he returns to the bench.

"Nothing." I smile.

His hand reaches for mine, and I shove the card in my pocket. "I don't believe you," he says.

Jude is attuned to my moods, but I'm an expert at pivoting and dodging minefields.

"How do you do it?" I ask. "How do you believe any of this is possible?"

"I'm not sure I understand what you're asking."

"This." I motion toward the tree. "People putting their prayers out there . . . on a street corner?"

He scoots in closer, the crowd around the tree growing, laughter and chatter filling the air.

"When I was in medical school, my father gave me some advice. I didn't understand it at the time, but it was pretty simple. He said when we stop dreaming, we die. I've taken those words with me, even when I refused to believe. And when we lost Mallory, I thought, *Never again.* No more dreams. No more plans.

"One night, Milo crawled into our bed, missing his mom. I looked at my grieving child, knowing I'd never be able to take away this loss." His voice quavers, and he collects himself. "I'd always tried to be strong for him . . . for all of them . . . but that night my son needed to grieve . . . and we cried together."

I'm listening to Jude with a well of grief in my own heart. For him. For Milo. And I'm struck by his sensitivity, his willingness to believe again.

"Our role as parents shifts with each phase of our children's lives. I knew I would have to love Milo differently because of his loss, and he would love me differently for the same. My father's words found me that day. Our dreams are the dreams we wish for our children. I had no choice but to keep dreaming. Keep believing. It kept me going. It kept all of us going."

Tears form in my throat, and I let the message in, recognizing how he found a way to trust in the universe again. "I wish I had your courage." We're hovering close together, and I understand how hard this must have been for him to share and how hard it had to be for him to let me in, too.

Our fingers lace together, and he pulls me up. "You're brave, Avery."

He's enjoying this too much. I hate to ruin it. "There's something I want to talk to you about."

"First I want to know what you wrote." And he smiles. "Then I'll tell you about mine."

I really want to tell him something else, but I've waited this long. What's another couple of minutes?

"I figured you put it so high so no one would see, because then it might not come true."

"I'm not superstitious," he says. "I put it that high so whoever pulls strings up there would pick mine first."

His eyes feel like they can see through me. They're beautiful and blue, and I want to give him the love he deserves.

"Don't tell me," I say, putting my hand up between us. "*I'm* still superstitious."

"What else makes you superstitious?" he teases. And before I can answer, he's wrapping an arm around me. "Tell me over lunch."

Every time I'm ready to start the conversation, *June 13* about to spring off my tongue, I get interrupted or afraid. We're having such a nice afternoon, I don't want to ruin it. I'm second-guessing myself.

We're seated outside a French café with tiny round tables shaded by trees. The checkered tablecloths hide our knees as they knock into each other, and it's quaint and romantic, and for a time, I forget about Oliver and Quinn. I forget about the past.

We talk about North Carolina and my time on the farm. He asks how my father's doing, and I share his progress. "He just wants to get back to his work. That's where he's happiest." And then he asks about my mother. "You hardly ever bring her up." I never bring her up. What could I possibly say? And I think this could be the opening, the great segue to the other loss. But he's asking because he's thinking about Elle, comparing our wounds, figuring out how best to navigate. So I share some insight on what it was like growing up without a mother and having an older sister to fill the void.

"I can tell from our phone calls that you've had an impact on her."

"It's the other way around." I sip from the champagne flute, placing it on the table, ready to take this step. "Here's the thing, my sister and I have been estranged . . . and you and the kids . . . I've always wanted a big family . . . ever since I was a little girl . . . but things . . . they just . . . they just didn't work out that way." I take a deep breath. I'm staring into the blue of Jude's eyes while he spoons the last of a crème brûlée, licking the sweet cream from his lips. The champagne has made me tingly, so when he leans over and brushes my lips with his, I let him. He tastes of vanilla custard, and I welcome his mouth, welcome him.

"I want to know more about you," he whispers in my ear, his breath tickling my skin, but we're interrupted by a call from the hospital, and the conversation eats into much of our lunch. I swallow the emotions. I was so close, but I'm certain we'll have more time. I listen as he goes back and forth between the patient and the hospital. Someone has to be admitted. There are problems with finding a bed. The hospital is at capacity. So we finish lunch and begin strolling down Main Street, and I can see he's distracted; he's forgotten I was about to reveal my secrets. But he clasps my hand in his, and we stroll like a normal couple, stopping at Kilwins for fudge, trying on silly hats in a gift shop.

On the drive back to Crystal, we are quiet, the taste of him still on my lips.

"You're different here," he says. "You seem more relaxed. At peace."

I am at peace. With him. Right now.

"I've missed you," he continues.

"I've missed you, too."

"We should talk about the proposal," he says.

He's not wrong, but I feel an immediate pang inside. All these emotions are colliding, and I want them, I do, because they mean risk and reward. I know that being away from Jude, being here, has made me realize more than ever that I need him. If I let him in, there's a chance I might lose him. But I'll never know if I don't try.

"Everything happened so fast that day," I say. "Then the call from Elle. I wish I'd had more time to explain . . ."

"You mean to explain why you didn't want to marry me."

"It's not that. Jude"—I turn to face him, tracing his profile with my eyes—"a proposal . . . a blended family . . . we needed more than a conversation. The kids . . . Mallory . . . the closet . . ."

"The closet?"

"Her clothes are all there, Jude."

He thinks about this. I let him. He should.

"I never would've pushed. Ever. But I wondered what that meant to you. And the kids. Did you ever discuss it with them? What it would mean to have me as their stepmother?" I face the window when I say, "How do you know I'd be any good at it?" When he doesn't respond, I say, "It's a huge step. We owe it to them and each other to discuss it more in depth."

He's picking at his scar, rubbing it with his hand while he drives with the other, and we don't talk for the next several miles.

"I saw your face. When the blond was asking me out."

"She asked you out?" The idea of Jude with someone else hurts. "Did you tell her you're with someone? That you don't even live here?"

217

"Am I?" he asks. "With someone?"

He's in my heart. Does that count?

"I still love you," he says. But then he gets upset. "Have you even thought about us? About what you want?"

"I have."

"And?"

"I think about you every day."

"Then what are we doing?" We are parked at the bed-and-breakfast when he turns to me and says, "Milo asked me why we're in time-out. I don't want to be in a time-out."

"Jude." It's a whisper. "You have no idea how badly I want to make this work." And my entire body bristles with energy, knowing it's now or never. "I want to tell you a story . . ."

But he doesn't hear me, perhaps I don't say it loud enough, and Jude, dear, sweet, Jude, he doesn't give me the chance. He kisses me. Full lips. Full heart. And the confession gets buried in our bodies, which have always been able to communicate. And because I may never have another chance to feel Jude inside me, because my truths may make him run, I let him lead me out of the car and up to his room.

Inside, he cradles my face in both hands and kisses me harder, and I remember why I love him, and I forget why I lied to him because I'm hungry for him, all of him. And soon we're undressing, our hands and lips speaking in the absence of words. Our bodies know exactly where to touch, how to please. And when we land on the bed and he spreads my legs to let himself inside, I'm not thinking about anyone or anything but him.

After, when we're lying in each other's arms, our fingers clasp tightly together.

"We can do this, Avery."

I want to believe him. And I allow myself to imagine the possibility, free-falling, wondering if he'd want to catch me. How nice if we could stay in this moment longer. No secrets. No lies.

But then his hand drops down on my belly. He whispers in my hair, "I'd love to see a little Avery in the world. A little girl who looks just like you." And I pop up from the bed and feel the memories pour down like rain. And I decide, if I'm going to do this, I have to be dressed for it. So I reach for my clothes at the same time his phone rings. It's the hospital, again, and I can tell by his tone, by his laconic responses, that the patient didn't get there on time. Jude is distraught. He gets off the bed and joins me in getting dressed.

I whisper, "I'll let you go," but he wants me to stay. He's calling someone, maybe the man's wife, daughter, I can't be sure. I hear a female's voice wailing through the phone. At first, I stay beside Jude, offering my hand, rubbing his shoulder, but then I feel out of place, like he needs to deal with this family alone. He covers the phone. "Let's talk tonight. After my dinner with Elle. You said you had something to tell me. It sounded important."

And I'm relieved that he heard, that he remembered.

I nod. I'll tell him tonight.

I kiss his cheek and whisper a faint, "I'm sorry."

Only a few more hours. I slam my car door and let out a breath. Squeezing my eyes shut, I think about the prayer stuffed in the pocket of my jeans, knowing I can do this: *Let me let go.*

CHAPTER 31

Driving back to the farm, I release a long breath, the weight of what almost happened filling the air. I open the window, the breeze skimming my cheek, and when I reach the gates, I long to talk to Willow the way we used to. Before the fire, before all our problems. She always knew the right things to say. She understood me; she understood this loss.

The house is quiet, and I collapse on my bed. Jude's scent fills my nose, his touch engraved on my body. After pointing out how he still hung on to Mallory's clothes, I know I'm a lousy hypocrite, or worse, for hanging on to Oliver. But I can't help myself.

"Ollie."

"Avery."

I'm staring at his words on the wall. Today, they scream brighter and louder. I recall Jude's face and the promises he made, and I touch my heart, remembering the way he made it feel when he held me, and I want to hold on to that feeling a little longer. I want to let this part of my history go. "I'm so scared, Ollie. I need to tell Jude what happened to us. To Quinn. All of it. The closer I get, the more I think of you . . . of us."

Normally, when I talk to Oliver, he lets me unload everything, my fears and insecurities, the anguish and regret I've held inside. He makes it so easy to hold on. He never pushes. He's an ally.

"You can't keep doing this, Avery. You've got to let this thing with us go. Jude loves you. And you love him, too. I'm telling you to go, or you're going to miss your chance."

"I have no idea who I am without you. Without Quinn. Everything is tied to the two of you, and I don't know how to cut myself loose."

"You know how. You're ready."

I close my eyes, repeating the mantra to myself. *You can do this.*

Beautiful Oliver. I see him there in my eyes. He's smiling, pushing me to move on. He's telling me he'll always love me, how I'm the only girl he'll ever love. "You're my honeybee."

I drown out his voice, trying to forget all that transpired and made it impossible for us to be together. There's no sense harping on what could have been. "Just tell me," I say. "Tell me I won't lose him. Like I lost you."

But not even Ollie can tell me that. I'd have to trust love. I'd have to take a leap.

"I know I have to do this . . . but what if he can't forgive me?" My fingers traipse along the black marker. I can feel his love through my fingers. "I love you so much, Ollie. I know I shouldn't . . . I wish I didn't . . ."

Oliver tells me he loves me, too, that he'll always love me, but he says it's time I tell Jude these things, not him. He says I've been holding on for too long, and all it's done is prevent me from moving on, from fully letting someone know my heart. "You have to trust him."

"Will I ever see you again?" I ask.

But he doesn't answer, and there's someone at my door.

CHAPTER 32

Willow storms in my room without knocking.

"Avery, who are you talking to?"

I sit up in bed and wipe my eyes with the sheet, refusing to meet her gaze.

"Avery, look at me. Who was it?"

"Leave me alone, Willow."

She comes closer, sweaty from the late-afternoon heat. "Avery, please, just tell me."

I don't answer, and this makes her furious.

"Avery, were you talking to Oliver again?"

The name splices the air, and I resist, a fresh set of tears trying to climb out.

"It's none of your business."

"Oh, Avery—"

"No," I say. "Get out of here, Willow. Just go."

"Avery," she begins, unsure. "Ollie's not here . . . You know this . . . The fire . . . You know he didn't make it . . . You know he died."

Her words slam into me, and I shout, "Please, Willow."

"Oh my God," she exclaims. "I thought you were better! I thought moving to Florida helped . . . That Jude . . . I thought you'd finally let Oliver go!"

When We Let Go

"It's not like that," I argue, and the tears spill. It's useless to stop them. They're always there. They're always waiting.

"You told me you hadn't heard from him. You lied."

My head hurts. A sharp pain digging into my temples. I try to massage it away, but it persists.

"I told you, it's not like that," I snap back. "I know he's gone. I live it every single minute of every single day."

Willow's eyes cloud with pity. She takes me in her arms and tries to shake it all away. "I know how difficult this is. I know being here makes it worse."

I try pulling away, which only makes her hold on tighter. "I won't let you go," she says, her musky scent sliding up my nose. "You scared me," she says. "I thought it was happening again."

And we're back in time, the curtains drawn. That terrible day when Willow caught me sitting on my bed, talking to Oliver. But back then, as the doctors eventually confirmed, the trauma was too severe to process, and I'd decided which memories to recall and which to let go. I had lost Quinn, but I really believed Oliver was there. I saw him. I smelled him. I refused to acknowledge that he was gone, because to me, he wasn't. He was right there beside me as we mourned Quinn together.

Frightened by my state, she ran out of my room and found a stack of newspaper articles and shoved them in my face. I slapped them away, slapped her away. But the headlines glared at me. *"Man Dies after Saving Pregnant Fiancée from House Fire." "Cabin Fire Kills Two, Including Unborn Child."*

I remembered the nausea climbing up my throat. Racing to the bathroom, I leaned over the toilet, the anguish spilling over. Willow came up behind me, holding my hair up off my face. She couldn't stop the tingling sensation of the milk that leaked from my breasts, and it only made me cry harder. "Let it out, Avery. Let it all go." I was too sick to fling her away. There was something about her presence that I needed and detested. When there was nothing left inside, she held my face in her hands. "I'm here. I'm not going to let anything happen to you. We'll get through this together. Like we've always done."

I was drained, and denial sputtered out of me, nothing making sense. "Oliver would never leave me."

It took all Willow's conviction to try to talk some sense into me, but I was adamant.

"Avery," she had said, full-on crying, "I wish he were here. We all do. He loved you so much, but he had to go."

I felt myself about to gag again. "Please, Willow. Please just stop."

She didn't react. The drip of the faucet the only sound.

That's when she made the decision to have me committed. My father was too distraught—she couldn't go to him with my condition—so she did what she'd always done, carried the weight of our world on her shoulders.

My sister dropped me off at Oak Haven, and I remember hissing at her, spit foaming from my mouth. "You can't take Ollie away from me."

But she did. Because after a few weeks at the facility, I had no choice but to accept what was lost to me for good. Oliver had promised me he'd never leave me, and I believed him. But leaving and dying were different things. And in some sadistic, irrational way, I blamed Willow for all of it.

For anyone who has experienced the mental anguish that comes from grief, there are necessary stages. However, there are some whose pain spirals, turning into a more serious condition. The therapist who sat me down and mined through my madness called it *complicated grief*. Simone attributed my inability to process Oliver's death to a combination of factors: early mother loss, the death of a child, the loss of my fiancé, and the lingering guilt for not properly extinguishing the candle. Any one of these single variables could trigger symptoms, but together, they were crippling. In managing my shock, she described an intense yearning, a rare form of denial, and an extreme culpability that made it impossible for me to accept the truth. Keeping Oliver alive was a coping mechanism.

Willow interrupts the memory, pulling back, waiting for me to say something that will allay her fears. I tell her there's nothing to be worried about. And I dial back some of the annoyance because she has a right to be concerned. I know Oliver's gone. The dull ache inside is a constant reminder. "Don't you ever talk to Mom? Isn't she that voice in your head sometimes? The one you call out to when you need some guidance?"

She hugs me as if her tiny body can obliterate the pain, her heart trembling against mine.

Pulling back, I stare into my sister's eyes as though I'm looking into my own. I see our history in the flecks of blue, our childhood. And I see Oliver, in the hospital, hooked up to dozens of wires and machines, his face unrecognizable, swathed in bandages, and his eyes, they don't open or close. They stare out, lifeless and dull. I'm begging him to fight. Screaming at him, pounding on his chest, but it's no use.

Willow wipes the tears sliding down my face, and then she holds me so tight I can barely breathe. She's hugging away the hurt, hugging away the awful memory.

My voice trembles when I speak. "I was so close . . . today . . . Jude . . . How am I supposed to tell him this? I know I have to . . . but what if he can't handle it? What if—"

Tears pool in her eyes. "It was an accident, Avery. He'll see that."

"What if it's a sign? You believe in that stuff. I tried twice to tell him . . . and something got in the way. Both times."

"You have to tell him," she says, her eyes beating into mine. "Or you'll never know what the two of you are capable of. If this is the one thing keeping you apart, let it be the one thing to bring you back together."

Everything she says makes sense. She's always made sense.

"Look at me, Avery . . . You have a choice . . . You've always had a choice. You can wallow in this . . . this . . . guilt and suffering, alone, or you can let him in."

"That's easy for you to say."

I might as well have slapped her across the face. Her hands come down by her sides, her eyes hardened in a blazing stare. "You think I haven't been hurt? You think losing my mother didn't scar me for life? I was five. One minute she was laughing with me, reading a story, and the next, she was gone." Her fingers snap in the air, and I watch her face morph into something unrecognizable. "Everyone said, 'She's young . . . Kids are resilient,' but I lost my footing that day, and it was *because* I was so young. My compass was gone. She was the one who made sure I had one foot in front of the other. She was the one who watched over me. I miss her every single day, and I imagine what it would be like if she were here today—who she would be, or would she like Jackson—but I'm living, Avery. I'm living the best I can with what I was given. And so should you."

"She'd love Jackson," I whisper, reaching for her until she softens.

We're hunched together on my bed, my head resting on her shoulder. "You've been carrying this burden for all these years. But who's paying the price, Ave? You. You're the one being punished. Over and over and over again."

I'm suddenly exhausted. I dry my eyes and place my hand over Oliver's inscription.

"I still love him, Willow. I love Oliver."

"I know you do. You always will."

"I don't want to hurt Jude, I never meant to hurt Jude, but he needs to know the truth."

A sound emerges from the hallway, and Willow and I look up to find Elle by the door. She's holding the cordless phone to her ear. I don't know how long she's been standing there, and an immediate worry grips me.

"Elle!" my sister says.

Elle ignores Willow and narrows in on me. "Daddy," she says into the phone, "hold on a second." Then she turns her rage on me. "I knew it! I just knew it! You . . ." She points at me, and her face contorts, eyes swelling with tears. "I hate you. I always have. I never liked you, and God knows, I could've never loved you. You . . . you're full of absolute shit. All of it. You never cared about us."

She's blinking back the tears, and the fear and dread I'd tried to avoid run through my veins. She backs away, tossing the phone in my direction. "Go on, tell him. Tell him about Oliver. Tell him why you said no to him. To us." Her cheeks are inflamed, her words like weapons. She races into the hallway, and it's not long before we hear the front door slam.

And before I have time to think, I'm on my feet, running after her.

CHAPTER 33

Elle breaks out into a run, avoiding the farm and racing in the opposite direction, toward the woods. I'm chasing after her, my heart pounding loudly. She's already crossed our property line and made her way down the side of the mountain, the dogwoods and oaks in her wake.

When the forest comes into view, I'm yelling, "Don't go in there," but Elle has a mind of her own, and my warnings don't have the power to stop her. Where she's leading us isn't an inhabited area. There are no marked paths, only an untouched stretch of land. She darts over rocks and knocks through branches falling in her path. She hits them with her hands. Punches them. Kicks.

"Elle, wait up."

"Get away from me, Avery. I'll run straight to New York if you don't leave me alone," she yells over her shoulder.

"New York is in the opposite direction."

"Well, I'm sorry I don't have my fucking map with me. I didn't expect to hear what a disgusting cheat you are." Her voice is steady, no signs of tiring out.

The forest is quiet but for the crackling of our steps. The trees grow taller and thicker; the air is dense, echoing each breath. But for a girl who wants to run away from her problems, the journey is effortless.

"Elle, come on, slow down."

"I'm not slowing down. You know I was on the cross-country team."

Of course she was. My stomach starts to cramp, and I try to breathe through it.

"Who the fuck is this Oliver?" she hollers. "Is that why we're here? Why you said no to my dad and made us come to this shithole?"

"I didn't make you do anything. And if memory serves me correctly, you saw something you liked here in this *shithole*."

She slows down. Not a lot, but enough for me to notice. Maybe it's the altitude, maybe it's the betrayal I've dropped on her, but her breaths are becoming louder. I take a moment to survey our surroundings, and a slow-building panic hitches to my chest. We are deep in the woods. *I have absolutely no idea where.*

And as though Elle senses my exhaustion and unease, she speeds up again, ducking low-lying branches and stems. Each step is a step away from me. All the progress we'd made dwindling into nothingness.

"Please, Elle," I pant, "we're really far. I'm not sure—"

"Oh, I can go on for miles."

But then she shrieks. "What the hell?" And I see her frantically swatting at her face and arms. "Fucking spiderwebs." She's squirming and jumping, swiping the silky threads off her skin, and just as I'm about to catch up with her, she takes off again.

The forest winds, sloping up then down, and soaring trees sprout beside mossy rocks. Twigs snap beneath our feet, bugs and snakes lurking beneath the surface, but I'm hell-bent on catching Elle and talking some sense into her. I don't even consider the bears. It's almost dusk, the bear witching hour.

Winded and out of breath, Elle slows down, transitioning to a fast walk. I'm breathing heavily, following about ten paces behind, while she hurls insults that fly through the air. "You suck! I hate you. Why can't you just leave us alone?" And I let her erupt, knowing she'll eventually run out of insults.

Night begins to fall, and slivers of moonlight pass through the thick canopy of trees. The forest echoes, and I'm sure we're smack in the middle of lost.

That's when she stops. She's bent over, gasping, and I slowly approach. "God, you're so annoying, Avery. Why can't you just disappear? Why do you always have to be everywhere?" Her arms come up, as if her little tantrum wasn't dramatic enough.

"Elle," I begin, completely winded. "What you heard . . . it's not what you think."

She turns to face me, cheeks flushed, a faint line of sweat dotting her forehead.

"I don't want to hear any more of your stupid stories, Avery. You're a joke. No wonder you came back here. All that BS about your dad. You came to see some guy. So you could cheat on my dad. What a disgusting liar."

I think back to the day I met her father. She's right. I am a liar. And a fake and a fraud.

"We should talk about this. Let me explain."

"I think we're past explanations," she fires back.

She positions herself on a fallen tree, its roots jutting out in all directions. I don't warn her of the insects that could potentially crawl inside her shorts. "We need to head back, Elle. It's getting late . . . Your dad will worry."

"What do you care about my dad?" she snarls. "You made it very clear how you feel about him." She's kicking at the dirt. "He was always too good for you, Avery. I never understood what he saw in you."

I'm beaten, worn down, and my worry about finding our way back mounts. Scanning the area for a familiar landmark, I find none, and we'll be lucky if we have a stick of gum between us.

"You know what's even worse?" she continues.

Worse than this? I can't begin to guess.

"I was beginning to like you." She pauses, digging a nail into the bark. "And I thought you liked me, too. Like you were so A1 freaking cool about stuff . . . the flower garden . . . with Luke . . . well . . . Your stupid advice is useless to me. You're useless to me."

Her cruelty burrows deep in my gut. Everything I'd ever feared rises to the surface, and I feel sick. "You know, you can be very hateful, Elle."

She lets that simmer, dropping her head and studying the ground.

"I'm willing to explain, Elle. You may not want to hear it, but I owe you the truth." And when I see what I've done, how I've affected all of them with my actions, I know it can't go on like this any longer. "But first we need to figure out a way to get back to the house. It's getting dark."

That's when it finally begins to click. The forest is soundless, and she carefully twists around until the realization sinks in. She doesn't say it, but her wide-eyed expression tells me she finally understands, too. We're lost.

CHAPTER 34

Neither of us talks as we inwardly assess the situation. I refrain from blaming her because the blame is on me. I should've been talking to Jude about my fears and worries, not Oliver. His memory has haunted me, held me back. This overt lie has cost me everything. Now Elle. Overhearing what I said had to have hurt, confused her. There's time to explain, but for now, we need a plan to get us out of here.

"Check your pockets," I say.

She doesn't argue, merely shoving her hands inside the back of her khakis, coming up empty-handed. "What did you expect me to find? A magic phone? Sure. I'll just go call us an Uber."

I dig into my jeans, the ones with the holes, which will hardly keep out the cold, and find the white card with my scribbly handwriting. *Let me let go.* I hold on to it tightly, drawing from its strength.

Before I can harp on the fact that we have no food or supplies and no means to communicate with the outside world, I tell myself to remain calm. Living in these parts, we were raised on tales of hikers getting lost, mostly being found without incident, but there were a few horror stories I try not to fixate on.

Elle's dipping her hands into her front pockets when she freezes. Looking pleased, she holds up a lighter, seemingly surprised by its presence.

I try not to be too elated, or concerned, by this discovery. "I'm not even going to ask why you have that." I don't reach for the lighter, and I avoid looking at it. "Hold on to that," I tell her. "We're going to need it later."

"Later?"

She hasn't fully figured out that we may be hunkered down for the night. One of the rules of hiking is if you find yourself lost, you remain in a safe location, waiting for someone to find you. And if night approaches, you wait for daylight to make any moves. I'm worried, but I don't let Elle see it. We need to get our bearings, some semblance of place, which means figuring out which direction we came from before the sky shifts to the inky black that means trouble. Unfortunately, I have absolutely no idea which direction that might be. Elle's roaming the area, careful to stay close, her arms crossed around her thin shoulders. The temperature has already dropped a few degrees, and whether she's cold or just afraid, I'm unsure.

Gathering a handful of sticks and branches, I mark the area by the felled tree. The trunk itself is a good starting point, the place I have now declared as base camp, our point of being lost. I don't like that word and all that it implies. It's never good.

The cackling sounds of nightfall crowd the air. Crickets and owls make it difficult to think. I know I'm expected to calmly come up with a strategy. Jude's face darts through my mind. My dad and Willow. Dad will want to storm the forest, though he'll realize he physically can't, and my sister knows better than to traipse into the woods alone after dark. Would she have any idea where we went? I stare up into the night sky, trying to figure out the time. If only I wore a watch, I'd know how much time has passed, but since that fateful day, I've had no use for tracking time.

"Do you know where we are?" Elle asks, her fear mounting.

Tamping down my uncertainty, I trace my steps, making a guess as to which direction we came in from, but it's no use. All I see is darkness.

There's no way I can make this decision on instinct or under these conditions. Doubt climbs through me and hitches on tight. I block it out, refusing to imagine what could go wrong. I'm turning my head from side to side, waiting for the answer to come. My body wants to head in one direction, toward home. Toward Willow and all that's familiar. Anywhere but here.

"Avery, say something. You're scaring me."

"It's okay," I say, though I am in no position to make that call. "It's going to be okay."

She tries to rein in the worry, but it's there, a slick hysteria lacing through her words. "It's getting so dark. How will we find our way back?"

I think about how to respond. It *is* dark. Too dark for us to even attempt wandering off. Elle needs to hear the truth.

"We may not."

"What?"

Never has one single response carried more weight. "We need to stay put. We can't make any moves until morning."

"No," she argues. "Don't give me that bullshit, Avery. Tell me how we're getting out of here."

"I'm trying. If you'd listen." And this quiets her, which allows me to proceed, bracing myself for the fallout. "We're going to stay here. For the night. We can't risk going deeper into the woods."

Elle slowly begins to unravel. She gets up from her perch and starts pacing, throwing her arms up. There may be whimpering and more swearing involved. "Mallory told me to join the Girl Scouts . . . that it'd teach me lifelong skills." She's definitely whimpering. And soon it will turn to deep sobs because I've told her we're going to have to set up camp for the night. "I can't believe this. I can't believe we're stuck here. OMG, I'm going to die in these fucking woods."

I make a move toward her. "Elle, we can do this."

"No. I can't do this. I can't spend the night in a . . . a . . . jungle. With bears and bugs and tigers and lions . . ."

"There aren't any tigers. Or lions."

She's glaring at me—though I can't see it, I can feel it. "This is all your fault. You . . . you . . . you lured me to this stupid little town. I should've just gone to New York. I could be on my way to a Broadway show. I should've known this would be a disaster. I knew it would suck, but I didn't think I'd . . . I didn't think I'd . . . die."

"We're not going to die."

"How do you know?" she shouts at me, her panic echoing against the trees.

It takes all my conviction, and I mean all of it, to reply. "Because I know. Because I would never let anything happen to you." All the feelings I've kept hidden, they're surfacing, and I understand what it means to be able to protect someone. Or to try. And seeing the fear cross Elle's face, I know I want to try. I have to try.

Mercifully, she doesn't doubt me.

"Stay here," I tell her. "I'm serious. Do not take one step away from this spot. No crazy notions about running away."

"Where are you going?" she asks.

"Not far. I just need to check out the area."

"I'll go with you," she says.

"No. You need to stay here. But you know what you can do for me?" This will go over well. "Sing."

"Sing?"

"Yes. Anything. Anything but Diana Ross."

"Diana who?"

"Don't worry about it. Just sing. Something loud. I'm not going far, I promise, but I want to be able to hear you."

It starts out as a low-pitched mutter, but with each step I take away from her, the tune gets louder. I've made a complete, colossal mess of things, but the fact that she chooses "I Kissed a Girl" is a small triumph.

Soon I'm singing along with her, making up the words as I go along, me, deep in the mouth of the forest, singing of cherry Chapstick.

The woods at this hour are misleading, playing tricks on the eyes and the mind. Sounds are amplified, difficult to tell if they're near or far, and shadows become threats, ready to pounce. It's why I'm cautious as I approach the anemic sounds of a stream. I don't think you can even call it a stream, more like a trickle, but it's water nonetheless, a small victory in getting us through the night.

I circle back to Elle, who's singing a new song I've never heard. But she's loud, and her voice is surprisingly good, and after tripping over a few stones and steadying myself on the uneven ground, I can make out the grainy hue that is her body. She's singing so loudly, this beautiful song, she doesn't hear me approach, and when my foot crunches the leaves right beside her, she shrieks.

"For fuck's sake, Avery!"

"I'm sorry. But I found water. You can grab some leaves to cup it, or just scoop it in your hands."

"Oh my God," she begins all over again. "Fucking *Survivor*. I'm stuck in the worst episode of *Survivor*."

We're going to have to do something about her language, but until then, I try to find the humor. "It could be worse. It could be *Naked and Afraid*."

"Gross, Avery."

After that, Elle settles down, the hours ahead of us beginning to mellow her. "My dad will send someone to find us, right?" Then she changes her mind. "Maybe not you, but he'd do anything to find me." She says this without an ounce of her usual sarcasm, and she's probably right, but no one knew what direction she took off in. Our land is surrounded by forest; it's a lot of terrain to cover. "Don't they have, like, rescue parties and dogs that will search for us?"

"They do, for missing people."

"Aren't we missing people?"

236

"Look," I begin, "I don't know how it works. I don't know if we have to be missing a certain amount of time . . . I don't know what they'll do, but Elle, nighttime in the forest is tricky. It can be dangerous and difficult to get around."

"My dad . . . we were supposed to have dinner tonight. He must be freaking out."

"We have to accept the fact that we're going to be stuck here a few hours. At most, until dawn."

Time passes, and the downed tree becomes our friend. Elle refuses to sit on the ground, preferring a deceptive distance from things that creep and crawl.

"There's no possible way you're going to be able to get any sleep on that stump without falling," I say. "Let me clear a space here for you to get comfortable. And Elle," I add, "it's going to get colder. We have to warm each other up."

It's June, but this part of the country could be cool at night, temperatures dipping into the low fifties or even forties. Her shorts and thin T-shirt won't stave off the chill. And so that she understands what it is I'm implying, I add, "Body heat."

Her response, which I'm sure is paired with an eye roll, is that she has to pee.

I fan out my hand, though she can barely see it. "The world is your toilet."

"I won't even ask about the toilet paper," she adds.

To which I smile inwardly. "Don't."

CHAPTER 35

Hours pass before the moon sets in the sky, and I can make out Elle's broken expression, her unblemished fear. By now, she's positioned herself on the ground beside me, where I've surrounded us with a makeshift bed of leaves and plants. The temperature dropped, as I'd predicted, and Elle's shivering beside me, her teeth chattering.

There's no minimizing my own anxiety, but I'm doing a decent enough job of pretending I have things under control, feigning calm when inside I'm quaking. *You can do this. This is someone's child. This is Quinn. Do whatever it takes.*

"Maybe we should start a fire," she finally says. And at first, it's easy to pretend I don't hear her, because I've been putting it off, but I know it's what we must do. "You're a mountainy person. You probably went to Girl Scouts. Earned yourself a bunch of those patches. Isn't starting a fire part of your training?"

The word itself sends heat down my neck. Living out here, we all knew how to start fires. Tonight, building one might be absolutely necessary, a means of survival, and I don't know how I'll manage to be close to the flames. The scar on my leg begins to itch at the prospect, and I place my palm over it while taking Elle's hand in the other. Her fingers are freezing.

"Come on, Avery. Maybe someone who's searching for us will see the smoke."

I remind her that it's pitch-black out, making the smoke difficult to see. I don't tell her about my aversion to fire. How I haven't lit a match in seven years; I don't buy candles.

She stands up, running in place to get the blood flowing. "C'mon. We have to collect sticks. That much I know. I can't sit here all night and do nothing."

I get to my feet, though I'm slow-moving. Whether Elle senses my reluctance or not, she's resolved to do this. Now is not the time to let my deepest fears impede our survival. Surrendering, I follow the instructions I know by heart, the ones my father had taught me when I was old enough to understand. The first one we'd already accomplished, building the fire near a source of water. Elle's busy snapping branches from a nearby tree, and I stop her with another rule. "Don't pull the branches off the trees. Search the ground for small twigs and sticks. Then gather a few larger ones. We'll also need to find some rocks."

We stack what we've collected, and Elle takes a break, bending over the stream, collecting water in her hands.

"I still hate you, Avery," she begins. "This doesn't mean I've forgiven you."

I hate myself, too. Had I told Jude the truth today when I had the chance, none of this would be happening. Maybe he would've forgiven me. And then I would have avoided Elle running away at what she thought was my love for someone else.

I set up the log cabin fire, the kind that's square in shape and promises to keep us warm throughout an eternal night. Elle's found enough sticks to last us for days, and after I encircle the pile with stones, I instruct her to go ahead and light it.

She looks at me curiously. "Isn't that your job?"

"You brought the lighter. And I'm not even going to ask why you're carrying one around." When she doesn't move, I catch her eyes through the darkness, fear coiling around my chest. "I can't do it, Elle." My tone leaves no room for question. "You need to do it."

There's little wind tonight, and I point her in the right direction when she snaps the head of the lighter. I wince, the slick sound a razor against my skin, and soon there is a flame. My pulse quickens. The bright orange is too close. I try backing away while she sets the sticks ablaze. The fire awakens and grows, but I've diminished in size. I hate the heat, the way the flames seem to taunt.

We're huddled close together, and I'm turned away, breathing deeply, maintaining a safe distance. She yawns, slumping down so that her head lands in my lap. And I feel my entire body responding to her nearness.

Minutes feel like hours, and I'm careful not to fall asleep. Elle dozes on and off, and I stare at her face, wanting so badly to save her. I lightly touch her skin, careful not to hover too long. I've disappointed her, I know, but if there's anything I can do to make it right, it's this. Protect her. The way I couldn't protect Quinn.

My little girl. She was so tiny. What they don't tell you when you lose a full-term child in utero is that you're forced to give birth and go through all the ugly steps that come along with it. Breathe. Push. A vigorous effort meant to produce joy, instead resulting in a terrible void.

Ollie tried to save us. He carried me out of the cabin, more than half of his body burned, my one leg dangling over the flames. But he got us out, even if it were to collapse on the ground, where the rescuers would find us. They said we were holding hands. Of course we were. Ollie would have never let me go.

Elle wrestles with sleep. I wonder if she can sense where my mind's gone, if she can feel misfortune through my skin. Her eyes open and close.

"Avery."

She's staring up at me, half-asleep, and when she realizes she's using my body as a pillow, she tries inching away. I recognize the suit of armor so well. I know. I wear one, too.

Finally, she speaks. "Why couldn't you love us?"

We can't avoid the conversation much longer. Tears burn the back of my eyes, and I blink them away. "I've made some terrible mistakes, Elle."

"You said you love Oliver . . . that you don't want to hurt my dad."

The fire brightens her face, and I can make out her precise features, the smudges of dirt. Elle is a beautiful young woman, and those stains on her cheeks reflect what lies beneath. No one would ever believe her suffering. But I know. And she deserves more.

"He's the one you've been talking about . . . that night at dinner . . . in the garden. Have you seen him? Are you, like, back together?"

"Oliver was my first love."

"Do you still love him?"

"I'll always love him."

She lets this soak in. "You know there are words for people like you."

I summon up the rest, unfathomable that she will know before her father. "He's dead, Elle." Then I say it again, so there's no mistaking. "Oliver's dead."

It's never easy to say those words, and I don't intend on making her feel bad, but I can tell by the way she silences that she's surprised, and maybe a little sorry. She rights herself, rubbing sleep from her eyes. I brush the few leaves from her hair.

"But you said . . ."

I can barely make out her eyes, but I stare into them, longing to sink inside and vanish.

Willow's whispering in my ear. So is my father. If I don't share the truth, I'll lose everything, and of all those things, I can't comprehend losing this complicated young girl I've grown to love.

"Ollie was my boyfriend. Like you and Luke." She waits for me to say more, and the fire hisses, forcing me to block it out. I open and close my eyes. "We were young . . . so young . . . and we were engaged. I loved him, Elle. There was no one else in the world for me. It's like we came from the same seed."

She takes a minute to process this because she knows how it feels.

"It's nice, right?"

She nods.

"And then I found out I was pregnant . . . We were being careful . . . It was just one of those things . . . and you know, nothing is foolproof . . ."

She interrupts. "We can skip the details."

"We were at his family's cabin in the woods. We'd go there on the weekends . . . He was starting a fly-fishing business . . . I was working on the farm . . . and I was really pregnant, close to my due date, and maybe we shouldn't have gone . . . but we did . . . and . . ."

I have to stop. Block the visual from my brain.

"I loved candles. I was always collecting them, lighting them, to the annoyance of Oliver. He'd have to remind me to blow them out because I had a habit of forgetting, but he always remembered. Except for that last night . . ." My voice trails off, and I hug myself tighter. "There was a storm . . . We were inside . . . and he was getting up to blow out the candle, to close the windows, and I stopped him . . . I distracted him. And then we fell asleep."

Putting this into words is the hardest thing I've ever done. Harder than I'd ever imagined. The grief is raw, sprouting from deep within, taking over like a wild vine. It circles my heart and squeezes.

When I try to swallow, it feels like sand is lodged in my throat. "Next thing I know, the cabin's filled with flames."

The gravity of what I've done grips her. She won't look at me. She's silent, and whether by choice or chance, she seems to plant herself between me and the fire.

242

"He tried to save us. He carried us out, but he was badly burned. He got us far enough, but then we slipped from his hands . . . and it was too much . . . too much for him. . . too much for the baby, Quinn." Reliving it makes my head feel dizzy. That's when I say, "Sometimes I wish it would've been me."

Sharing the story is letting that rock out of your shoe, pulling a splinter from your finger. The acute pain turns into a dull, throbbing ache. I'm half crying, focused on the memory, making sure I get it all out.

Sparing her the agony of my hospital stay, I describe the guilt, how I could never let it go. "When I got to Miami, I was twenty-three and, for lack of a better word, a widow. I broke ties with my sister, my best friend, and was entirely alone. And I believed I deserved it. Being alone meant no one to hurt, no one to disappoint. I didn't want your father to know. How could he love someone like me? How could he trust me with you kids?" Her back is to the fire. I can only make out the silhouette of her head and shoulders. But she's listening, and she hasn't run away.

"I was wrong. Your father deserved to know the truth. And then he proposed, and all I could think about was how I'd misled him, how I wasn't the person he thought I was." I'm picking up sticks and tossing them into the air. "Relationships are complicated enough to begin with—I told you that—but they're far more complicated when they're founded on lies. I asked you to be honest with Luke, and all this time, I haven't been honest. I'm sorry for that. In some ways, you're braver than I ever was."

"Daddy would've understood. If you'd told him . . . if you hadn't waited all this time."

Hearing her say it like that, I cower, letting the crackling fire fill the silence. I'm embarrassed Elle has to see my imperfections, but it's long overdue. "I know that now. I think. But when you love someone and lose them, you find yourself a little lost. And afraid."

"That's really sad."

"I know. And I know this is a lot for you to hear, but I want you to know who I am." I pause because I'm welled up and having a hard time letting it out without completely breaking. "I want us to know each other. I want to be there for you. I may lose your father, which breaks my heart, but whatever happens, you need to know what you mean to me. You're a remarkable young girl, Elle. The last few weeks . . . our flower garden . . . watching you blossom and fall in love . . . all your holding on . . . and being scared . . . there's so much of me in you . . .

"I'm going to talk to your father. You have my word. I'm going to fight for you. And for him. You can push me away, but I'm not going anywhere. I love you. I didn't give birth to you, but I'd do anything for you. You just have to let me."

CHAPTER 36

Elle stands up, pacing around our little fire, not knowing what to do with my confession. I imagine it's hard for her to accept my love, just as it was for me to accept Jude's. So she does what she does best. She pushes me away.

"I'm nothing like you, Avery."

"Please sit," I warn, trying to keep her from getting too close to the flames.

She backs away, and from this angle, I see the struggle on her face, the tears she keeps from escaping. Her voice comes out strained, hurt lining every word. "I'm not some loser who lies to everyone she knows. I don't keep things from people I love."

"You don't," I say, swallowing the shame, "but you're angry. And there's the drinking. And the pot—"

"I haven't touched that stuff since we got here. The lighter is for the bracelets. That's how we seal the ends."

"You've been afraid of letting Luke in, of sleeping close to an open window or door."

"You don't know what you're talking about. None of that means anything. I'm a teenager. That's what we do."

"I'm not talking about any teenager, Elle. I'm talking about you. Do you realize how much energy you've expended on hating me? And when you've succeeded at turning me against you, you dangle a carrot. And I take a step . . . and you slam the door. You've been afraid to let me in, but I've been just as afraid."

Silence stretches. It unravels with more questions than answers.

"I know this might be difficult for you to understand or take in, but I've really grown to care about you this summer. I'd hate to see you making the mistakes I've made, pushing people away, especially the ones who love you the most—"

She's laughing, a loud, cackling laugh that echoes through the forest, but I'm determined. I have nothing left to lose. I need to give it my all.

"Holding on to pain, Elle—what I've done and what you've been doing—it's no way to heal. We can't love or be loved with all that anger inside. Or regret. Or fear. We have to let it go."

She quiets, shifts in place, then plops down beside me and drops her head into my lap. My hand comes down to touch her, then draws back, afraid to spoil the moment.

"She'd be seven," Elle says, and the loss hits me again. *My daughter. My child.* I'd learned to stop focusing on what she'd look like, each passing birthday, an eternal infant wrapped in that soft, pink blanket. Oliver wasn't there holding my hand when I was in the hospital. He wasn't shouting in my ear for me to push, kissing my tears away, wiping the strands of damp hair from my face. But I willed him there so that we could mourn her together, give her the proper goodbye.

I know this is a lot for someone like Elle. She's already had her fair share of loss, and this likely stirs an array of already-mixed emotions in her. "I was eleven when Mallory died."

"Why do you do that?" I ask. "Why do you call her by her first name?"

"That wasn't the point."

"She's your mother. She'll always be your mother."

And because this is difficult for her to process, she jumps to a different subject. "What if we die out here?"

"Nothing's going to happen to you," I say.

"You don't know that. What if a bear finds us and he's hungry? We have no way to defend ourselves."

Years of living in these parts, I know. "If we don't bother him, he won't bother us."

The darkness and cold are making her delirious. Her sentences run into each other. Hurried and breathless. "What if nobody finds us? What if . . . I'm not ready to die, Avery. I haven't even had sex yet." There's no mistaking the tremble in her voice, which sends a tremble through me. "I'm really scared." She burrows deeper into my lap, and my arms come around her. We'd both been cheated out of a mother's comfort, but I'm beginning to understand how that loss can join us together.

"I promise you with everything I have . . . it's going to be okay."

"You can't promise that."

I can't, but I hold her tighter, stroking her hair, untangling the knots. Her skin feels chilled, and I do my best to provide warmth and comfort.

When she speaks, it's more like a whisper.

"I miss her."

"I know you do."

Missing someone you've loved and lost doesn't come with a roadmap. There's no knowing when the ache will creep in, knocking you flat.

"I wish she was here," she continues weakly. "I wish she was the one telling me everything's going to be all right. No offense."

"None taken."

"That morning . . . she went for a run . . . we'd had a fight."

She struggles with what to say next.

"Over brushing my teeth." She waits for my reaction. "Do you believe it? Colgate. That's the last thing we talked about."

"You had no way of knowing, Elle. None of us do. Especially not an eleven-year-old."

"Colgate," she says again. "I lied to her. I went back to my bathroom and pretended to do what she asked. I hated brushing my teeth. And washing my hair. Sometimes I'd sit in the bathroom and let the water run so she'd believe her daughter had the cleanest teeth and hair on earth."

"I think every little girl has done that once in her life." I know this. Willow used to expect the same from me.

"Yeah, but their moms didn't leave."

"Whether you brushed your teeth or not, your mom had an underlying condition that no one could have predicted. It could have flared up anytime, anywhere. You didn't cause this, and it had nothing to do with Colgate."

She brings her fist up to her forehead and pounds it. "I just want her back, Avery."

"I know you do. And I wish I could make that happen for you. I would. If I could."

And then she begins to cry. It's not hysterical, and it's not calm. It's a subtle release that means acceptance of something that's been long out of reach. I'm reiterating what Willow said only hours ago. I'm telling her to let it out, telling myself, too, tears forming at our bittersweet connection. I tell myself to inhale the future, exhale the past, and soon we're holding on to each other tight, our arms encircled around each other. I love this girl, love what she's come to mean to me. Love her as though she were mine, and it's terrifying and it's scary, but it fills me with hope, too.

"Is this okay?" she asks.

I nod; she can feel it against her face. She has no idea how much.

Though it's her loss, her letting go, I feel everything alongside her. This courageous young woman is drawing me back to life. Our tears collide, and I let her in, let the feelings in.

"Say something," she says.

"I don't want to frighten you, Elle."

"It can't be worse than all those creepy noises."

"You . . ." I draw in a breath, nervous energy shooting through my body. "You can't even begin to understand what having you here has meant to me. How you've made me feel things I didn't think possible. I never thought I could be a mom, or a stepmom, or take care of anyone after what I've done, but you proved to me that I can. I know this because it wouldn't be possible to feel this way without having another chance. You've made me believe that I'm not too broken. That I can survive this."

And though I can't see it, I feel her smile.

"You're very brave, Elle Masters. And all that you've experienced is going to make you stronger than before. You can be sad and you can be scared. But you can move on. And let people love you."

"What about you? Can you do the same?"

"I hope so. I know I'm going to try."

The trees rustle in the wind, creaking and groaning as though they're listening in on our conversation. Before, the sounds frightened me, but now I find the hum of the forest freeing. I share with Elle the funny stories of Willow and me on the farm, detailing our mudslinging matches and the time I left horse manure in both her sneakers. I tell her about the day I met Oliver (in my bright-purple onesie) and about, all those years later, when he got on his knees and proposed, and I screamed yes, because love was boundless and full of hope. I admit how afraid I was when I met her dad. And how scared I was of her. Beneath my fingertips, her body becomes less rigid, more relaxed, and she laughs and asks for all sorts of details, until I've described every last one.

And then she reciprocates by telling me about Luke. All about Luke. That failed first kiss and the burning desire that lingered. How she wants to let him touch her. "I can't tell my dad any of this."

"Nor should you." I half laugh.

"Is it normal to feel like this?"

"I hate to be the one to break it to you, but yes," I say, thinking of Oliver, thinking of Jude's fingers on my skin. "Love, in its many forms, guarantees two things. It can burn us, but it can also surprise us. In the best possible way."

"What's going to happen when I leave?"

I'm careful to choose the right words. "Sometimes summer romances are fleeting, but that doesn't mean they aren't real. Or that the feelings aren't big."

"Someone always leaves," she says, which brings her back to Mallory. "Avery," she begins, her quavering signaling that this is difficult for her. "I can't call her Mom. It just makes me too sad."

I hold her tighter than before, and I make sure that in my arms, she feels completely loved. Because I can say the words, but they'll just slip through her fingers if they're not actually felt. That's what Elle needs right now. She needs to feel the embrace that only a mother can give. And while I'll never take the place of her actual mother— would never try—I'll do everything I can to give her something that resembles it.

"I miss her a lot. I want to talk to her. And when I talk to you . . . or when I need you . . . I feel bad . . . because . . . if I love you . . . does that mean I love her less?"

She's tired. Her thoughts jumble together, but they make perfect sense, and my emotions are all over the place.

Elle has become so much more to me than Jude's daughter. She's an ally, a friend, and now she's showing me things I could never see for myself. For too long, I thought loving Jude meant I was being disloyal to Ollie and Quinn. But I couldn't have been more wrong. I know that now. She showed me that. Our hearts are big; there's room enough to let others in.

"Elle, what you share with your mom, no one can ever take away. No one will ever take her place."

Under normal circumstances, and if we weren't stuck in the woods, she'd be giving me a piece of her mind—probably, *As if.* But she refrains. "I don't like needing you, Avery. I hate it. I'm not a needy person . . . and it just makes me feel like a loser."

"You're the furthest thing from a loser."

"Oh please, I've made it an Olympic sport, picking on you."

"I may have deserved some of it."

The wind swells, sweeping leaves into the air and a chill through my bones. I'm wondering if we've crossed into the next day. Tomorrow. When everything is new and possible. I'm sure I hear the footsteps of rabbits and deer or hedgehogs and skunks, and I tell myself, *I'm not afraid of the dark.* The fire, to my surprise, feels somewhat reassuring. With Elle here, the flames don't frighten me as much.

"What about you and Daddy?" she asks.

"I held on to this part of me I didn't want him to see, and all it did was hurt us. I don't want to live my life without him. I know that. And I know when I tell him everything, I still might end up alone, but I have to put it all out there. And it'll be up to him to decide if he can forgive."

She nestles her head deeper into my lap. "I'm so tired, Avery."

I tell her to close her eyes and get some rest. I assure her I'll stay awake and watch over her. I'm not afraid of what lurks in the forest. I've already faced worse. Far worse. And just before she drifts off to sleep, she lets out in a whisper, "Candles don't just burn down houses. The wind could've blown the candle over. An act of God. It's not your fault. You shouldn't blame yourself." And before her eyes close, she adds, "Whatever happens out here, Avery . . . I don't hate you. I don't hate you at all."

The hours pass slowly, my body cramped and stiff from Elle pressed against me. She sleeps fitfully, tossing and turning, and I watch her, aware of every sound, every movement around us. When I do take my eyes off her, I try not to look too much at the bright-orange flames.

I look up toward the sky. When you spend long hours in the dark, your eyes adjust to the blackness. Focus becomes clearer; awareness intensifies. I see the stars dotting the sky, and they flood me with some relief. Highland thunderstorms come on rapidly, packing a punch and producing gusty winds. Seeing the stars means clear skies, and I breathe a little easier.

By now, Willow and Jude must be frantic. My father, too. I'm sure they've contacted Sheriff Floyd, and Willow's shouting in the diminutive man's ears, *But this is my sister!* Though he's small in size, Floyd's presence in Crystal is well-known. There was hardly a kegger or evening of cow tipping without Floyd showing up. His were the eyes I remember from that night in June. When Quinn and I were taken to the hospital in the rescue vehicle, Floyd left his patrol car down the road and climbed in beside me. He knew my mother. He was friendly with my father. He understood that my broken family couldn't shoulder another loss.

On the drive to the hospital, I was in and out of consciousness. *Smoke inhalation*, they said. But when I half opened my eyes, the bright lights burning my pupils, it was Sheriff Floyd staring back. "There you go, Avery. You don't go giving up now. Stay with me."

Fatigue settles in, and it's an effort to keep my eyes open. I don't dare go to sleep while the fire's burning so close, but I notice that it's beginning to wane. We need to add more sticks, stoke the flames, snap the lighter. I'm tired. My head hurts, a sharp, hollow thud behind my eyes. My fingers and toes ache from the cold. Pins and needles pinch my legs. I'm about ready to topple over, exhaustion settling in, Elle's intermittent breaths lulling me to sleep.

That's when I hear Ollie's voice.

"Avery, you need more flame. You'll freeze to death out here."

"Oh, Ollie."

Elle tosses.

"I love you, Avery. You have to stay awake."

I'm trying. I don't say it aloud. He's in my mind, where he's always been, his voice leading me through the toughest of times.

"You're ready," he says. "I'll be here watching over you, but it's time to move on."

A reel of memories plays. Ollie and me on the river, tossing stones into the water. Ollie dropping a slimy fish down the back of my shirt. I hear the laughter, mingling with the flames, and I realize how badly I want to live. Really live. Not the fearful, inhibited pretending of the last seven years, but a full life. If there's anything I've learned this summer, holding on to those you've lost means you're living in the past. And if you're living in the past, you're not really living.

"Ollie," I whisper. "I'm going to let you go now. Is that okay?"

And this time, he doesn't answer. Oliver is gone.

Our big, beautiful love story has come to an end.

I must have nodded off, because I'm roused awake by the smell of smoke. My eyes pop open, and I check to be sure Elle is there. She is, curled on her side in a ball, head resting comfortably in my lap. The fire's gone out. The gray dewiness to the hour means it's almost dawn, and if help is near, I have to arrange the sticks and light a new fire to lead them in our direction. I nudge Elle, but she's in a sleep too deep to reach. I can make out the outline of the lighter in her back pocket, and so I take a deep breath and grab it. It's like a hot coal in my fingers, but I know what I must do.

Without disturbing her, I manage to align the sticks to form another square. After a few tries, my thumb presses against the spark wheel, producing a flame.

Elle stirs, a light whimper as she opens her eyes.

She immediately sees the lighter in my hands and the fiery hue. She seems to know how incredibly hard this is for me, though she doesn't utter a sound. She sits up, stretching, leaves sticking to her arms and legs. Her hand comes down on my leg, just beside the scar, and she has no idea what that gesture means. She watches me light the fire. And when it's a beacon between us, she smiles with her entire face.

We hear the dogs first, their barks jolting Elle from sipping water from the stream, me squatting in the dirt to relieve myself. Fear crawls inside her eyes as she goes through different scenarios in her head. "What is that?"

"It sounds like a dog," I reassure her.

And then I hear the unwavering terror in my sister's shrill voice. "Avery! Elle!"

I open my mouth, but no sound comes out. Relief washes away everything, including my strength. It's no different from when you're dreaming you're being chased, and your legs refuse to move. Any sounds escaping my dry, cracked lips are garbled and unintelligible. Elle hears me struggling and gets up from the stream, wiping down her shorts and cupping her hands over her mouth. "We're over here. Help! Help!"

"Hallelujah," finally squeaks out of me, and I silently thank Elle, her smile eclipsing what we'd just gone through. She stops complaining about her breath and the yuck taste in her mouth, how she'd do anything for a cheeseburger and steak fries. The idea of civilization accentuates my own hunger, but there is something I have to do first.

The dogs become louder, as do my sister's shouts. And that's when I hear Jude. I momentarily allow myself to imagine a happy ending. Elle hollers back, "We're over here." And a pale sun climbs through the forest, shining light on our makeshift bed of leaves, and I see my sister approaching with an entourage. Jude, Sheriff Floyd, Cole, Luke, and a pair of dogs. And I've never been happier to see all their faces.

CHAPTER 37

When my sister wraps her arms around me, she smells of patchouli, and I'm sure I hear the clinking sounds of crystals in her pockets. Willow despises patchouli, so this must have been an attempt at one of her miracle potions—one that helps locate missing loved ones.

"I can't believe you're here."

I'm not sure which one of us says it first. Our bodies are fused together like one.

"I was worried sick about you." This is definitely Willow. "You have no idea what went through my head."

Elle is wrapped inside Jude's arms, and I can tell he's squeezing hard, kissing the top of her head. He makes no move in my direction. He doesn't look at me, something wounded in his eyes, and I wonder if he knows. But Willow wouldn't dare. This is my story to tell, so I remain hopeful it's something else, hopeful because I'm watching Elle as she lets go of her father and crashes into Luke with all her might.

Sheriff Floyd radios the station with the news that we've been located while Cole calls my father. Jude examines Elle, searching for signs of injury or harm, before it's my turn. He seems annoyed to have to give me the time, cold and distant, and neither of us speaks. They offer us packs filled with energy drinks and snacks, but I've already lost whatever appetite was there. I watch Elle bite into a granola bar while Jude covers her shoulders with a blanket. He makes no effort to comfort me.

Jude is conferring with Sheriff Floyd when Willow's relief turns into something else. She slinks over to Elle, who's rubbing the dogs' fur. "What on earth were you thinking?"

"It's not her fault," I interrupt, putting myself between them.

"She could've gotten you both killed."

I look to Elle, who is neither smug faced nor her usual haughty self. She hasn't thrown one expletive in Willow's direction, which is shocking. I make sure Elle hears me over the chomping of her bar. I home in on her eyes, a little less blue this morning, and say, "You've got it all wrong, Willow." Elle stops chewing. Jude watches the exchange, listening, too. "Elle saved me."

Smears of crimson stain Elle's cheeks, and she quickly takes another bite.

Jude's eyes travel up and down my body before settling on my eyes. There's disdain written there, confusion that smacks of hurt.

Sheriff Floyd extinguishes the fire, and Willow's unusually quiet.

"I was worried sick," Willow says, more to me than to Elle.

"I'm sorry," Elle begins, moving toward her, shoulders bent. When she's in Willow's face, she looks down at her. "That was a dumb move." This isn't Elle acting before an audience. This is Elle letting us know how much she's grown to love us. "I'm really sorry."

Willow pulls her into a hug. "You crazy kid." She's holding on to her tight. And Elle hugs her back, apologizing over and over.

Sheriff Floyd wants to know if we're able to walk on our own, and it's Luke who responds for Elle. "I've got you, Elle. You can get on my back."

"It's about a mile or so," the sheriff adds, and it sinks in how far we ventured off, and Willow and Cole both offer to escort me, carry if needed, but not Jude. He stays behind, a dog on each side.

The walk home takes us about an hour, though none of us complains. Elle's wrapped around Luke for part of it, the two of them smiling, her cheeks aglow, and my sister has hitched her arm through mine, and we're walking close together. Cole and Jude watch us from behind, and someone starts telling jokes about bears and skunks, which are funny now but wouldn't have been hours ago. Every so often Jude speeds up to check on Elle or comment on the terrain, which is stunning at this early hour, but he fails to include me in any conversation, and it slows down my pace.

I hear the details of what happened after we left. How Willow assumed, with good reason, we were outside arguing, but as time passed and Jude showed up at the farm to pick Elle up, Willow had the unpleasant task of meeting my ex while having to explain that she didn't know where we were. The two of them set out on foot to find us, but there was too much terrain to cover. And with night approaching, there was little they could do. They had to wait until daylight.

I had imagined Jude experiencing the forest, but not like this. With each step, the realization of what I've done seeps through. Jude didn't deserve this. Jude and his wishes and prayers, his goodness and vulnerability. All he did was love someone he thought he could trust. All he did was take a chance. If this was the end, I had no one to blame but myself, and that notion haunts me every step toward home.

When we arrive, my father's waiting outside and gathers me into his arms. "I knew you'd be okay," he whispers in my ear. "I taught you to be strong." I hug him hard, and we thank the sheriff for his help while Willow scampers off to cook breakfast. My father climbs into his Polaris, ready to begin his day in the fields. Luke and Cole hitch a ride, and Luke lets Elle know he'll see her later, but Jude has another idea. He tells Elle to hurry and get showered because he's taking her back to the Albemarle. I try to get him to look at me, but he refuses, and a knot of desperation runs through my belly. His face is drawn, the exhaustion and worry darkening his eyes.

Elle pouts. "But, Daddy—"

"No *buts*, you're coming with me. We're going home."

Her face drains of color. "I'm not going home. You can't do this. I have a job . . . I have . . ."

Jude expects my support, but I can't give it to him. I don't want them to leave. Then Elle pleads with me. "Please tell him . . . please tell him I have to stay."

If there is that one moment I will never, ever be able to fully believe, or ever forget, it's watching Elle beg her father to stay in Crystal. And though I'm certain it has more to do with Luke than me, I can't help but believe I am a small part of it. "We'll have dinner tonight," she says. "Just the two of us. And tomorrow I'll show you the farm and the chicks . . . I started a garden! I milk cows! I'm friends with a goat named Baxter . . ." But her pleading doesn't make a dent. "Milo and Henry would love it here. They can come to visit." She crosses her arms in defiance. "I'm not leaving."

Jude, speechless, steps aside and lets Elle pass.

"I'm going to take a shower and try to get some sleep," I say, though I'm really hoping he'll ask me to stay so that we can talk.

"I'm taking her home, Avery."

I know I should fight, but I'm fatigued and out of sorts, preparing for another goodbye. When I disagree, it's barely a whisper: "You're making a mistake."

"My daughter just spent the night in the woods. How could you let this happen?"

The swipe hurts, but I'm stronger now. "That's not fair." And it's hard to reconcile this man with the one who embraced me so lovingly only hours ago. I want to reach across and touch him, have him comfort me the way he did Elle, but there's a divide between us that may be too wide to cross. Besides, I'm not yet sure what he's mad at. This, or something else, but what comes out of his mouth next plays on my deepest vulnerability. "It was stupid of me to think you could take care of her."

Stupid. And there it is, the insult I've been waiting for all this time. Stupid. Irresponsible. Untrustworthy. Once it would have shattered me, knocked me flat. Today it has the opposite effect.

"I'm not going to let you do this. I may not have done everything right, but I did everything I could. *She* followed me to North Carolina. *She* begged me to stay. *She* was the one who ran off into the woods without looking back, forcing me to chase after her."

It feels like minutes pass before he decides to answer. "I really thought we had a shot. I thought . . ." He stops himself. "Never mind."

And I don't know where it comes from, but it does, something deep inside of me spilling out. "Yesterday, there was something I had to tell you. Something important. We kept getting interrupted . . . and then your patient . . ."

His eyes are fixed on mine when he says it; there's no mistaking. "I know about you and Oliver."

I'm not surprised. I saw his disappointment, and I hadn't forgotten he was on the phone with Elle when she singled me out, calling me a liar and a cheat. But he didn't know all of it. "It's not what you think."

"Not everything is," he says, shaking his head. "Not even you."

The last few hours have taken their toll on all of us, and his shoulders noticeably sag. "There's really nothing more to say, Avery."

"So that's it? You're not even going to hear me out?"

He glances at his watch. "I'm going to get changed. Let her say her goodbyes, but we're leaving. I'll come for her this afternoon." And then he's gone.

The shower's stream awakens me, reminding me I'm alive, but it doesn't wash away the hurt. I haven't endured this summer and finding out who

I am only to lose the man I love. I scrub at my cheeks and hair, taking time to linger on the scar on my leg. Over the years, it's turned from dark black to splotchy pink. The skin indents, the scar nubby with thick tissue. I'm thinking about Jude, about the time he asked about it. The one time. Perhaps it was my response, how I shut him down. *It looks like a burn, Avery.* But I was firm, omitting the details, only saying that he'd be amazed at how the tread of a spinning tire could badly burn someone. Respectfully, he acquiesced, never asking again, which had become a pattern for us.

I scrub my skin until it stings, which is ironic, after the years I'd spent erasing the pain and all the sensations that came along with it. I'm wiping off the dirt and grime, and once I allow my brain to wrap around what we just went through, I break loose and cry. There's the finality of my relationship with Jude and what that means. I may never see Elle and the boys again, and it hurts my heart in a different way than saying goodbye to Jude. There's Oliver, dear, sweet Oliver, and Quinn, reminders of what could've been. But there's also a shred of hope. There's my sister finding happiness with Jackson, a new garden filled with life, and a way for me to finally break free of what's held me back. The water mixes with my tears. Some of those tears are happy ones, the kind that mean freedom and new beginnings, but the others weigh on me, and I drop to the floor and let the drizzle tap against my skin.

Pulling myself together and swathed in a fluffy robe, I meet my sister in the kitchen, where she's preparing a feast. She looks up from a pan of eggs and smiles at me. Her eyes are puffy, and she's still in the same clothes as last night. I'm sure she didn't sleep either, that she fought herself from venturing out in the dark to find us.

I reach for a muffin, freshly baked, and shove it into my mouth. When I'm finished, I back up against an adjacent cabinet and tell her how sorry I am.

"And to think Cole falling off that horse was going to be the big news of the summer. That little stunt wasn't your fault," she adds.

Wiping my lips with a napkin, I turn. "No, it's because of me."

My sister, God love her, she's defended me, she's aided and assisted beyond measure, but I must hold myself accountable. Blaming Elle isn't going to repair the damage, correct what I've done.

She turns off the gas and stands beside the worn-down butcher block. The smell of bacon fills the air, and she waits for me to continue. "You were right all those years ago," I begin. "When you insisted I go the hospital. Get treatment. I needed the help."

She abandons the counter and inches closer. Once, I'd have backed away, but today I don't. "I'd been holding on to the guilt . . . the horrible memories . . . thinking I didn't deserve love . . . couldn't be loved . . . but last night . . . this summer . . . even you and Cole . . ." I feel my voice cracking. "I finally understand what it all means. Love comes with risks. We can't always protect the people we love, but we do our best. Because we really don't have any other choice.

"Jude knows about Oliver . . . I'm not sure exactly what . . . He heard Elle screaming at me . . . about being a cheat. Did he mention anything to you?"

"Nothing. He was worried sick. He spent most of the night on the couch, alternating between pacing and demanding to go out and find you guys. He was really shaken up."

He wasn't worried about me. This may be the tipping point, and the feeling deflates me. "Elle's right about one thing, I'm a liar. I've lied to everyone who matters."

"Talk to him. Make him understand."

I shake my head, tears brimming in my eyes. "Yesterday . . . I thought we could survive this. But now he's just furious . . . blaming me for Elle getting lost in the woods." I swallow back the hurt. "Maybe if I'd told him everything earlier, we could've worked through it, but hearing it the way he did . . . I don't know . . . I'm pretty sure we're through."

"Jude seems like an understanding guy. He's had his own share of pain."

"I never realized how much I loved him. Not until I lost him."

"You don't have to lose him."

"It's not up to me," I say.

I fall on my sister and release the tears. She does what she does best and pulls me into her arms, squeezing the pain away. "I'll be here with you every step of the way." Which only makes me cry harder.

"I've missed you so much," she says. And I know she doesn't mean the last twelve hours we were gone. I've missed her, too. Because I haven't been the same person. Not since the accident. And even though cutting her out of my life was necessary, a casualty of my brokenness, I can't do it anymore. It's time to open the door.

She prepares me a plate, and when I'm finished, I tell her I need to sleep for a couple of hours. I collapse on my bed, my back to Ollie's message. When I can't do it for much longer, I turn around and trace the words with my finger. "Goodbye, Ollie."

CHAPTER 38

Hours later, the house is empty and still—Willow and Dad on the farm, Elle with Luke—and I'm dragging a brush through my hair and touching up my face. A whisper of tension nips the air, a wiry thread of anticipation that I dread and welcome. It's hard to believe that hours ago, I was stranded in the forest. There's a calmness in my cheeks, a weightlessness that wasn't there days ago that I can only attribute to one thing: the truth.

Jude is on his way. That's what his text reads. He's picking up Elle to take her back with him. I'm scrolling through the missed calls and texts from last night when his name pops up, and if I expected him to write anything more, I'm disappointed. I give him the thumbs-up emoji and return to the notifications that have piled up. There are several missed calls, one after another, from Jude, my sister, and a text from Lloyd asking how I've been, with a picture of my blooming buttercups. Jude's messages are crammed with worry and concern, the traces of fear hard to miss. My sister's are much of the same, though she's louder, more desperate.

When I hear his knock, my heart accelerates, and I take my time getting to the door, as though I haven't been waiting for this all day.

His back is to me, and the first thing I notice is his size. He seems bigger, even more imposing than this morning, though I know that's impossible. He's wearing a powdery-blue polo that hugs his arms, and I think to myself, regretfully, how I've messed everything up.

When he spins around, he appraises me, taking me in, but there's an unmistakable hurt.

I open the door wider for him to walk through, and we both start talking at the same time. I'm asking if he wants something to drink; he's asking if he can go to Elle's room to get her stuff. "We're leaving in the morning." This news saddens me, though I have no recourse, so we're left in an awkward clash, and I lead him upstairs and down the hall. When we reach the open doorway of my old room, he stops, peering inside. "I didn't get the tour last night. This yours?"

I nod.

He steps through the threshold, and a swell of intimacy greets us. Suddenly, I feel like a little girl, wanting to hide the underwear that's balled up on the floor by my dirty clothes, pull the blanket over the exposed sheets. Having Jude in my childhood bedroom brings up a whole host of feelings, reminding me that I was once a young woman with big dreams.

"This is nice," he says.

"If you like horses."

I follow his eyes to the wall. It's hard to miss, and not even the bunched-up blanket hides the black strokes of the marker. I let him take it in, unmoving. He would soon know the truth. All of it. "Her room is just across the hall." And I'm about to turn to show him the way, but he stops me, locking my eyes with his.

He walks toward the bed for a closer look at what Oliver's written while I take in a deep breath. The room feels small and crowded, and I brace myself for what's to come, anxiously awaiting the right moment to reveal myself. There's a bristling tension. As if he doesn't quite fit in this space.

"I tried to tell you everything. Yesterday. We kept getting interrupted."

But he's not interested, and he retreats from the bed and passes me, en route to Elle's room. Our arms brush against each other, though there's nothing deliberate about it.

I take the stairs down to the living room, knowing our relationship is over, knowing he may never let me see Elle again, and when it's too painful to consider, I slide the back door open and step outside. The fresh air feels good, and I sit there quietly until I hear him approach. He drops Elle's suitcase on the deck, but I don't turn away from the gorgeous view. He notices it, too, looking out, taking it all in. "You were right. It's beautiful here."

"I think so."

"I'm surprised you stayed away this long."

There's suspicion in his voice, and it sets a divide between us, but then he takes the seat next to me.

"You misunderstood about Oliver," I begin. "Let me explain."

"You had two years to explain, Avery."

I shuffle in my seat, unable to get comfortable. "I know what you think you heard . . . I'm not cheating on you. Elle was confused. And—"

He casually crosses one leg over the other, though his gaze is set. "I know you're not cheating on me," he says, "at least not with Oliver." If he's trying to be cryptic, it's working. "I know about the fire, and I know about your baby."

The walls come tumbling down as everything I've desperately hidden rises to the surface. Minutes pass with unpleasant silence, the rippling disappointment in being found out. The day is windless and warm, no sounds of leaves rustling, nothing to distract from the tension between us. I hadn't considered Jude hearing about all this from someone other than me. "Who told you?"

"Does it matter when it wasn't you?"

My hands are in my lap, and I'm studying them because I can't face him. My bare finger mocks me, all the promises out of reach. I feel his eyes pleading with me to say something, but I can't bear the disappointment there. When I don't answer, he does. "Would you believe I googled you?"

I look up. "You what?"

"I spent all night thinking you were a cheater, wondering how I could be so off about you. Then I got back to my room this morning and googled you. I'm not sure why I never did it before . . . It just never occurred to me to have to check. There was no reason." He makes no effort to hide that he's upset. His voice strains for composure, and it comes out forced. "How could my girlfriend keep a secret like that . . . for so long?"

I turn away. The dismay in his voice too much for me to take. I train my eyes on the stitching in the seat cushion instead.

"I'm terribly sorry that you went through such a horrific ordeal, Avery, I am. Such a senseless tragedy. But I'm sorry, too, that you didn't think this was something you could share with me. Something that important." He releases a deep exhale. "I never knew you. You never let me."

The crack in his voice forces me to look up.

I can hardly manage a word, let alone a sentence. "That day you proposed—"

"June thirteenth. I figured that out. And I'm sorry for that. I would've never proposed on that day if I'd known."

He stands up, and I know this is it, the end of us. And I know I should stop him and beg for his forgiveness, but I don't.

"I could've forgiven the engagement, Avery. We could've worked through this, had you really come home to figure things out. But the dishonesty, all these years, when I was as vulnerable as a person could be . . . that's not the kind of person I want in my life or around my kids."

Those words, like darts, prick my chest and make it impossible for me to speak. And the worst part? They're true. Everything I avoided staring me in the face. *What kind of person am I?* I'm circling the drain, about to disappear, when he adds, "That doesn't mean I didn't love you, Avery. I loved you . . . I would've married you. The last few years were the best I've had in some time."

I'm sick, my insides turning, thinking how the last few years weren't real. Because I wasn't real.

The front door slams and I jump, knowing it's Elle and that these are our last few moments. She will find us here together, but separate, her bag signaling goodbye. An urgency spills through my body, the pull of unfinished business, fighting for love, begging to be heard, but soon Elle's waltzing through the door, lunging into her father's arms. She hugs him, but he hugs her harder, and I, the outsider, envy their closeness.

When they separate, Elle immediately spots her suitcase, and her smile quickly fades.

"I'm not leaving," she says. "I told you . . . you can't do this!"

"We're going, Elle."

She's shaking her head in denial. "What about my job? The kids have field-trip day tomorrow! Who's going to make stupid beaded bracelets with them?"

Jude eyes me, more out of habit than necessity, and I almost smile because Elle is still funny when she wants to be.

"Please don't do this." And I see the tear slip from the corner of her eye, which makes me want to cry, too.

"How about you clear out what's yours from the bathroom and see if there's anything I forgot in your room?"

"I'm not leaving!" She's pacing back and forth, then unzipping her suitcase and flinging her clothes onto the floor. "You can't do this. It isn't fair! I have friends here. I have Luke . . ."

Jude doesn't seem to care about any of that. "Go get your stuff, Elle. That's the last time I'm going to say it."

Elle stomps away, leaving us with little left to say, and I feel the chasm between us growing wider. I'm heartbroken at the prospect of them leaving, just when I'd figured out this thing called love, just when I was finally ready to trust it.

And that's when I find my courage. "You're right. I kept things from you—"

"That wasn't just a thing, Avery—"

"Let me finish." If we were going to lose each other, two people who loved once, big and tender, he needed to know.

"Neither of us may have been ready . . . for all this. I'll own my part. I hid this side of myself, but it wasn't to be cruel. It was because I found myself loving you so much, I didn't want to lose you. I thought you'd leave, just like they did . . . and I couldn't bear another goodbye, Jude. I couldn't."

"I can't be in a relationship with someone who's this closed off."

And I think about us playing house, precise days of the week, tip-toeing around Mallory's blouses, a schedule and a wall that inhibited us from growing together. "You don't see it now because you're upset—"

"This is more than upset," he says.

"You're closed off, too, Jude. We both are. Two injured people. Holding on to things we can't let go. I wished you'd have asked about my past."

"I asked."

I'm on my hands and knees, picking up Elle's clothes and stuffing them back into her suitcase. "I'd give you the short answer. You never dug deeper."

"So this is my fault? For trusting your answers?"

"No. But maybe you were afraid, too." I pause to zip the suitcase, stand it up on its wheels. I hate what this means. I hate that they're leaving. "Marriage is a big step. The kids should've been a part of it. It's not just me and you. It's all of us."

He doesn't argue. He doesn't disagree. "This was such a betrayal, Avery. You lied so freely."

"You think that was easy?" I ask, my voice rising. "This was the hardest thing I've ever done. And you know something, I didn't tell you for this very reason. This. Right here. You walking out. Everything I'd feared . . . it's happening. You're still leaving. This is exactly why I couldn't tell you."

The door swings opens and Elle appears, staring at us curiously.

She's carrying a Target bag, and Jude grabs her suitcase. There's silence as he walks around the side of the house to his car.

"I'm not going home," Elle announces again, though she's lost some of her fervor.

Jude turns around and tries to talk some sense into her. He suggests dinner, a place they can talk, just the two of them. "Sushi?" he suggests. "You love sushi."

"Good luck," she asserts, crossing her arms. "The sushi's marginal at best here." She glances in my direction as if to apologize.

I'm just relieved to see she hasn't lost her spunk, and it breaks up some of the sadness I'm feeling.

She stomps her feet in his direction, and I'm following behind, watching them for what might be the last time. I'm angry. At him. At myself. At the situation. An accumulation of feelings that grab hold of me and squeeze.

This goodbye is a lot more difficult than I'd expected. I watch Jude get in the car without even a glance back in my direction. The rejection climbs from the tips of my toes to the length of my fingers, and I feel burned and bruised, but I refuse to let it show. Because there's Elle. Beautiful, captivating Elle, the sadness crossing her cheeks, and I need to be strong.

We're standing on the sidewalk, Elle reverting to her old, tough self, biting on her bottom lip to make the uncomfortableness go away. I make a move toward her, Jude watching through the window, and pull her into my arms. At first, she's rigid, fighting me, fighting back the emotions, but then she quickly gives in, releasing herself into me, hugging me back. "Remember what we went through together," I say. "You're a remarkable young woman, Elle. You're tough and you're strong. Never forget this . . . you saved me."

Her body shakes, and I know she's crying. I step back and cup her face in my hands. "I'm here for you. Whenever you need me."

She swipes at her eyes.

"And road trips," I add, because I'm losing her, and I'm desperate to hold on. "Whenever you feel up to taking one . . . I'm your girl. You got that?"

She doesn't answer. She just nods, because she can't speak, and a lone tear spills down her face. Then she reaches inside her pocket and drops something round and slinky into my hand. She squeezes my fingers around it, and I hug her again so that she can feel my love, how much I'm going to miss her.

She opens the car door, and I watch as she slumps inside.

Jude's staring straight ahead. I hear him telling Elle to put on her seat belt.

I don't look at him. And soon I don't have to because they're gone. And when I open my hand, there's a bracelet, the kind she makes with the campers. This one has red and blue beads, and it reads *KEEP FUCKING GOING.*

And all I want to do is cry, but I laugh.

CHAPTER 39

The days following their goodbye, I keep expecting to hear Elle's voice down the hall, her shouting at me for something inane. Even though she'd undergone a radical reformation, there were some fundamental aspects of her personality that remained. And I don't want her to be anyone else. Elle is fierce and opinionated, and the world needs more women like her.

That first night, when they landed in Miami and she finally got her cell phone back, I received a text: I haven't cursed in eight+ hours

Good, I texted back. Potty mouths are for the uneducated.

And Jude. I kept thinking he'd heard what I said, really heard, and that he'd call me and we could talk civilly, without blame. That didn't happen. I suppose I thought having Elle with me, Jude wouldn't be able to cut me out of his life, but with her gone, there's nothing holding us together. I started and stopped no less than twenty-seven texts and emails, drafts that I cut and pasted, thinking one day I'd hit "Send."

Willow and Jackson, my father, they all saw how the absence of these two turned me inward. As much as Dad wanted me to stay in Crystal, he knew my heart was somewhere else. "Go after him," he had said. Willow did her part by loading me up with teas to cure my blues. She said her new concoction promised to make me miss Jude and Elle less, but it had the opposite effect.

During that time, I spent hours in the garden, tending to the blooming flowers, talking to them about my plans. Some days, Willow would join me, and we began to feel close again. I regret how I treated her, how I turned my back on her and lost precious years, but sisters love wholly and unconditionally, and she forgave me as I forgave her.

My sister and I are united as we sit in the garden on the stone bench our father had purchased. He had all of our names engraved across the back. A quote about flowers and life. "I'd forgotten her middle name was Mabel," I say to my sister, referring to our mother.

"It's awful," Willow says, not even trying to hide her laugh. She sits back, her sundress hugging her thin arms, the heat reddening her skin. "She and Dad argued about your name for weeks, but we all knew it was Avery. Even if it was a boy. Dad just liked to challenge Mama."

Willow prattles on wistfully about Mom's maternity dresses and how she matched her headband to the colorful fabrics. How she'd dance around the house to the Jackson Five, rubbing her belly. And I hear her voice skip, a thready tremble. "You would have loved her, Avery. Not because she was your mother. She was just . . . she was so much fun . . . so alive." This memory haunts Willow. I can tell by the way she folds into herself. And it occurs to me that in all these years, through my grief and selfishness, I never once comforted my sister.

I slide my arm around her, and she drops her head on my shoulder. Our roles have reversed, and I get a glimpse into her loss. "I should've known," I tell her. "I wasn't the only one grieving. You were hurting, too. Long before me."

"We all hurt, Avery. Some of us more than others. But I had you. You became mine. And I loved every minute. I swore I'd never let anything happen to you."

"I felt that."

"I dropped you," she blurts out. "Once, on a cold, hard floor. I lost you at Tweetsie Railroad, that amusement park with the creepy llamas. I wasn't perfect. None of us are. But we do our best. That's the way I honored Mom."

"You gave up everything for me. For Dad. The farm. You wanted to move to the city . . . go to law school . . . and Cole—"

"I told you to let that one go. Everything happened the way it was supposed to happen. You didn't know . . . and besides, the Ouija board told me it would've never worked."

A tiny laugh escapes, and I go on, pulling her tighter. "I know how sad it must've been for you to lose her. You're that person for me."

And she takes my hand into hers, and I see how similar they are. And I admire the diamond and all that Willow has ahead of her. And she admires the bracelet Elle left me with. "That girl may be smarter than all of us," she says. "Red and blue. Fire and forgiveness." And I wonder if it's possible that she chose the colors on purpose, and I hold on to that.

We grab our gloves and get back to the business of flowers.

"You know you have to be my maid of honor at the wedding, right?" she says with a grin, patting the soil.

"That sounds like frilly dresses and a lot of pink, if I know my sister well enough."

"So you'll do it?" she asks.

"You know I'll do it. I wouldn't miss it."

"Maybe you'll catch the bouquet, too."

"Maybe." And I can't help myself, so I ask, "Did you do any of your voodoo to get me to come home?"

"You think I'd send Dad flying off Georgie?"

Of course not, but she had ways to intervene.

She winks. "I didn't need any spells, Avery. You were always going to find your way back home."

And we work side by side, and the years we were apart disappear, and everything that was broken between us finds its way back together.

CHAPTER 40

Over dinner, I let Willow and my father know I'll be leaving for Miami soon. This is met with disappointment, but it's something I need to do. Being here has been cathartic and refreshing. It's healed old wounds and brought the three of us closer than ever. And as much as I love the farm and being with the two of them, and now Jackson, in Crystal, I will always be the girl who started the fire, the one who made that fatal mistake. I understand now that it was an accident, but it's still a history I need to distance myself from.

The next few days are spent on the farm, my father and I taking rides on the Polaris. He's fully recovered and basking in having me by his side. "Don't stay away too long, honey. Or I'll have to come up with some way to get you back again."

I smile, leaning into him. "Please, nothing involving a hospital."

The day before I leave, I know there's one place I need to go. I've been avoiding it, pretending it doesn't exist, but the game of pretend is over, and I'm driving the winding roads to meet it. I think about Jude along the way and whether I'll call him when I get home or just show up at the house, refuse to let him turn me away. Every part of me misses him. And with the weight of my secrets all but vanished, there's an openness in its place that's liberating and exciting.

I see now how the fear kept these feelings away. I see how its presence made it impossible for me to grow. But now I want him, that love, so much, I can hardly breathe.

My cell phone dings, and I see Elle's name on the screen, so I pull over.

I miss you, Avery. It makes no sense. You're *OLD* and you broke Daddy's heart. I finished the paper. The teacher's going to fail me. I didn't choose! There's good and bad in all of us right? Guess what? LUKE IS COMING TO MIAMI. OMGOMGOMG!

My smile is met with a string of worries. I worry about Elle growing up. I worry about her falling in love and falling apart. What if she has sex? What if, like me, she gets pregnant? I want to be there for her. I want to guide her, hold her hand.

Elle: Avery?

Me: I'm here. Just missing you. When's he coming?

Elle: October. He has family in west palm.

And before I can respond that I'm happy for her and that she needs to be smart and safe and NO DRUGS, she writes, Do you think we should tell my brothers I got them high when they were little kids?

Not now. Maybe at their weddings.

I'm about to get back on the road when I see she's typing something. Do you think you and daddy will get back together?

It takes me a minute to digest what she's asking, but then I tap into the keyboard. I'm not giving up. I'm going to keep F---ing going.

As I get back on the road, the skies do a sudden shift, and it begins to drizzle. It's no coincidence. I'd been waiting for the rain and the cleansing and renewal it brings with it. Rain also brings growth and revival, and it hides the tears that come with goodbye.

As I get closer, my nervousness mounts, because that's what letting feelings in does to a person. You're forced to experience them fully.

When Oliver and Quinn died, I couldn't get out of bed, no matter how much coaxing from Willow and my father. Oliver's parents took charge, I was told, and there were rumblings of a memorial set up by the river. It's where we were happiest, and that's where they scattered the ashes. I was in terrible shape, vacillating between the hysteria over losing my daughter and the refusal to believe I'd lost her father, too.

I know the exact whereabouts of the memorial, miles along the Watauga, where the river meets the lake. In a small town, people talk, and the location trickled through my ear like a stream of music I could neither turn down nor turn off. It was always playing.

The road leading toward the spot narrows, the soaring trees closing in, bowing as if in greeting. As I pull off the shoulder, the rain tapers off.

I collect myself, taking another deep breath before getting out of the car. I'm afraid, for a moment, that I might run into Oliver's parents, though I'd heard from the same people that they rarely came back.

Just as I'm about to step onto the stone footpath, the sun appears, turning the remaining drops into sparkly glitter. I stare up at the sky and feel him all around me. Every which way I look, the sky is an ominous gray, but here, right here, there is a ray of sunshine.

My legs are shaky as I make my way toward them.

Had I imagined what it would look like, had I given myself the permission to truly mourn back then, I would have known that this was the ideal resting place for Oliver. A fine, welcoming bench, polished in deep green, shaded by a sprawling beech tree. When I sit, one of the low-lying stems tickles my skin.

A large stone sits in front of me with a plaque that bears his name. Beside it, there's a smaller stone with hers. It's startling and real, and I hop off the bench and drop to the ground, touching my fingers to the polished metal. I trace each letter of Quinn's name, wondering who she'd resemble, wondering if she'd be mouthy or subdued. Would she have his eyes, his laugh? I say a silent prayer for her, that she's resting easy beside her dad, and I tell her to look out for her grandmother, the red-haired angel. There's a small comfort knowing she's up there watching over my little girl, over Ollie, when I can't.

I trace each letter of Oliver's name as though they embody his spirit, and I remember how carefully he'd draw on my back, sending me special messages.

"Oh, Oliver," I begin. "I'm sorry I haven't visited."

And I expect myself to cry. I expect anger and tears and for him to say something, anything, but I only hear the gentle breeze, the sounds of the water trickling past. I know it's Oliver assuring me that it's okay; he's telling me by way of this peaceful moment that he knows I'm ready to move on, with his permission.

"I love you," I whisper. "I'll always love you." And there's something so freeing about letting the pain go and letting the happy memories live. "Take care of our little girl."

CHAPTER 41

Airplanes howl above when my father and Willow drop me off at the airport. Dad insists I ship the car home, his treat, and I let him do this for me. Besides, the drive won't be as much fun without Elle. This time, saying goodbye is markedly different from the last. I'm not running away and I'm not blaming. I'm razor focused, strong, and ready. Dad's back to his normal self, and he swoops me in his arms, my feet lifting off the ground.

I may have lost everything, but I found this, and I hug him hard, promising to return in the spring for the wedding.

Willow's hug is long and mighty. I feel her love through my sweater, and the path that led us back to one another, culminating in this deeply intimate moment.

"You promise you'll take care of the garden," I remind her.

"I promise," she says, backing up first. "Even though you're much better at it."

We've discussed it a dozen times since I made the decision. Crystal was my childhood, but Miami has become home. The future. Her ocean pulls me in, the balmy weather, and I enjoy my work at the museum. It's different from the farm, but it's mine. And I'm eager to begin again, fresh.

Who am I kidding? I want Jude. And I can't reach him, convince him to forgive me, when miles separate us. We've already been distant for too long.

Willow places her hand on my shoulder and forces me to look at her. "You deserve this, Avery, and even though I'm going to miss you like crazy, your beautiful story waits for you." She stuffs her magic tea bags in my purse. "Go on and get it."

I'm convinced the gardens look off-kilter when I arrive my first day back. Lloyd whispers in my ear, "You'll have it straightened out in no time." And when he says "straightened," he's being rather literal.t

Sure, no one can trim hedges like I can, but that's not what I'm seeing. The roses are a deeper red, the lilies in the pond a crisp white. I rub my eyes, the sun sharper than it's ever been. The plants and shrubs are every possible shade of green, and while I'd always been able to take in the rare beauty of this place, something's different.

It's me.

I make it through those first few weeks back without wallowing in Jude's absence. Elle and I are quick to avoid the subject of her father, texting instead about the therapist she's been talking to, the C plus she received on her paper, and how Milo and Henry have been asking her to *drive* them to the gardens. I tell her I'm not sure it's a good idea, but she insists, Elle's natural response to any pushback.

PUH-LEASE. We're coming.

I'd be lying to myself if I didn't admit that I hope they'll show up. Just because everything between their father and me shattered doesn't mean I have to lose my relationships with Elle and the boys. My affection for them is real. And what Elle and I experienced this summer transformed us.

I think about these changes as I trim bushes and fill flower boxes. I know now that it's okay to paint outside the lines, to be vulnerable, make mistakes. In deference to the new me, I leave one of the shrubs crooked, setting my shears down instead of snipping away at a wayward stem. Ignoring the illusion of control feels strange, though I'm getting used to it. And the garden appears happier, like it's having a good time.

I stop what I'm doing and stare out at the bay. I'm thinking about Jude. I do that a lot now that I'm back. Today I'm remembering the day we first met, how I was drawn to someone I deemed safe, someone who wouldn't expect too much. Perhaps he chose me for the same reasons, and we were only guilty of protecting ourselves. I don't want to descend on him too soon. I'm giving him time to think about what I've done, what he's done, and for the shock to wear off. But I miss him. I'm terribly afraid I may have lost my shot, but I'm practicing patience. I'll know when it's the right time.

Upon my return, I spoke to Delilah about an idea that had formed while I was in Crystal. The Prayer Tree, sprouting with dreams and wishes, standing up to the ashes of the great fire, had stuck with me. I was the tree that survived. And I wanted to be the one to spread that same courage into the world. Or at least I'd try. I showed Delilah the article about the shop that perished, how the trees allowed strangers to release their deepest desires and heaviest burdens. "Who doesn't need hope in their life?" We were always thinking of ways to build community, capitalizing on what Vizcaya has to offer, so the concept was a natural fit, only I'd suggested calling it the Dreaming Tree.

Delilah loved the idea, and soon there were workers carving out a spot near the water, a cluster of trees that would make for the perfect canopy of wishes. Their presence was a reminder of where I've been and what's ahead.

It's a spectacular October morning when I'm entering the rose garden. The property is waking up, slowly coming to life, the staff scrambling in preparation for an afternoon wedding.

That's when I spot him walking from the main house and in my direction. Jude. He's here. Handsome and tan, the kids on either side. And Luke.

My heart skips a beat as he walks toward me. There's a purpose to his stride I want to believe belongs to me.

They approach, and I drop my shears and gloves. The boys have sprouted. "My goodness, what did your grandparents feed you?" I realize how much I've missed them. Milo moves in closer, and I do what I should've done a long time ago, I grab him in my arms and squeeze. I don't recall hugging the boys often, letting them this close, and the thought fills me with regret. Henry stands back, teetering on teenage-boy adolescence, which means hugging older ladies isn't a thing.

"Hey, Avery." He waves.

And then there's Elle. She's glowing and gorgeous and smiling. Luke's smiling, too, and she untangles herself from his grip.

When we hug, my head reaches her chin. "Are you getting taller or am I getting shorter?"

She blushes, whispering in my ear, "Don't make a fuss or emote like I know you want to, but I'm in love. I just wanted to tell you. And we're being smart and taking things slow, so don't lecture me."

Elle being in love spreads through my body. The parts of me long numb come alive, and I remember what it once felt like to fall. The exciting newness of possibility, the hint of expectation, the longing that feels so good it makes you ache.

She unleashes herself from our embrace and our secrets, and Jude waits awkwardly. He's more handsome than I remember, as though he's lighter and brighter. Butterflies flutter in my stomach when he approaches.

"What are you all doing here?" I ask.

Milo answers, each word enunciated with a marked eagerness. "Me and Henry have a class on birds, and we're going to do art."

"That sounds like the perfect morning." I smile at him.

"Guess who drove here?" Jude finally speaks.

Elle holds up the keys, and Jude looks on proudly. I notice she's wearing the watch I bought her for her sixteenth birthday last month, the one with a compass, sent with a card that read, *So you always find your way home.*

"Daddy yelled a lot," says Milo.

I try to make eye contact with Jude, but he's careful not to linger too long in my direction. A lifetime has passed since we were last here, when he proposed. But being back also has me remembering how we came together and the pieces of him that never went away. Elle's watching us, but she's also spending a lot of time observing the wedding decorations. Staff members are arranging the chuppah, covered in pale pink and white roses, lining the gold Chiavari chairs, and before I know it, Elle and Luke are shuttling the boys off to the main house for their instruction, so different from the girl who called them morons that first day.

Which leaves Jude and me alone.

I should be anxious, my heart going a mile a minute, but I love this man. I know that with the utmost certainty. I've been waiting for this moment for weeks. Longer.

"Hi," I say.

"Hi," he says back, meeting my gaze. It's powerful and packed with emotion.

"How've you been?" I ask.

He nods his head, his thick, wavy hair sexy as all hell. "I've been good."

Our eyes lock, neither of us willing to move. "What about you?" he asks.

"Good." I laugh. It's a nervous laugh. He still makes me nervous.

"The family's doing okay? I thought maybe you'd stay . . . I saw how happy you were there."

"They're great. Dad's back at the farm full-time like he never left. Willow and Jackson are getting ready for a spring wedding."

"That's nice. Elle told me she keeps in touch with you."

"I hope that's okay. She's been a gift."

"Are we talking about the same person?" he jokes.

"We both had some growing up to do." I smile. "Do you mind taking a walk with me? They're setting up for a wedding . . . I don't want to get in the way."

He looks around at the grounds, seemingly just noticing the wedding decorations. "Sure."

Birds fly above, and the estate is buzzing with activity. As we walk, I let Jude update me, listening attentively, practicing patience. "Elle's been working hard with her therapist, overcoming some challenges . . . The boys go sometimes. It's been beneficial for all of us."

I let him know that's great, because it is. I might have spared myself quite a bit of suffering had I continued speaking to someone.

When we reach the water's edge, I stop to face him. "I owe you an apology, Jude. I kept so much from you. That wasn't fair."

"I owe you an apology, too."

"Let me go first." I inhale the fresh ocean air, knowing this is it. "That day we met, I was about to walk into the grief workshop. I wasn't like you, Jude. I didn't know how to deal with the feelings. I was a coward, and I bailed . . . and I buried the feelings . . . from myself . . . from you, and sometimes it worked, not always. There were some difficult days . . ."

A brisk wind whistles around us. "No one can do this perfectly," he explains. "I had three kids in pain, three kids who could barely function . . . missing their mother. I had no choice but to be strong. And I still fell short."

I'm silent, thinking about all our imperfections and how they bonded us in difficult ways, but also the most profound.

At this point, there's no sense hiding anymore; there's no use pretending to be someone I'm not. I take a seat on the nearby seawall and motion for him to join me. I lift the cuff of my jeans and show him the scar he's seen a million times, touched, caressed with his bare hands. He doesn't hesitate. He brings a finger to the dimpled skin. "The fire?"

"Yes."

"You're lucky your injuries weren't worse." And I know he means the physical wounds, and because his eyes are sullen and sad, I forgive the mistake.

His hand rests on my scar, and it feels different, as though all the secrets are traveling through our skin, as though everything I've hidden is released by his touch.

"I would've been there for you," he says. "Or at least tried. We could've helped each other." I expect him to say I didn't give him a chance, but he doesn't. He waits, taking his time. "I knew that wasn't a burn from a bicycle tire. And I sensed you were uncomfortable talking about it, so I didn't ask. It was easier that way. And that was wrong."

My eyes glisten with long-held tears. How could Jude ever know me unless he knew the one thing that made me who I am? "You had three kids to take care of. Why burden you with more problems?"

He takes his time in answering, his fingers running through his hair. "I was devastated when I read the articles about you. I admit, at first there was shock, like I was reading about a stranger, and then there was an awful sadness. For you. For your losses. I couldn't imagine how you survived. But then I couldn't grasp how we had lain next to each other in bed with this thing between us."

I find my voice, and it's thick with regret. "Telling you, saying it out loud, would've made it real, and I didn't want it to be real. Loving you . . . letting you in . . . I know this is crazy . . . but it felt like I was being unfair to Ollie and Quinn. Disloyal. If I loved you," and I hear Elle's voice, "did it mean I loved them less?"

"I had a wife, Avery. If anyone understood that way of thinking, it was me. I guess what I'm trying to say is that I get it, to some extent, your struggle. And I didn't help the situation." I don't like that he's taking the blame. I've been accustomed to holding all of it in my hands.

"The fire . . . I don't know what you read in the articles . . . I'd left a candle burning . . . and there was a storm . . ."

He doesn't have to respond. Everything he's thinking shows up on his face. His lips slightly part, then close again. "You've been blaming yourself all these years?"

"Wouldn't you? That candle . . . it destroyed my baby . . . my fiancé . . . not to mention the forest. Do you know that Elle was one of the only ones who saw it from a different perspective? She was the one who helped lessen the blame, made me see that it truly was an accident. A freakish, once-in-a-lifetime fluke." Hearing this moves him. It's there in his eyes. "I've learned to accept that now. A horrible accident. Blaming myself was useless. But it kept me from falling deeper in love with you. It kept me guarded, and it kept us distant. If I was a few steps away from you, I couldn't get hurt. I couldn't hurt you."

He doesn't say it, but I know he's thinking about Mallory, about his own guilt. They were different circumstances, the same awful out-come, but he has his own burden to carry. A cardiologist who should've known, could've prevented his wife's death.

"Terrible things happen. To all of us. To think you had a hand in this—"

My eyes burn, but it could be the salt coming off the ocean. "For a long time, I wished I had died in that fire, too."

He moves closer, an arm coming around my shoulder, and I collapse against him. "I'm sorry. I should've told you. I should've been better at this . . . I wasn't very good at letting go."

His lips brush against the top of my head like they used to do, and I remember our happiness. I miss him and I want him. And I close my eyes, wishing it didn't feel so good.

"I thought if I told you, then you'd judge me. You wouldn't feel the same way about me. You'd think I was some monster . . . and you'd never trust me with your kids . . . if I . . ."

"Don't say it. Just don't."

He ducks his head, so I can't see his eyes. "You were right about all of it. The proposal . . . the kids . . . my holding on to Mallory . . . There was a lot we needed to sort out . . . so much we were both holding on to."

"I thought it didn't bother me," I say. "But that was part of the problem. I think I may have resented it . . . I don't know . . . or maybe it justified my need to keep this part of me hidden."

A bird lands beside us, a robin, feathered in red, darting aimlessly on the rocks. Jude turns to me with his beautiful blue eyes. "I've done my own share of soul-searching, and I heard you, and I recognize how I contributed to our problems. You were right about the closet, what holding on to her things meant for me. The kids and I went through her stuff. They chose what they wanted to keep; so did her parents. Then we donated the rest to a women's shelter."

"That couldn't have been easy for any of you."

"No," he says, "but it was time."

And when I see the pain we've collectively endured, the battlefield we crossed, I can't help but feel the deepest form of love for him. For being here. For listening. For admitting he's as human as the rest of us. I didn't think I could love someone the way I loved Oliver, but what am I feeling if not love? "I appreciate what you're saying, but just know how sorry I am, Jude. I wish the apology could cover the mess I've made."

He searches the ground in front of us. "I came here today because I needed to see you." And the way he says it touches my entire body. "I needed to apologize, too, for how I contributed to your holding back . . . how I treated you in Crystal. Some of the things I said were pretty harsh, but I was terrified when I heard about you two stuck in the forest. I honestly couldn't imagine what I would've done . . ."

"I wouldn't have let anything happen to her."

"I meant you, too," he says. "If something happened to you . . ."

I want to reach for him, but I wait.

"But then I was so angry about the secrets you'd kept from me. From us. My hurt got in the way. I wish we could've figured out a way to help heal each other."

"I needed to heal myself first. So did you. We couldn't be the missing pieces for each other. I, for one, needed to come to you whole."

"You're right. And I know that for next time." Which catches me off guard, and I realize maybe he's not here to reconcile, as I'd hoped. He's here to apologize but also to say goodbye.

The breeze picks up, the nearby trees and flowers dancing around us in rhythm. "Are you happy, Jude?"

He clasps his fingers in his hands. "I'm trying, Avery. Aren't you?"

"I don't regret our time together," I say. And it's as though we're staring down the barrel of memories, remembering the thrill of us, torn between holding on and letting go. I think about these two men I loved. How one kept the flames of my youth alive; the other offered a future. One was reckless and irresponsible. The other meant taking a chance.

"Neither do I," he says.

My phone dings, and I tell him I have to get back to work, desperate for this moment not to end.

He smiles and I feel myself melt, like I'm seeing him for the very first time. But that's not the case. This could be the last time. And it hurts. "Go on," he says. "I'm going to sit here for a bit and take in the view."

Walking away, I feel his eyes tapping up and down my skin. I turn one last time, not ready for him to go. "Stick around and watch the wedding. It's for Delilah's daughter. Everybody's invited. Free lamb chops and mushroom canapés."

There's a shimmer in his eyes, from me or the glow of the sun. "I'm starving," he says. "We just might."

CHAPTER 42

The sky is an endless blue, the temperature hovering in the low seventies, and the gardens are an extraordinary backdrop to the intimate ceremony.

After the happy couple exchanges vows, the guests move to the terrace for a buffet against the bay, the waves mingling with the music and mimosas, goat-cheese omelets and raspberry muffins.

Music plays, and I see Elle and Luke swaying to the rhythm, absorbed in conversation. Jude stands off to the side, and Milo and Henry, finished with their class, pull their father onto the dance floor to join.

Lloyd approaches, looking handsome in his dress shirt and slacks. He hands me a glass of champagne and we toast. "Don't go blowing a second chance with that hunk of a man," he says with a wink.

Elle works her way in my direction, the pale-blue halter top accentuating her shoulders. There's a tug on my heart when she reaches my side. I drop the glass on the table, and she doesn't reach for it. "I'm driving." Which leaves me impressed with her maturity.

She dips her fingers into the bowl of chocolate-covered almonds instead, grabbing a handful. And that's when she stops. "Avery . . ." She's leaning over the flower arrangement, inhaling. "That's it. I smell her. Mal—" And she points. "That's my mom."

I search each flower and know at once. Plucking the bud from the vase, I hand it to her.

"Gardenia."

She closes her eyes and breathes it in. "Oh my God, it's her." Then she drops the flower behind her ear and turns to me. "Thank you, Avery."

I tell her she doesn't need to thank me.

"But I do. Not just for this. I never thanked you for all you did for me this summer. There were a few times I was pretty hard on you." She stops herself. "Fine . . . a lot of times. And you never gave up on me."

My mouth curves into a smile. "You gave me as much as I gave you, Elle. Maybe more."

She bravely asks, "What about you and Daddy?"

He's across the way, horsing around with the boys, when he catches us staring and waves.

"I'm hoping your father and I will remain friends. We have something in common."

"What's that?"

"We love you."

She doesn't say she loves me back, and that's okay. But she drops into my arms, letting her head burrow into my shoulder, and I hug her with everything inside of me. "Your mother would be so proud of you, Elle. And if I've learned anything this summer, the people we've loved are always with us, even when they're not. Hold on to that."

I feel her nodding her head, taking it in.

"Always remember where you came from. And the many people who love you. And even if you're not driving, stop stealing booze from random wineglasses."

She laughs. "I'll try."

She backs up. Her beautiful blue eyes, full of depth.

"You would've been a cool stepmom," she says. And then she points at the bracelet I wear every single day. It never comes off, not even when I take a shower. *Keep Fucking Going.* "Don't give up, Avery. Fight." And then she's off, meeting the boys and Luke, who smiles brightly when she returns to him and his kiss.

The party is in full swing. Lloyd and Delilah are smiling for a picture. Luke, Elle, Henry, and Milo are standing by the water, chasing the birds, laughing together, and the bride and groom are mingling with their guests, visiting each table, arms around each other, smiling.

And then there's Jude.

He stands beside the rose garden, his back to me, and I wonder what he's remembering when he stares at the long stems, the vibrant colors. My steps take me in his direction, and when I reach his side, he turns around, surprised to see me there.

I apologize, a nervousness creeping through my skin. "Hi, again."

He's watching me, the feel of his stare warm like the sun.

This is it. This is my moment. I give him my hand. "I'm Avery. Avery Beckett."

He squeezes my hand. "Jude Masters."

Every cell in my body is drawn to him, and I keep going. "I love you, Jude Masters. I'm not backing down. Not anymore. I'm fighting. I'm going. And it may not always be easy, and we may hit a few bumps, and there are no guarantees, but I'm not giving up. Not on you. Not on us. I lost love once before, but I refuse to lose it again. I refuse to lose you."

He smiles. It starts out subtle, but then it covers his face. "I've been wondering what you've been waiting for."

The words brush against me, or it's the wind, something magical and soft that tickles my skin, awakening something deep inside. The band

293

begins playing a song, "Here Comes The Sun," and he reaches for me. "Dance?"

I take a step forward, and he wraps his arms around me. They fit as though they never left. His voice is a whisper when he breathes into my ear, "Are you scared?"

I whisper back, "Not anymore."

The Farm, Crystal, North Carolina
Spring

Willow and I are in her bedroom, finishing up the final touches on her dress and makeup. She knows I'm not very good at this, and that's when Elle magically appears, brushing Willow's cheeks with blush, smoothing out her hair.

"Not bad for an old lady," she says, stepping back, admiring her work. We laugh, happy to be together again.

"You look beautiful," I say.

"I do, don't I?" says Elle, posing in pale pink.

Willow playfully shoves her aside, the three of us reflected in the mirror. "We've come a long way, girls, haven't we?" she says.

Elle and I exchange looks. "Here we go again. Brace yourself for *a moment*," she says.

"It's my wedding day, Little Mermaid. I'll have whatever moment I want."

But I decide, watching my sister, being here with Elle, that I want to be the one to give her the moment. There's champagne on the counter, a pair of flutes, and I pick one up. Willow reaches for the other. "To my sister, Willow. For loving me when I didn't always deserve it. For making every day an adventure. For saving us with your special teas and spells, for being there, for everything, good and bad . . . Now it's your turn . . . May you live the life you dreamed of, always with honesty, always with a gorgeous view ahead of you . . ."

"Always with us," Elle adds.

"With us. And I know Mom is smiling down on you, sprinkling her fairy dust, or tea leaves, or sage; she's so proud. Cheers to you and Jackson, Willow. To a lifetime of love and laughter . . . and a truckload of kids you can spoil as you did us."

We clink glasses and sip, the sweet liquid tingling inside. Willow wipes away a tear, and Elle tells her not to ruin her makeup. I hand Elle the glass, but she refuses. And that lasts all of three seconds when she sees it's not a test, that we want her to join us. "Oh, heck . . . if you insist!"

Willow and Jackson are reciting their vows, and I'm staring at Jude from beneath a canopy of flowers. He's as handsome as I've ever seen in his cream-colored suit and white button-down, and we can't take our eyes off each other.

Crystal is flaunting her beauty, her gorgeous blue sky, a slight nip in the temperature. Willow beams in form-fitting white lace, and Jackson stares at her as though she's an angel on earth. And she is. I couldn't have imagined it any other way, standing there beside her, my sister, my heart, my protector, finally getting her happily ever after.

Dad's bawling like a baby, wiping his tears in his handkerchief for all of us to see. Beside him sits Jan, his *girlfriend*, and there's Elle, tall and beautiful, Luke never letting go of her hand. And Milo and Henry. They wear matching slacks and dress shirts, already so grown-up, looking more and more like their father.

I stare out at the people I love. There's Cole and Skye. Sheriff Floyd. Our farm family. And I breathe a little easier, excited for the future.

It's been six months since Jude and I danced at Vizcaya. Six months since we decided to start over, from the very beginning, no secrets, only truths. During that exciting time, we found a groove that included the kids, giving them a say, letting them in on our growing feelings. And Elle. She was so happy, but she was afraid, too. I could sense she feared I'd leave, or worse, but we promised each other we wouldn't let our fears get in the way of what could be. And we leaned on each other for support. And we listened. And we cared.

When the plans for the Dreaming Tree were finished, the five of us made a special trip to drop our wishes on the branches.

The boys couldn't think of just one, so they wrote a bunch: a PS4, the Miami Heat to win the NBA championships, a lot of pizza, school to be canceled for the foreseeable future. Elle's wishes she kept private, and I watched her lovingly place them on the tree as though her fingers had the power to make them come true.

And Jude. He said he'd go last, so it was my turn. And I scribbled: *Let this family love me. Let them feel the love I have for them. Let us live a beautiful life, safe and healthy, while special angels look over us.*

We stood around the trees, admiring the size and length, the dreams tacked to the stems. Who are we without our dreams?

And just when I thought we were done, I remembered it was Jude's turn, and he handed me his wish. "It's the same one I had all those months ago when I visited you in Crystal. It hasn't changed."

"But—"

And he knew me, knew what I was about to say. "I'm not superstitious, Avery. I'm not afraid to tell you my dream. Take a look."

I took my time reading his words. *Let her say yes next time.*

And as if on cue, the kids gathered close and clasped their arms around us. Milo and Henry hollered, while Elle was a whisper of hope, and Jude got on his knee.

"Marry us, Avery Beckett."

And I looked at their glowing faces, the love there in their eyes.

"Yes," I said. "I'll marry you. All of you."

The smile spreads across my face; I have no way to stop it.

He smiles back. Jude.

I'm twisting the diamond, witnessing love in the place that I love, and later, after I've caught the bouquet, when Jude and I are dancing under the stars, and we're making plans to spend our summers here on the farm, because he's ready to slow down, cut back his hours at the hospital, I figure now might not be the right time to tell him my news.

But we promised, no more secrets.

We walk toward the flower garden, the beautiful Avery & Elle Garden, which Luke and Willow have tended to so lovingly.

We take a seat on the bench, and I reach for his hands.

"There's something about being here," he says. "I don't know how to describe—"

"Anything is possible?"

"That's it." He's smiling at me, more with his eyes than his lips. I don't want anything to ruin this moment.

"Jude," I begin, whispering in his ear. "There's something I have to tell you."

And this time, he allows for no hesitation, drawing me closer. "Whatever it is . . . you know you can tell me."

And I begin, saying the words I'd practiced all week, choosing the right ones, and he tilts his head, as though he's unsure he heard me correctly.

"Wait. Can you say that again?"

I repeat myself. This time with more conviction, no chance of him misunderstanding. And when I say it, my heart explodes, for him, for us, and all the people we loved and lost.

"We're having a baby."

He's a mixture of joy and uncertainty. His hug is hard; no misunderstanding there. His happiness is real. "We're having a baby," he says.

And I think of all the storms we weathered to land in this place. The broken dreams. The prayers we cast off into the sky. And I know now that endings bring forth new beginnings, and letting go means you're alive.

ACKNOWLEDGMENTS

They say it takes a village, and nowhere is that statement more applicable than when you're a writer. This is the book that almost leveled me. Almost. I was so close to giving up, but then this mix of angels-on-earth surrounded me, and I dusted myself off—dusted off the doubt and uncertainty—and I kept going.

Kim Lionetti, I don't know how many drafts you read—and there were a lot—but you plodded through and gave each one your best. Tiffany Yates Martin, you're my pinch hitter, the one who clears the forest so the story can shine. Alicia Clancy, you brought Oliver to life, and I thank you for that. Danielle Marshall, you'll never understand, or maybe you already do, what your commitment to me and this book has meant. I am deeply grateful for your enthusiasm and passion.

Thank you to the entire team at Lake Union for a seamless publishing process, with special thanks to Nicole Burns-Ascue for the eagle-eyed editing and Kirsten Balayti, Brittany Dowdle, and all the other expert hands who shaped this manuscript. Gabe Dumpit, you're always there, wherever that is, answering the most inane, annoying questions, and I appreciate it when you tell me that I'm never a bother.

Ann-Marie Nieves, publicist extraordinaire, you are a calming force and someone I'm happy to call a friend.

A special thank you to Dr. Ron Berger, Dr. Pete Coleman, Due South Outfitters, Paige Harnick, and Dr. Elizabeth Etkin-Kramer for sharing your knowledge and expertise, whether it ended up in the final draft or not. Your time and experience matter.

Authors rely upon the generous support of the bookstagram community, book bloggers, Facebook groups, podcasters, and early reviewers, and I am grateful to each and every one of you for the continued support. I only hope I have shown that gratitude year-round, not merely here.

Readers, my words mean nothing without your reading them. Thank you for choosing my stories when you have many options out there. I know I say this with each book, but it's worth repeating. It's because of you that I write.

A special thanks to Lauren Margolin and Jamie Rosenblit for your endless support of all authors—and for the friendship I deeply value.

Andrea Katz, besides my appreciation for Great Thoughts' Great Readers, thank you for being that battle-ready friend. You showed up day after day—armed and willing—with just the right amount of pink and blue. Thank you also to Jay, Stanley, Sophie, and Jenny for sharing you with me.

Camille Di Maio and Lisa Barr, we've been through all of it together. The career highs, the challenging lows, and everything in between. In your own special ways, you've been there for me with support, pride, and the extra hand when I most needed it. Your friendship is a bright light for me.

Samantha Woodruff, our friendship is new, but it already feels old (unlike us). I look forward to the day we are dressed in coral and green, hugging in person. I will then be able to appropriately thank you for your endless support.

Tracey Garvis Graves, Colleen Oakley, Allison Pataki, Liz Fenton, Allison Winn, Pam Jenoff, Jane Healey, Kristin Fields, Barbara O'Neal, Elizabeth Blackwell, Susie Schnall, Lea Geller, Rebecca Warner, Sally Koslow, M. J. Rose, and Samantha Bailey, whether I asked for your help or needed your advice (at a pivotal time), you gave it. Willingly, without hesitation. I am forever indebted.

Our author community is generous beyond measure. There are so many of you I am blessed to call friends, and at the risk of leaving anyone out, I am grateful to each and every one of you for your acts of kindness and for "getting it" when no one else ever will.

Merle Saferstein, I love being on this journey with you.

Thank you to my family and friends for your unending support and love. Even when things are tough, you give me the comfort and strength to move forward.

Last and definitely not least, Steven, who continues to think I'm more than I am, and our boys, Brandon and Jordan, who make me want to be that person.

BOOK CLUB QUESTIONS

1. Avery keeps a secret from Jude because she fears the truth will make him leave. Has there been an event in your life that has forced you to keep a secret from someone you love? Would you do it again?

2. Nature is another character in the novel. For many, it can be a great healer. Where are you most at peace?

3. As Avery's dad explains, there are lessons in gardening that apply to life. Is there a hobby you enjoy whose lessons have stuck with you? Give examples.

4. Themes of loss and letting go are woven throughout the story. What is your own experience with both? What advice would you give to someone who is struggling with either?

5. If you were able to spend a day on Watauga River or the farm with one character, who would you choose and why?

6. Do you believe in fate and circumstance? Signs and spells? The power of positive thinking? Have you ever had an experience that felt otherworldly? Explain.

7. Throughout the story, Avery holds on to Oliver. Is there someone in your life who has stayed with you even though they're gone? Do you feel their presence? Explain

what connects you.

8.   Avery returns home to North Carolina to confront her past. Do you live where you grew up? If not, have you ventured home? What keeps you away? What does being home bring forth in you?

9.   Avery and Elle have clearly come into each other's lives for a reason. Is there someone other than family and close friends who you've met or come to know who has touched you or shared an impactful life lesson with you?

10. The novel depicts the tender relationships both of mothers and daughters and of sisters. If you were Willow, how would you have handled Avery's decision to leave Crystal? What do you believe is the most valuable part of a mother-daughter relationship?

11. Several of the characters in the novel have lost loved ones. Did any of their handling of grief resonate with you? Were you able to learn anything about yourself through their experiences? What would you say to these characters if you could?

ABOUT THE AUTHOR

Photo © 2018 Hester Esquenazi

Rochelle B. Weinstein is the *USA Today* and Amazon bestselling author of emotionally driven women's fiction, including *This Is Not How It Ends*, *Somebody's Daughter*, *Where We Fall*, *The Mourning After*, and *What We Leave Behind*. Rochelle spent her early years, always with a book in hand, raised by the likes of Sidney Sheldon and Judy Blume. A former entertainment industry executive, she splits her time between sunny South Florida and the mountains of North Carolina. When she's not writing, Rochelle can be found hiking, reading, and searching for the world's best nachos. She is currently working on her seventh novel. Please visit her at www.rochelleweinstein.com.